GENESIS GIRL

JENNIFER BARDSLEY

This book is a work of fiction. Names, characters, places, and incidents are either products of the author's imagination or are used fictitiously. Any resemblance to actual persons, living or dead, business establishments, events, or locales is entirely coincidental. The author makes no claims to, but instead acknowledges the trademarked status and trademark owners of the word marks mentioned in this work of fiction.

GENESIS GIRL by Jennifer Bardsley

ISBN: 978-1-944816-75-9

Published by Month9Books, Raleigh, NC 27609
Cover design by Beeitful Book Covers

PRAISE for GENESIS GIRL

"A thought-provoking read with a wish-I'd-thought-of-that premise. At its core, *GENESIS GIRL* is an exploration of power. Not simply the power that technology wields over us, but the power we must wield over ourselves."
—Jeanne Ryan, author of *NERVE* and *CHARISMA*

"A totally original sci-fi thriller, *GENESIS GIRL* plunges readers into a future world scarily like our own, where private lives are warped into commercial spectacles. The story of feisty heroine Blanca's battle to reclaim her identity kept me up late—with the computer and the TV off!"
—Joshua David Bellin, author of the *SURVIVAL COLONY 9* series

"Fast-paced, thrilling, and action-packed, *GENESIS GIRL* is a debut that will make you think about how the ways we use technology today could come back to haunt us in the future. The perfect start to a powerful, entirely original new series."
—Laurie Elizabeth Flynn, author of *FIRSTS*

To Doug, for everything.

GENESIS GIRL

Chapter One

My boot hits him in the nuts at the same time as the flash goes off, but it's too late. The Virus has already taken my picture. He was aiming for Fatima, but I pushed her away just in time. I sideswipe his legs and topple the Virus over while he moans in agony from my kick to his groin.

"Nobody takes my picture, you freak!" I stare at his tattooed face. There's something familiar about the snake inked around his eyebrow, but I can't quite place it. We're in the underground parking garage at school, and the fluorescent lights shade everything ugly. I crouch down and flip the Virus onto his stomach, bashing his nose against the pavement.

Ever since I was little, teachers have warned me about Viruses. They're paparazzi scumbags whose sole purpose in life is to destroy privacy and expose secrets. I'd never seen one in person, until today.

"Hand me your belt," I tell Fatima. I hold the Virus in place by grinding my knee into his back while Fatima slips off the cinch from her black spandex uniform. I wrestle the man's arms behind me with both hands. Surprise, surprise—security doesn't show up until I'm already hog-tying the bastard.

"You're not so special now, Vestal!" the Virus says as they haul him off.

He's right.

Until about two minutes ago, I was a Vestal postulant. A blank slate. An Internet virgin. There were no images of my moniker floating around cyberspace. My parents hadn't blogged about my every poop. It had been planned that way from the beginning. They had castrated my virtual identity for the promise of a better life.

In one week I'm graduating from Tabula Rasa. Today was my chance to shine while I'm interviewed by companies. Only nobody will want me now.

With one flash of his thumb-camera, that jerk destroyed my life.

"Don't worry," Fatima says, helping me to my feet. "You've still got a face that can sell soap. I knew it the first time I saw you. Your skin's your best feature, and that hasn't changed."

The sound of the security gate opening drowns Fatima out. We watch as a white car enters the Tabula Rasa garage. A flash of sunlight taunts me before the gate closes. All my life I've lived in this twenty-story fortress of protection. Today was going to be my first day in sunshine, being interviewed by bidders.

But that Virus ruined it all. How the hell he snuck in, I'll never know.

"You're the girl next door," Fatima says, a bit louder. "Couture might not want you, but the average American will."

I nod because I've heard it all before. Not everyone can be the seductress. I'll never be like Fatima, I don't begrudge her that. A clear face, green eyes, and brown hair are what I have to work with, and that's fine. But there's no fixing a picture of me on the Internet.

"It'll be okay, Blanca," Fatima says again.

But we both know that isn't true.

For a Vestal, a clear Internet history is the most important thing. Without that, I'm nothing. Our elusive privacy is what makes us valuable.

I've watched our class shrink from two hundred eager postulants to a graduating group of ten. The infractions were usually unavoidable: their memory was spotty, their temperament was bad, or worst of all, they turned out ugly. But once in a while, somebody was thrown out because of an online transgression.

Everyone left is bankable. Ten perfect human specimens who could sell you anything.

Even Ethan, with his poufy hair and scrawny build, is a sure thing. He wears glasses now despite his perfect vision, and goes around in bow ties and suspenders. "Nerdy, but in a good way," the teachers say. "This one's going high-tech."

Beau can write his own ticket too. He's six feet tall and can out-bench press every other guy in the group. America will drool.

And then there's Fatima, standing next to me. With her dark

eyes and svelte figure, she'll have her choice of any fashion house.

I had been hoping to sell cosmetics. That's prestigious too, and I really had a chance. But nobody will bid on me now. The auction is a week away, and I'm ruined!

"Blanca?" A woman approaches us right as a dark black limousine pulls through the gate. "That car isn't for you. Good luck with your interviews, Fatima."

Fatima waves at me sadly and slides into the vehicle.

"Let's get this disaster under control," says the woman as the limo drives away. Her billowing skirt makes her look ethereal in the shadows of the parking garage. I have never seen her before. But she's wearing white like our teachers and has a platinum cuff, so of course, I follow her.

She takes me to a room on the twentieth floor of Tabula Rasa that boasts a wall of windows. "Darkened for privacy," says the woman when she sees my apprehension.

I approach them hesitantly, unaccustomed to the glass. I see a tiny patch of sky surrounded by glowing billboards. On every rooftop is an advertisement featuring a face I already know. Vestals stare down at me from all vantage points, hawking perfumes, cars, and weight-loss supplements.

"You'll be up there too, Blanca. There's still hope." The woman stands at my elbow.

I peek and study her this time. She's fortyish with blue eyes and a heart-shaped face. I know she's a Vestal because of her white outfit, but I don't recognize her.

Weird. I know all the Vestals. Everyone does.

The hydraulic doors hiss open, and we both turn to look. The

Tabula Rasa headmaster enters in a swirl of white cloak.

"Blanca," he says, "you have a problem."

"Yes, Headmaster Russell. I'm sorry, Headmaster Russell."

"I don't know how you let this happen." He strides to the enormous windows, holding a manila file folder. None of the Tabula Rasa faculty is permitted computers, including Headmaster Russell.

"You mean you don't know how *you* let this happen, Russell."

I brace for impact. Nobody talks to Headmaster Russell that way and gets away with it. I know that better than anyone. He grits his teeth. "Security is being questioned as we speak. Sit down, Ms. Lydia. Please."

"I will *not* sit down." Ms. Lydia's stare could cut glass. "Not until you apologize to Blanca. She deserves better, and you know it."

There is audible silence. Headmaster Russell rubs the golden cuff on his wrist. "Blanca, I'm sorry that this happened to you." His eyes don't meet mine.

Ms. Lydia snaps her fingers.

Headmaster Russell clears his throat and tries again, this time meeting my gaze. "I'm sorry that *I* let this happen to you. I should have protected you better. I will do everything in my power to make sure you are still harvested at the auction." Then he turns to Ms. Lydia who stands resolute and icy. "Are you satisfied?"

"Perhaps." She shrugs. "Let's see what's in the folder."

A few moments later we are seated at the table in the center of the room. Headmaster Russell shows us the picture of me that is now plastered all over cyberspace. I fight back tears.

FIRST LOOK AT NEWEST VESTAL, the caption reads. Then there's me executing a roundhouse kick, my hair flying back, my face a perfect mask of rage.

"This is what we are dealing with," says Headmaster Russell.

"It could be worse." Ms. Lydia presses her lips together. Right then an old-fashioned phone hanging on the wall rings. "Well, Russ? Aren't you going to answer that?"

Headmaster Russell jumps to answer the phone. I can hear him say "Blanca" and "photograph," but that's it. My future is muffled as he whispers into the receiver.

Ms. Lydia extends her hand to me. Her touch is very cold, but her shake is firm. "My name is Lydia. I'm the elected agent of all Vestal graduates. I lead the Tabula Rasa board of directors."

"What was your company?" I ask. I still don't recognize her. But I notice her platinum cuff. That means she was top pick.

"I didn't have a company. I went Geisha."

I try to keep my face blank. Really, I do. But what she said is so shocking that my eyes widen for an instant. Ms. Lydia notices.

"It's not as bad as you think," she says. "Maybe it's better. There are many ways to be a Vestal, and they all have honor."

"Of course," I answer. "It says so right in the Vestal Code of Ethics."

Most Vestals leave Tabula Rasa with major corporations, but on rare occasions they enter contracts with private individuals as Geishas.

Nobody wants to go Geisha. Giving up privacy for another person's pleasure is creepy. Selling out to a company is so much better.

Headmaster Russell hangs up the phone with a loud *click*. He smoothes his cloak over his barrel chest. "Blanca has five bidders," he says. "That picture has whipped up a frenzy."

"Good," says Ms. Lydia. "You're redeemed."

I'm not sure whom she's talking to, but I brave a smile anyway.

Barbelo Nemo founded the Vestals fifty years ago after the Brain Cancer Epidemic rotted humankind via cell phones. Bluetooth scanned sensitive neurons. Wi-Fi washed over weakened gray matter. Before the medical community realized what was happening, millions of people were dead.

Scientists promised finger-chips were the solution, but Barbelo forged a different path. Why risk another tech-induced health crisis? Barbelo set Vestals apart and kept us safe. Eighteen years of schooling at Tabula Rasa behind lead-lined walls, and then twenty-five years of service to the Brethren. We have a sacred duty to remain digitally pure.

If it weren't for Tabula Rasa, I'd be tech-addicted like everyone else. I'd expose my private thoughts to total strangers. I'd be too engrossed in my finger-chips to pay attention to my friends. I'd judge people by scanning their profile before I met them in person. I wouldn't buy anything or go anywhere unless the Internet told me it was a good idea. I would let my finger-chips rob me of forming real relationships with the actual people who matter in my life. What's worse, I wouldn't know I was ruined. I'd willingly give up my humanity one byte at a time.

But as a Vestal postulant, I'm sheltered from that. Chaos swirls around us, but Vestals are constant. We are loyal. We keep secrets. We remind the world there is a better way to live. Because we are so trustworthy, the public buys anything we sell.

No wonder corporations lust for us.

It's been seven days since the Virus stole my picture, and I've made it to the auction after all. I'm sitting on stage with the other Tabula Rasa graduates, safe inside the lead-lined walls of school. The Harvest is minutes away. We're about to auction our purity to the highest bidder. In front of us are Silicon Valley elite. Many of them are flexing their palms, frustrated that their finger-chip connections won't work.

Fatima's hand is on my thigh, and my hand covers hers. Sweat trickles down my back, tracing the curve of my spine as I arch my shoulders in perfect posture. I curl my toes inside their black leather boots, trying to release the pressure.

My whole education, my entire existence, has led up to now.

This morning I woke up in the metal bunk bed of my cloister. In a few days I'll move to my new home, the Vestal quarters of my business sponsor. I'll represent a company, a product, and a lifestyle. The world will follow my life through carefully released images. Whatever my company chooses to share will become my new identity.

Where I eat, who I date, what I do, it will all be for one purpose—to sell my company's products.

I'll never beg my friends to like my pictures. Total strangers will hang on my every word. I'll be a Vestal, and millions of people will care about who I am.

Even better, I'll have a family. Older Vestals will be my mentors. I'll join their manufactured family in print, media, and billboard campaigns across America.

If I'm lucky, the company will have at least one Vestal in their roster close to me in age. Hopefully a guy, and preferably one who looks more like Beau and less like Ethan. I've been waiting eighteen years for a boyfriend, and he had better be good.

"Fatima," the announcer says. My best friend squeezes my hand and winks at me. Then she walks to the stage. She's gorgeous, like always. Ever since we were little, I always knew Fatima would be the top pick. Fatima has a body that can sell anything. She's smart too. It will say that in her portfolio.

But while Fatima stands at the podium next to Headmaster Russell, there is only a shuffle of papers in the audience, heads bent over still placards. Fatima glances back at me in panic.

No one is bidding.

A woman wearing a white suit scrambles on stage and grabs Headmaster Russell's arm, whispering into his ear. It's Ms. Corina, from charm and deportment. She doesn't appear so polished now.

Ms. Corina points to me, and Headmaster Russell looks too. Then he cringes.

"There has been a change of plans," he announces to the audience. "Bidding on Miss Fatima will wait. Bidding on Miss Blanca will now begin."

Fatima gazes at me from across the stage. I know what she's thinking without her saying one word. Fatima's the seductress, and I'm the girl next door. She's the one people drool for, not me.

I try to smile placidly, like Charming Corina taught us. But watching the audience freaks me out. I'm used to the black uniforms of students and the white robes of teachers. Now all I see is the ambiguity of color.

I try to focus as Headmaster Russell says something about my education.

"Poetry, literature, music," he says. "Blanca is the perfect package. She's well versed in the seven liberal arts and entirely ignorant about science and technology. A Vestal Virgin for the modern age."

Headmaster Russell regards me with dark eyes. Then he turns back to the sea of faces. "Blanca's the perfect image for your company. Born and bred in Nevada and groomed right here at Tabula Rasa. Let's start the bidding at five million dollars."

A deep breath. I fight to be calm when I see arms shoot up and numbers wave. But I don't think about the auction or my impending future. I think about my past.

Until now, I had no idea I came from Nevada.

Were my parents still in Nevada? Were they scanning the news feed on their palms at this very second? Were they trying to guess which name was mine, eagerly anticipating their cut from my sale? My parents were going to make a lot of money off me.

But my so-called parents aren't important. All that matters is right now: the bidding war. So many people shout that Headmaster Russell appears stressed. He uses the sleeve of his cloak to wipe sweat off his forehead.

"Thirty million? Do I hear thirty-one?" he asks. That's when I feel the skin on my arms prickle. Companies don't pay that much for a Vestal. But private individuals do.

"Thirty-one-and-a-half?" Headmaster Russell asks loudly. Another arm goes up. Then another. "Thirty-two? Thirty-two going once? Going twice? Sold," says Headmaster Russell, banging the gavel. "Sold for the highest price ever paid in Vestal history. Sold to Mr. Calum McNeal for thirty-two million dollars."

And just like that, I've gone Geisha.

A middle-aged man stands. His hair is brown but graying and longish around the ears. He's smiling so hard, it looks like he's going to burst.

I'm finally wearing white, but I don't feel like I deserve it. Instead I feel dirty inside as I stand with my fellow graduates around the Pool of Purity. My unlit candle weighs heavy in my hand, and I nervously finger its waxy edge. Everyone has been sold to a company but me. Fatima won't make eye contact.

"On this the most private of nights," Headmaster Russell says, "we celebrate the blessing of one more class of Tabula Rasa graduates. The brothers and sisters who came before you surround you with their guidance and welcome you to our ranks."

I feel their presence before I see them. Older, experienced Vestals step from the shadows and flank us in a larger ring. Together we form two concentric circles, our billowing white robes hovering over the pavement, reflected in the water.

"The candle please." Headmaster Russell turns to look at Ms. Lydia, who stands nearby.

She is beautiful in the moonlight, her heart-shaped face a mask of serenity. When she reaches out her candle to touch his, the sleeve of her gown slips down below her elbow, exposing a platinum cuff against creamy skin. "The beacon of light," she says. "We are a sacred fire that will not burn out. Those who came before you welcome you into our Brethren."

Soon the flame is passed from candle to candle. The dark circle of Tabula Rasa graduates illuminates in a warm glow. When Fatima tips her candle to mine, she struggles to smile. She hasn't spoken one word to me since the auction. My harvest price was double hers. But I know that's not the real problem between us. It's because I've gone Geisha.

Headmaster Russell's voice is solemn. "Vestals are a beacon in a dark world. We alone stand together. We are living sacrifices for all that is pure and all that is sacred."

An older Vestal steps forward with a silver tray. Nine golden cuffs sparkle in the candlelight. The single platinum cuff beckons to me. I am the top pick.

Ms. Lydia selects a golden cuff. "It is time for the vows. Master Ethan, do you solemnly swear to uphold the Vestal order?"

"I do," says Ethan, stepping forward.

"Will you consecrate your body? Will you promise to never be marked by ink, stain, piercing, or technology? Will you give your highest self to our cause?"

"I promise," says Ethan, holding out his arm.

Ms. Lydia snaps the golden cuff on his wrist.

"And now, for the sealing," says Headmaster Russell, who approaches with a small blue flame. There is total and utter silence for this, the most sacred part of the ceremony. Headmaster Russell singes the metal, searing it shut. Ethan's golden cuff now marks him for life. The whole world will forever know he is a Vestal.

The sealing happens eight more times until finally, I am the only graduate who remains.

Ms. Lydia picks up the platinum cuff and holds it to the light. "There are many paths a Vestal can take, but one thing is constant: the world relies on us. We are the last guardians of private living. When we sell our reputation, it is with purpose and thought. We do not give it away freely like the masses of humanity. To be purchased privately is a holy act within itself."

My tears start when she says this. They roll down my cheeks, washing away the shame. It's like a window has opened in my heart, releasing all the pressure. I feel joy again. Joy and pride for being a Vestal, no matter what.

This is my time. This is what I have lived for. When Ms. Lydia snaps the platinum cuff on my wrist, it is the happiest moment of my life.

Chapter Two

My new identity as a Vestal Geisha begins today. The road to McNeal Manor is about a million miles long, and it's lit up like a candelabra. There are cameras everywhere, and they are terrifying. Somebody is watching. It's a good thing my Tabula Rasa limo has dark windows.

Eventually the driver parks, and I have to get out, pretending like this smile on my face is genuine. Before I know it, I'm standing on the threshold of my new home. The mahogany door in front of me is massive. The limo is already driving away.

I lift my fist to knock, and the door swings open.

There, standing in front of me, is my purchaser.

Mr. Calum McNeal is shorter than I realized. My white leather boots have two-inch heels, and they put me at eye level with him. He's simply dressed in wool slacks and a button-down shirt. There are lines around his eyes, his face cracked from too much sun. But his smile is kind.

"Welcome to McNeal Manor." He steps backward, inviting me into his space. When I walk past him, I smell the soft, woodsy scent of his aftershave.

"I'd shake your hand, but —" Mr. McNeal wiggles his fingertips. "I had surgery yesterday. All my finger-chips were removed. I lost a day at the office, but I thought you would be more comfortable this way. Now you know I'm not connected."

I smile quickly, fleetingly. At least he can't take pictures of me with his hands, no matter what else he does with them.

The great hall is gigantic. There are three stories of innately carved wood. Tapestries hang from the ceiling. An enormous fire burns in the hearth. The whole room is warm, and heat radiates through the marble floor.

"You have a beautiful house," I say. It's the truth. Everything about this place is stunning, except for the security cameras in the corners. Mr. McNeal notices my glance.

"Deactivated. Nobody needs to see you but me. At least for now. I'm sorry, but there was so much retrofitting needed for your arrival that the workers didn't get to those yet. But I want you to know that when you're in the manor, your privacy is completely secure. That's as important to me as it is to you. The indoor cameras will be removed tomorrow, but the security cameras will remain outside. Let me show you around."

He offers his elbow, and I link my arm with his. It's strange to be so close to the person who controls my fate for the next twenty-five years.

Mr. McNeal leads me down the hall. "All of my employees have gone through the strictest security clearance and are entirely trustworthy."

"That's good to know, Mr. McNeal."

"Please, call me Cal."

"Yes, Cal. Of course, Cal."

We move through room after room, all filled with artwork and antiques. Most of the rooms seem quiet, as if they have been unused for some time. Boston ferns grow in porcelain planters by every window. The red carpet cushions my footsteps.

"The house is still connected, I'm afraid," Cal says. "There's no way to run a household Net-free anymore without major remodeling. That set-up you have at Tabula Rasa is practically archaic." He looks at me quickly. "I don't mean any offense by that."

"None taken."

We're on the second floor now, approaching a metal door that appears newly installed.

"I want you to be comfortable, Blanca, so this suite is all yours. Your rooms are lined with lead. No electronic device will work inside them." Reaching into his pocket, Cal pulls out a key.

I guess this is the part where I get locked up.

"My own cloister?" I ask.

"Yes." But then Cal does something shocking. He places the key in my palm. "You have full access to the entire estate. I hope you will be happy here." He smiles again, kindly.

I don't know what to say or do next. We are both silent for a moment, his hand still in mine. I know I don't have a choice.

This is my lot in life as a Vestal Geisha. It doesn't matter that Cal's over fifty.

That's when the silence is broken by a buzzing sound coming from his wrist.

"My old chip-watch," he says. "A high-school graduation present from my parents back in 2030. The staff had to dig around in the attic to find it, but it still works great." Cal glances down at the message and scowls. He types something quickly with his knuckle, his fingertips too bandaged to function.

"I'm sorry, but I have to go. There's a problem at work. I'll be back for dinner, okay? We'll get started then." Cal leans in and kisses me on the cheek. "I'm glad you're here. I've been waiting for someone like you for a long time."

As soon as he turns away, I shudder.

I don't completely relax until I've deadbolted the door behind me. Cal said I have free range, but maybe that's a test. I'd better stay put.

My new room is quiet. One entire wall is full of books, the old-fashioned kind with actual pages. Another wall has windows, shielded by a massive stone-wall courtyard below. A third wall is completely mirrored. In the center of the room is a canopy bed with a velvet coverlet. By the door is a glossy white desk, stocked with stationary.

Somebody has thought of everything.

I take off my traveling cloak and lay it across the bed. Then, looking down at it, I lie down too, burying my face in the fabric. I can still smell the faint scent of Tabula Rasa. I'm cut off from everyone, exhausted by the unknown. Thinking about the familiar brings tears. But when I wipe my eyes with the hem, I feel a folded sheet of paper slip out of my cloak pocket.

Dear Blanca,

My favorite words Barbelo Nemo ever spoke were: "See with your eyes. Hear with your ears. Listen for the directions that will come."

I share that wisdom with you now because anticipating your purchaser's wishes is the most difficult part of being Geisha.

But remember: clarifying questions are your friends.

Follow your Vestal training. Keep yourself private, and everything will be all right.

You are lucky, my dear girl. Nobody will ever know if your life is a success or a failure. Whichever path your life takes, it won't be your fault.

I'll make sure you get invited to the Vestal corporate banquet in a few months, one way or another. Hold on till then.

Ms. Lydia

I fall asleep with Ms. Lydia's letter in my hand. I dream about her heart-shaped face blessing me and my new life.

Sometime later when I finally open my eyes, the afternoon is fading. Dust motes float in the air as the last rays of sunlight pour through the window. That's when I notice hardware handles on the wall of mirrors. They're actually doors, and they open to a large dressing room. There's an entire wardrobe of white! At least I'll be able to honor my Vestal vows of dress.

Vestals forsake all color. We wear white as a symbol of purity and trust. If Cal had dressed me in color, I wouldn't have been able to return to Tabula Rasa when my contract was fulfilled.

But maybe these clothes hold other keys to my future.

I walk past each row of clothes and run my hands across the garments. There are skirts and dresses of every length, plus leggings and jeans. Each item hangs neatly on a wooden hanger. These clothes tell me nothing about what Cal wants from me.

Maybe I'll have better luck with intimates.

The top drawer of my new bureau is lined with cedar. Silk, lace, and chiffon are nestled in sachets of lavender. Everything is much finer that what I'm used to, but again, I learn nothing.

From my bedroom, a clock chimes five o'clock. It's time to prepare for the night.

When Cal knocks on my door about an hour later, I'm sitting at my desk, wearing a silk skirt, camisole, and cashmere sweater. I've spent the past ten minutes trying to compose a letter to Fatima, but the words won't come.

Cal is wearing a tweed jacket, the kind with patches at the elbows. He seems nervous as we walk through a series of drawing rooms to dinner.

Neither of us says anything.

Before we turn into the dining room, Cal stops. We pause in front of a beautiful painting of a young woman. She has brown hair, like me, and is standing barefoot in a field of flowers. A golden pendant hangs from her neck.

"My wife, Sophia," Cal says. "A beautiful person, on the inside and out. She could play the cello and harp. She could," Cal stops himself, without finishing his sentence. "She's gone now," he says simply. Then he clears his throat and leads me into dinner.

When Cal pulls out the chair for me to be seated, I see small beads of sweat at his temples.

Dinner is not the plain fare I'm accustomed to. Fish, vegetables, the occasional piece of fruit; Vestal training dictated every morsel of food I ever ate. The spandex Tabula Rasa uniforms are unforgiving.

Now that I've been harvested, I'm supposed to eat whatever my purchaser provides. There are platters of roast beef smothered in gravy, golden yams, and Caesar salad. Cal's eating a dinner roll lavishly spread with butter, so I do the same. The taste is so rich that I forget my fear. I lose myself in the pleasure of eating.

But before long I remember who I am and what I'm here for. So I put down the bread and get to work. I give Cal the full force of my smile. "I really appreciate everything you've done for me, Cal. I've never had my own room before."

"I'm glad you like it. I used Sophia's old decorator. She has exquisite taste." Cal takes a large drink of wine. When he sets down his wineglass, it hits silverware, making a clinking sound.

"I need to show you something. Will you be offended if I show you a website?"

My silence is so thick you could cut it with a knife. Cal activates his chip-watch and displays *Veritas Rex*, the blog that broke my picture. I can see myself now, floating on the silvery screen coming from Cal's watch. If he moves his arm to the right, it will look like I am kicking my water glass.

There are a bunch of non-Vestal advertisements on it and other junk like that, but the thing I notice the most is the inky black snake that slithers across the page. I've seen that snake before. It was on a face, staring up at me from asphalt.

"That's the Virus who took my picture!"

"Yes," Cal says, "and now he's in jail."

"Good."

"It's more complicated than that."

"How can it be more complicated? That Virus can rot forever, as far as I'm concerned. He stunned two security guards, broke into Tabula Rasa, *and* stole my privacy. Jail sounds like justice to me."

Cal winces like I struck him. "That Virus is my son."

Well then. I scrape my fork across my dinner plate like there's something left to eat. "I'm sorry," I say. "I didn't know."

Cal scrolls the pages until his son's picture appears. Of course I look at it. I have to.

The Virus is dressed in leather, covered in tattoos, and sitting astride a motorcycle. Dark hair sticks up every which way, and there's a defiant edge to his face.

"So that's your son."

Cal nods. "Yes. He calls himself Veritas Rex now, and has been a viral blogger for the past five years. But his mother and I, we named him Seth." His voice catches a little bit. Then Cal taps his watch and closes the visual. He pours himself another glass of wine but doesn't offer me the decanter. "There's no easy way to say this, so I'll come out with it and leave it at that. I purchased you as bait."

Bait? My stomach feels too full. The rich food is catching up with me.

Cal sweats harder. He speaks in a rush. "My son hasn't spoken to me in five years. But I know, *I know*, that with you living in my house, it will be impossible for him to stay away. A blogger like Seth won't be able to resist easy access to a Vestal."

I consider this. Before I can say anything, Cal hurries on.

"We'll say you're my daughter," he says. "That I'm adopting you."

"But really you want me for your son?"

"Exactly! I want you to bring Seth back into my life, one way or another."

A Vestal should never be with a Virus. But Cal's paid thirty-two million dollars to say otherwise. And I'd gladly play with a son instead of an old man.

"Pull up the picture again, please."

Cal shoots off the picture of Seth one more time. I lean across my dinner plate to examine it closely.

Seth's eyes are dark, not like Cal's at all. They are rimmed with black, almost like he's wearing eyeliner. A scar cuts across the bottom corner of his chin. A pendant hangs across his neck, tied with a red cord.

I've seen that necklace before. It's the same lion-faced snake medallion that Seth's mother was wearing in her portrait. It's the same animal on his website and on his face.

"What happened to your wife?" I ask point-blank.

Cal takes another long drink of wine. "She left us too soon," he says. And then he tells me the whole sordid story.

Sophia McNeal is never coming back, that much is clear. But maybe Cal is right. Maybe his plan will work. Because I can be anyone Cal wants me to be, especially a daughter. Ms. Lydia made me practice that role extensively.

I can do other things too. I've been trained for every possibility. I can hurt, I can heal, I can hook, and I can release.

If Cal wants me to lure Seth back into his life, I can do that.

The only thing I can't do is fall asleep on my own.

My cloister is quiet and darkened by shadows. I know the door is bolted shut, but it doesn't help. There's no murmur of breathing, no shuffling of feet.

Rolling on my side, I pull the covers up tightly around my shoulders. If I concentrate hard enough, maybe I can still picture it. The Tabula Rasa bunk beds. My old black sleep shirt. Ms. Corina wandering the aisles, giving instructions.

"Relax your forehead," she'd say. "Then your cheeks, then your smile." Ms. Corina's voice was always sickly sweet. *"Lie back and straighten your spine until you feel yourself lifted from above. You're a little cloud floating in the sky above the whole world. And you're*

placid. Perfectly placid."

Fatima used to mock her for using the word "placid" so often. *"Charming Corina is such an idiot,"* she'd say. *"Why can't she say 'calm'?"*

But I'm trying not to think about Fatima or Ethan, Beau, and the rest. It's too hard, thinking about my friends.

So maybe if I try hard enough, I can still do it. I can be calm, I can be placid, and I can fall asleep all by myself.

I'm still a Vestal even though I'm alone. I'll always be a Vestal, no matter what happens.

I have everything I need to achieve happiness.

Chapter Three

Vestals don't usually free people from jail. But if this is what Cal wants, I have to do it. He asked Headmaster Russell to send over the paperwork this morning, dropping all charges against Seth for the crime of trespassing on Tabula Rasa property with the intent to cause harm.

Thankfully the car Cal's provided me with is pretty opaque. That's good, because I've never been out in daylight before, except that one ride from Tabula Rasa to my new home at McNeal Manor.

I've been dreaming about sunshine forever. But usually, those dreams are nightmares.

Back at Tabula Rasa, they infused our water with vitamin D so we wouldn't get rickets. It's better that way. The outside world is dangerous for a Vestal. Somebody might see us and tell people where we are. Or worse, they might take our picture. Then we'd be overexposed like everyone else, unable to control our own profile because our privacy was gone.

Vestal purchasers pay good money for our digital purity. Cal has taken every precaution. This limo has dark windows, a lead-lined interior, and a vetted driver named Alan.

"As soon as you close the windows between us," Alan tells me, "you are completely cloistered. Mr. McNeal made me guarantee your privacy. So tap on the window if you need something because I won't be able to hear you."

But I don't close the window between us. Driving through Silicon Valley is overwhelming, and it's nice to have the company.

All the newsboards offer support too. Each one we pass shows a Vestal I know. It's only a matter of weeks before my friends are up there too. Beau leaning against a truck with his arms around Fatima; Ethan looking totally smart, like he actually knows how to make finger-chips.

A truck company, a fashion house, a chip manufacturer; the only surprise at our Harvest was me. I wish I could be like my friends and still feel normal.

Right now it feels like my scarf is strangling me. I rip it off my neck and gasp for breath.

It took me forever to decide what to wear. Dressing for criminals was not covered in school. I finally settled on a bundled-up number with a scarf, tank top, leather jacket, and my high-heeled boots. With my hat and glasses, I'm almost entirely shrouded in white.

By now we're in the parking lot of the county jail. "Good

luck then, Ms. Blanca." Alan opens the door for me and nods.

I smile back weakly and step into the light. Heat hits my cheeks, and I feel like I'm on fire. The sunshine is blazing! I can barely see it's so bright. I stumble a bit as I walk up the path.

Grime, sweat, and desperation; the odors assault me as soon as I enter the precinct. The public waiting area is packed with people, some of them so covered in tattoos that their skin is no longer visible. Most of them stare at video screens coming from their finger-chips. The rest gaze into space, totally wacked out on drugs.

I head straight for the VIP section because Headmaster Russell made some calls before I came over. He knows all the right people. Even though I'm protected by privacy glass, I pull up my scarf anyway. I keep my glasses on too, like I'm an old-time movie star.

But the VIP section isn't as a great as it sounds. The officer on duty is middle-aged, nondescript, and lumpy in places she shouldn't be lumpy. She sits at the counter, too engrossed in her palm game to do her job. I hear tinny music emanating from the speakers in her thumbs. She completely ignores me after several minutes of me patiently waiting.

That is her first mistake.

I clear my throat. "I'm here to drop charges against Seth McNeal."

"Name?" she says, clicking on her palm. She's got fake purple eyelashes and insolence emanating from every pore.

"Blanca."

"Last name?"

"I don't have a last name. I'm a Vestal."

"Don't be a wise-ass," she says.

That was her second mistake.

The officer holds out her hand, trying to scan me.

"I can't be scanned because I don't have finger-chips," I say. "I told you, I'm a Vestal."

Finally, the officer looks up. "No way." Then realization dawns as her scan fails. "You're unreadable!" she blurts, examining me closer. "Show me your wrist."

I fight to stay composed. I smooth my expression and hold out my left arm, pulling back my sleeve.

She picks up my wrist in her technology infested hands and rubs my platinum cuff. "Oh my God! It's really you! You're the Vestal from the picture!"

I withdraw my hand and wipe it on my clean, white jeans. I'll have the maid bleach them when I get home. This tech-addict never should have touched me.

That is her third mistake.

"4-3-8-5-7-2-9."

"What?"

"4-3-8-5-7-2-9," I say again. "Your badge number. I'm memorizing it."

"What do you need to know my badge number for?"

"I have a responsibility."

"Huh?"

I look at her right in the eyes. "Technology is no excuse to be rude. I hope you get help for your addiction."

"What?"

"People matter, not your palm. Now please get me what I need so I can drop the charges against Seth McNeal."

Paperwork, forms, an old-fashioned pen—she has to hunt them down because I refuse to type. She scrambles, but it's too late.

Tech-addicts need to be cleaned from the inside out. That's what Barbelo Nemo wrote. *Vestals have a responsibility to avenge all wrongs, especially when our honor is assaulted.* When I get home to the manor, I'll write Headmaster Russell a letter and tell him Officer 4385729 ignored me, called me a "wise-ass," and touched me without permission. He'll want to know.

But right now, I need to focus.

The new officer who leads me through the corridors to the jail cells is refreshingly obsequious.

"There're no cameras in here, Ms. Vestal. And the walls are lined with lead, so you'll be safe." The officer pauses and smiles at me shyly. "I've never met a Vestal before. My mom told me that they bless people. Is that true?"

"Yes." I smile. "Would you like to be blessed?"

"If you don't mind," the officer asks, sheepishly.

"Of course not. What's your name?"

"Stanley Francis."

We are standing at the door to the jail cells. The room is gray and stale.

I look at Stanley full in the face. "Stanley Francis, you have a hard road. In so many ways, it's difficult being you. But I know that you can do it. You have everything you need to achieve happiness." I bring my cuff to my heart, and the moment is complete.

"Thank you." I think there might be a tear in Stanley's eye, but I pretend not to notice. "Let's get you on your way," he says.

"If you don't mind, I'd like a few minutes to talk to the Virus first, while he's still locked up."

"Of course, Ms. Vestal. I'll be a few feet away. If you need anything, let me know."

I walk through a river of catcalls. Every last dirtbag I pass hoots and hollers. Cal was upset that his only son was surrounded by criminals, but I'm going to make things right. My very presence will make these prisoners suffer. I let my scarf fall down and show some skin.

"Hey, baby! No need to wear white after I'm done with you."

"Bring some of your blessings my way, sugar!"

"You only thought you knew what private meant!"

The only inmate not saying anything, not noticing me, is Seth. When I stand right in front of his cell, he still lies slumped on the ground.

I crouch down, wrapping my arms around my knees, but not letting my butt hit the floor. "Veritas Rex?"

"Who's asking," he mumbles. But when Seth finally sees me, he scrambles to sit up straight. "Holy shit, it's you!"

"Yes. And you're the Virus who took my picture."

Neither of us says anything further. I search Seth's face for some sign of his father, but all I see is his mother. Brown-black hair bolts straight up and matches the dark eyes from Sophia's portrait. Seth's muscular forearms stretch the confines of his orange jumpsuit. I struggle not to inspect his tattoos. When Seth slowly starts to smile, the way his mouth turns up at the corners reminds me of Cal. But then his smile turns acrid, and any familiarity is gone.

"What are you doing here, Vestal? Have you come to gloat?"

"Not at all. I'm here to release you."

"Yeah, right."

"No, really," I say. "That's what I'm here for."

"Then why am I still locked up?"

"Because I wanted to talk to you first."

Seth clenches his fists and gives me a once-over. "Hey, are you still a Vestal? Did that picture get you kicked out?"

I hold up my wrist so he can see my platinum cuff.

"Top pick, huh? I guess you're here to thank me then." Seth smiles wickedly. There's a spark in his eye that's incendiary, like I could be his fuse.

"It turns out that your picture was the best thing that ever happened to me," I say.

"Yeah? Which company have you sold your soul to?"

I take a deep breath. If Seth ruffles me, then it's all over.

"Vestals don't sell their souls." I try not to sound annoyed. Instead, I launch a different tactic. "Vestals don't always get harvested by companies."

That catches his interest.

"You mean you went Geisha?"

I nod and look away, my cheeks burning. I know what people whisper about Geishas, but it doesn't matter.

Now I've got his attention. Now the fun can really start.

"It's better than I could ever imagine. He's so sweet to me, and kind and thoughtful. I never thought I could be this happy."

"Some old guy buys you and you're happy?"

I grip the bars, and my face is as close to Seth's as possible. He leans in too, and our noses almost touch.

"Does age matter when you feel like you've known someone your whole life? He makes me feel seen and heard. That's the most important thing."

"Only a Vestal would say shit like that." But Seth doesn't pull away. He puts his fingers on the bars right below mine, so that we're closer than ever. I feel his eyes linger on me, on my eyes, and then my mouth.

"I'm here to release you, Rex. It only seems fair. You made me the happiest Vestal ever. So yes, I guess I am here to thank you. And to make things fair." I pull away from the bars and look down at the white tips of my boots. This next part is critical. The most important part. "There's just one thing," I practically whisper. I shake my finger between us both. "This has to be our secret."

"Why?"

"My purchaser does not know I'm here."

"You didn't tell him?"

I shake my head. "I'm not sure he would be forgiving. So do we have a deal? I have to know you're not going to blog about this to the world."

"But the truth never hurts anyone," Seth protests.

"Total privacy," I insist. "Take it or leave it."

Seth stares at me. His face has a weird sheen to it, like he's diseased or in pain. Tech-withdrawal is taking its toll. "I can't sit on the truth," he says.

That's when I get up to go. "If you're not interested, goodbye."

"Wait!" Seth calls after me.

I'm already headed toward the door. The other inmates mark my departure with a fresh round of suggestions.

"I promise!" Seth yells after me.

I pretend not to hear.

"Blanca, wait!"

Finally, I pause.

The dirtbags around me are practically frothing now that they know my name. The thing is, I don't know how Seth ever learned it. He's been incarcerated since he was hauled away. How does he know my name is Blanca? That information wasn't released until after my Harvest. By the time it was blaring on every newsboard in the world, Seth was already locked up.

I turn around and walk back to Seth's cell. This time, I don't crouch down to his level. "How do you know my name, Rex?"

Seth stands up and peers down at me. He's a lot taller than his dad. He holds up his hands so I can see the chips. "I'm a Virus, sweetheart. Ordinary measures of protection don't keep me out."

"Then why have you been locked up in this jail all month?"

Now it's Seth's turn to flush. I must have hit him where it hurts. I'll be sure to remember that for the future.

"I heard you and that other Vestal talking," he says, "before I took your picture."

"So you're not only a thief, you're also a sneak."

"I'm sorry."

I don't say anything. I don't need to. I let my silence weigh in on Seth for a second so he can't be sure if I will help him or not. I want him to know that there are consequences to being a toad.

Finally, Seth wags one of his hideously maimed fingers between us. "Private," he says. "I won't tell anybody about this."

"Anything about me ever," I correct. "I'm completely off limits."

"Okay."

"Swear it."

Seth holds up his mother's pendant, the lion-faced cobra, and kisses it. "I promise," he says.

And like a fool, I believe him.

Seth's hands shake the whole ride back to town. There's a sticky stench in the car, and it's not coming from me. It emanates from Seth, the tech-addict sitting to my right, who probably hasn't showered in days. Alan has already put up the lead-lined divider, and we're completely cloistered.

"The batteries are dead," Seth mumbles. "I can't charge them in here for some reason. Couldn't we pull over for a minute?" He's practically incoherent. "I need to check my feed. I need to —"

"No," I interrupt. "I've already been gone too long."

"It's been almost forever." Seth wiggles his finger-chips. "I need to see my hits."

"*You* need to take a deep breath." But I can't ignore the fact that he's suffering.

I look down at my cuff. The blank slate of my arms is a crazy contrast to the wall of tattoos covering Seth's biceps. Sometimes physical comfort helps, so I grab Seth's hands in mine. The shaking goes right through me. I'm totally clueless about tech-withdrawal, but I do know about comforting someone who's hurting.

When we turned fourteen and had our operations, Fatima was a mess for weeks. Every night in our cloister, I'd hear her crying on the bunk right above me. I'd climb up with her and lay my head on her pillow.

"It'll be okay," I'd say. But Fatima would sob and sob.

"I'll never have children," she'd weep. "I'll never be a mother."

"That's not true," I'd whisper. "When you're harvested, your company will assign a family to you. Someday they'll harvest a Vestal for you and then you'll be a Vestal-mom."

"To a teenager, not a baby!"

I never knew what to say to that. *Sterilization is for our own good,* Barbelo Nemo wrote, but Fatima didn't care. So I would put our wrists together and say the Vestal blessing.

"Fatima, you have a hard road. In so many ways it's difficult being you. But I know that you can do it. You have everything you need to achieve happiness."

I wonder if the blessing would help Seth too.

"Can't you drop me off on some corner?" he begs.

"So you can go online? You're so desperate to get your finger-chips charged that you can't spend five more minutes in the car with me?"

Seth laces his fingers around my hand. I feel his sweaty arm press into mine. He stares at me with glazed eyes. "Please, Blanca. I need to see what's happening with my site. I need to see my hits."

I try to let go of his grasp, but I can't. "Fine. I'm due at McNeal Manor anyway. Cal will miss me."

I rap on the divider with my free hand, but Seth stops me. Muscles rope through his neck, and he takes deep breaths through his nose.

"Who's Cal?" he asks, his voice rising.

"My purchaser, Calum McNeal. What's the matter, Rex?" I've been very careful to call him "Rex" and not "Seth."

He doesn't say anything for a minute. Seth stares at me, examining my every inch, right down to the yellow specs in my green eyes. I fight the urge to grab my scarf, to wrap myself up in fabric so I can't be seen anymore.

"You were bought by Calum McNeal?"

"Harvested," I correct. We're still holding hands. I wish I could let go, but Seth's grip is strong.

"And you're happy?"

"Happier than I ever thought possible." I smile knowingly.

Seth slumps back in his seat. His shaking has stopped, but I can feel his pulse pound through his fingertips.

Now's the perfect time to turn the screw.

"Cal is wonderful," I say. "He's so kind and generous and attentive. He makes me feel like a princess." I lean in close to Seth and whisper in his ear. "Thanks to you, I'm a happy woman."

When the car stops at a random corner downtown, Seth is still. He turns and looks at me with eyes filled with so much kindness that I can almost overlook the ugly snake inked across his face. "Be careful," Seth says. "The world isn't made for Vestals."

"I don't want to be part of the world. Cal provides everything I need."

Seth swallows hard. "Like I said, be careful." He holds my hand for several moments too long before finally letting it go.

"Thank you," Cal says to me when I tell him the whole story. "I know that must have been difficult." We're in the dining room, eating a cozy dinner for two.

"I've never been so close to tech-addicts before," I say. "Seth and that precinct officer could barely function without their finger-chips."

Cal laughs. "It's how the world works. Everyone's a tech-addict."

"You're not!"

"Of course I am. I'm just not as bad off as a Virus."

"That's not true. You don't have finger-chips anymore."

"But I'm totally reliant on my chip-watch. Without the Internet, my entire company would go under."

I take a knife to my lamb. The mint sauce is disgusting.

"You're nothing like Seth at all," I say, "despite your chip-watch. He destroys people's lives for a living. He digs up dirt. He publishes secrets. *Veritas Rex* is the dirtiest virtual tabloid I've ever seen."

"And how many online tabloids have you seen?"

I stab more veggies. "Only this one. But I've read all about them in my textbooks."

Cal smiles, and the corner of his mouth twitches. "Textbooks? Printed pages are yesterday's news. That's why Viruses like Seth are so successful. They're on the front lines of stories. Yes, sometimes they go too far and sometimes they break the law, but they share information that people care about."

"More like steal information that's none of their business."

"Sometimes, yes."

"Viruses hurt people," I say. "Some of them are violent!"

"Seth's not. He'd never assault anyone to get a story."

"Physical violence isn't the only way to cause harm." I think about the Tabula Rasa parking garage and the instant when Seth ripped all my future plans away. "Viruses hurt people. I can't believe you're defending them."

"I'm not defending them, I'm illustrating a point. What Viruses do isn't black and white. In many cases, they're public workers. They bring knowledge out into the open. And even if they were entirely in the wrong, Seth is still my son. Virus or no, he'll always be my flesh and blood."

I take a deep breath. I hope I haven't offended Cal. I know better than to have argued with my purchaser. Thankfully Headmaster Russell isn't here to witness my infraction. I shiver, remembering my training.

I have to be sure. Can I trust Cal? Can I trust him to know what he wants?

"You want to be a father again," I say. "But just to Seth, right? You're not looking to start over?" *It never hurts to clarify.*

Cal's eyebrows shoot up and then furrow. "No," he says quickly. "I want a second chance with Seth, that's it. One kid who hates me is enough."

Okay then. *Now's the time to make Cal feel important.* That's what Barbelo Nemo would say. *If you want to control somebody instead of be controlled, tell that person what they want to hear.*

"Then you need to stop thinking of yourself as a bad father," I say, "and start thinking of yourself as a good person who's on the road to getting his son back into his life."

Cal doesn't say anything. He stares down at his asparagus.

"A grand gesture," I continue. "You're showing Seth that you're the type of father who will do whatever it takes to win back his son. How can Seth say no to that?"

"Do you think it will work?"

"Of course it will. If you want to be a good father, then I want that too. I'm going to make it happen."

I say that because I have to, never mind that I still don't know where I fit into all this. Cal wants to be a father to Seth. Not to me. What will happen when this is all over? Does Cal want me to *lure* Seth or *be* with Seth? Is there still a chance Cal wants me for himself afterward?

"Do you think tomorrow night will work?" Cal asks. "I know that if I invite the McNeal Solar Enterprises board of directors to a party in your honor, they'll come. But what about Seth? He's never bothered to show up before."

"He'll come," I say, tapping on my platinum cuff. I fake a confidence I'm not sure I deserve.

"I hope so." Cal folds his napkin. "I'm banking on it."

Chapter Four

Wrap me in silk, twirl me around, and tie up my chest with diamonds. My bare arms are cold, even though Cal has every fireplace in the house burning. I lean into his shoulder and drape my wrist around his arm. His wool jacket is scratchy but warm.

"I didn't think I'd be so nervous," Cal says as we descend the stairs. There are executives everywhere, filling up the great hall. The McNeal Solar Enterprises board of directors is out in full force, watching my every step.

"You'll be fine." I try to sound reassuring, but I'm not used to so many strangers. Invisible butterflies beat in my stomach. In mere seconds, an older lady in a sequined top approaches, her black hair pulled tight in a French twist with a fleur-de-lis inked on her neck.

Cal whispers in my ear. "Here comes Nancy Robinson, my attorney. Don't let her manners fool you. Nancy is a shark, and the whole board listens to her opinions."

"Cal, darling!" Nancy gushes. "I've been dying to come as soon as I got the invitation." She holds out her hand to be kissed, which Cal does, graciously.

"Nancy, I'd like you to meet my new daughter, Blanca."

"Daughter?" Nancy's tattooed eyebrows arch. "Is that what you're calling her?"

"Yes," Cal answers.

"How … unexpected," Nancy says. There's an uncomfortable pause. Other guests join the circle, hungry for information.

I want to tell Cal he doesn't have to say anything. His private business is just that— private. But Cal's not a Vestal, so he keeps talking. "My wife, Sophia, was fascinated by the Vestals."

Nancy's jaw sets into a fake smile, and her teeth glisten. "Sophia was a wonderful person," she says. "A true genius."

I feel Cal's arm flex right below my elbow.

"You'll get no arguments from me. My wife was the most brilliant anthropologist Stanford ever had. And she was mesmerized by the Vestals. Sophia wrote her dissertation on Barbelo Nemo."

"That quack," Nancy says, her face flat and shiny.

"He's not a quack!" I say.

"She speaks!" somebody from the back of the crowd pipes up.

Cal places a hand on my arm, already linked with his, and gives a little pat. "Sophia was inspired by Barbelo Nemo," he says.

"She was amazed that he could create something so powerful in forty-five years."

"Fifty, now," I correct.

"Whatever happened to Barbelo Nemo?" Nancy asks. Her gray silk skirt swishes around her.

"That's private," I answer. Barbelo has retreated to Plemora now, his estate at an unknown location. But that's nobody's business either.

"You mean you don't know or you can't say?" Nancy asks.

Heat prickles up my spine as I feel everyone watch me. I know these strangers are hungry for information, but there's no way I'll betray my Brethren. So I offer a placid smile, straight from Ms. Corina's lessons in charm and deportment.

Cal clears his throat. "The mystery enchanted Sophia. She wanted to know the unknowable. Vestal secrets fascinated her. That's why I knew Sophia would have been concerned about that picture of Blanca gathering unfavorable attention before her Harvest. She would have felt responsible. She would have wanted to do something."

"Because it was Seth who took the picture?" somebody says.

"So it's true then?" another guest asks. "Veritas Rex is Seth?"

"Oh, please." Nancy swats the air with her hand. "Everyone's known that for ages."

"Yes," Cal admits. "That's not exactly privileged information."

"Seth's picture really caused chaos," Nancy says. "He stirred things up."

Cal nods. "I couldn't let Seth ruin a young Vestal's life. Sophia wouldn't have wanted that."

Inwardly, I flinch. My life wouldn't have been ruined, no matter what Cal thinks! *There are many paths a Vestal can take, and they all have honor.*

Nancy looks right at me. "The news feed said there were several men after you." I feel my skin turn clammy. "That man from Korea with the plastic surgery, a time-share billionaire from Florida, and the senator who got in trouble a few years ago with his intern."

I see delight in Nancy's eyes as she witnesses the effect her words have on me. I fight harder to stay composed.

"So happily for all, I get a new daughter instead," Cal says, a little too brightly.

The other party guests aren't looking at me anymore. Their eyes are on Nancy, waiting to see how she responds. The wait seems endless.

"Excellent," Nancy says at last. "I'm so happy for you both." Then Nancy throws her arms around me, and her earrings tangle in my hair. "Welcome to the McNeal Solar family, darling!"

"Thank you," I say, extracting myself.

After that, everyone wants to take my picture. Most people spend their whole lives and never meet a Vestal in person. But Cal doesn't let them.

"Part of Vestal culture is not to be photographed," he explains. "Unless it's to sell a product."

Vestals give blessings freely, but never their image. Vestal privacy belongs to their company. Or in my case, to Cal. But he doesn't want my picture out there either. That would ruin everything.

"Are you the new face of McNeal Solar?" a guest asks me.

I shake my head. "No."

"I want Blanca to have a normal life," Cal says. "There's no need for her to do anything but simply be," he lies.

So the party continues. I eat shrimp, I drink water, and I sample strawberries. I shake hands as Cal leads me through the room. But I'm not here to make conversation.

I am here as bait.

I feel his stare before I see him. The whole room goes silent when he enters the room. Probably nobody but Cal and I expected Seth to come.

He stands by the fire, dressed in a black tuxedo. He's so cleaned up he's practically a different guy than the one who was in my car a few days ago. Seth's hair is slicked back, and the tattoos shoot up his neck from a starched white collar. His hands are in his pockets as if he's trying to be causal, but his face is like iron.

I don't have to fake it. I'm completely stunned.

It's like I'm finally seeing Seth for the first time.

And he's blinding.

Fast as lightning, I tell my hormones to shut down. Sure, Seth looks different from every other guy I grew up with from Tabula Rasa. Yes, my pulse races at the sight of him in a way it never has around Beau or Ethan. But I am a Vestal, and Seth is a Virus. He's forbidden to me—unless my purchaser instructs me otherwise.

Tonight I have a job to do, and that's it. My heart pounds as

I lean into Cal and stage-whisper, "Who is he?"

It's showtime.

Cal squeezes my arm. Then he leads me across the room. "Blanca," he says. "Meet my son, Seth."

Seth stares at me, at my shoulders and at my neck. Then he glances at his father with the coldest chill ever. "Blanca and I have already met."

"We've met? Right. If stealing my picture and getting kicked is your idea of an introduction, then we're old friends. Too bad you didn't bother telling me your real name."

Seth smirks. "I was kind of busy."

I turn to Cal and glare. "You knew?" I pretend to accuse him. "You knew Veritas Rex was your son, and you didn't tell me?"

Cal feigns hurt. "Blanca, I should have told you. I'm sorry." His eyes meet Seth's. "You've seen her, okay? Now it's probably best if you leave her alone. You've done enough harm to Blanca already, so let her be and stay away."

I don't wait to hear Seth's answer. I flee.

The white silk of my dress billows after me like a sail. When I get to my room, I leave the door open, on purpose.

I don't have much time.

My skirt's detachable, and I rip it off. Underneath I'm already wearing my white spandex pants. They match perfectly with my strapless silk top. I throw on my leather jacket, zip on my boots, and start to climb through the open window, right as Seth walks in. Exactly like Cal predicted he would.

"He'll do precisely what I tell him not to," Cal told me before the party started.

"Where're you going?" Seth demands, bursting into the room.

"To get some air."

"What are you gonna do, jump? It's the second floor."

"There's a ledge," I counter.

Seth crosses the room in about two strides and slides his arm around my waist, pulling me back. "I've got a better idea." He sets me on my feet. "Let's go for a ride on my bike."

That wasn't the official plan, but Cal did say I could improvise. Maybe this will be easier than I thought.

Ten million stars light up the night. I can hear music piping out of the manor, but Seth and I are outside, standing in front of the biggest motorcycle I've ever seen. It's got the Veritas Rex cobra painted across each side.

"Here you go, princess." Seth hands me a helmet.

A *red* helmet.

"I can't wear that."

"Safety first, angel."

Again with the mocking! I wish Beau were here to teach Seth some manners. Or Fatima. She'd probably say something cutting.

"Sorry, Rex or Seth or whatever you name is. But there's no way I'm wearing color."

And just when I think I've lost, like I've totally failed my mission tonight and am going to have to walk back to the party in shame, Seth reaches into a saddlebag and pulls out a white helmet. "Try this one."

That's when I realize I haven't lost. But it's also when I realize my target is a lot cagier than I knew.

When I put on the white helmet, it's a perfect fit.

So that's how it happens. I'm on a motorcycle behind a Virus zooming through the night at top speed, my arms holding on to the guy for dear life. And Seth's jacket isn't scratchy like his dad's; it's smooth and tight, like him.

Adrenaline rushes through my brain, flooding out lucid thought. I fight to remind myself of my mission. But it's difficult because this is the first time I've ever really been outside. There's no car, no lead, and no security force protecting me. It's simply me, Seth, and the night. The freedom terrifies me, and I grip Seth tighter.

Occasionally Seth stops, when we come to a red light or an intersection, and people snap my picture. Am I a real Vestal or a copycat in white? They scan me to find out and shake their hands when their finger-chips register nothing. I have no virtual profile to bounce back.

Hopefully most people can't tell which Vestal I am under this helmet. But the possibility makes me quiver.

Sometimes the other drivers don't see us at all. They're driving away and finger-chipping at the same time. Seth swerves more than once so we don't get hit by idiots.

When Seth rolls to a stop at the top of a canyon, every square inch of my skin tingles with excitement. He takes off his helmet, so I pull off mine too. Nobody can see us up here. There aren't any eyes watching, only a cozy bench to sit on, under an ancient oak tree.

Seth helps me off the bike. "So you and my dad … "

"Yes." I take a steadying breath, and my chest heaves against the boning of my corset.

"He's a real douchebag."

"No. He's not."

Seth snorts and loosens his tie. "You don't know what you're talking about."

"Of course I do."

I sit down on the bench, and Seth joins me two seconds later. Warmth radiates between our touching legs.

"Isn't my dad, like, thirty-five years older than you?"

"So what?"

"*So what?*" Seth scratches his jaw. "Doesn't that creep you out?"

"Oh wait. You think —"

But before I can finish my sentence, Seth types the air. He pulls up *Veritas Rex*, and then I see the video.

There's Calum McNeal and a redheaded woman in bed. There are twisted sheets and nakedness everywhere. Seventeen-year-old Seth walks in on them, shooting video from his hand.

"What the hell are you doing, Dad?" teenage Seth yells.

The redhead turns away. You can't see her face because she tugs up the sheet. Cal looks guilty. Sweaty.

"Son?" he starts to say. "It's not what it—"

But then the video cuts out, and you never hear what Cal says next.

"I did *not* want to see that," I say, with all sincerity.

Seth shakes his fist, and the image disappears. "That was a

week before my mom died. The asshole was screwing another woman when my own mother was dying of brain cancer!"

"Seth—"

"And now you're doing him too!"

"I am not!" I leap to my feet. "It's not like that at all."

"Yeah? Then what's it like. Tell me. Why does an old man spend thirty-two million dollars on an eighteen-year-old Vestal?"

"Because he's lonely. Because he wants a daughter."

"A daughter?" Seth flexes his neck. "I don't believe it."

"It's true. He misses you. He misses your mom. He's lonely, and—"

"Don't talk about my mom!" Seth jumps up and kicks the tree trunk with his dress shoe.

I follow him, and we stand underneath the branches.

"I'm sorry," I say. And I genuinely am. What happened to Sophia was awful.

"You have no right to talk about her, and neither does my dad!"

I wait a second, not saying anything.

"She was a good mom," Seth whispers. "The best."

I put my hand in his. I'm not sure he notices.

"She didn't deserve any of that crap. That's why I posted the video online. That's why I started *Veritas Rex*."

"She deserved better."

Seth thinks I'm agreeing with him. "Yeah." He nods. "She did."

It's hard not to get riled up when the conversation has turned to everything I stand for as a Vestal. "It's not only the video, Seth.

Your mom didn't deserve to die in the first place. There never should have been a cancer epidemic. As soon as people realized cell phones were evil, they should've stopped using them."

Seth looks at me, bemused. "I wouldn't go so far to say cell phones were 'evil,' but they were shitty technology."

Even now, he's completely brainwashed.

"Shitty technology that killed people! And the tech companies didn't care. They wanted money, and the customers wanted tech. It's disgusting! The Brain Cancer Epidemic was the whole reason Barbelo Nemo founded Tabula Rasa to begin with."

"Is that why?" Seth asks. "I thought you guys were fancy spokespeople or something."

Irritation coils inside me. "That's only a small part of it."

"So what's the rest?"

"We follow a sacred calling. We are beacons of light in a dark world that's forgotten what's important."

Seth rolls his eyes. He clearly doesn't get it.

So I inch closer to him. "For centuries holy people … nuns … monks … hermits … they locked themselves away and took on the sins of the world. They were living sacrifices of prayer, and it made the whole world better. They kept knowledge alive through the Dark Ages. Vestals are living sacrifices too. We are reminders that you don't need chips and you don't need texts, and you shouldn't give away every last piece of yourself for one more hit."

"Because selling yourself is so much better?"

I square my shoulders. "Yes."

"But you'll never have a normal life. Doesn't that bother you?"

"Of course not. Not when 'normal' is so messed up. Not when 'normal' gave a whole generation of people brain cancer."

"*That* I get." Seth rubs the cord of his pendant. "My mom was always talking about you guys. Did you know that? She loved all things Vestal. That's why I took your picture."

I wonder what Seth's mom would say now.

We stand there in silence looking out across the city. The whole world feels huge and empty. If I reach up my arms, they'll touch sky forever. There's nothing holding me in and nothing protecting me. The only person between me and disaster is Seth.

"I should get back," I say. "Your dad will hate me being out so late."

Seth looks at me suddenly, like he's remembering why he brought me up here in the first place. "Why worry about a liar like him?" He steps closer and encircles me in his arms. "We've got all night." Seth smiles a wicked grin and bends down, brushing soft lips against mine.

I know what he's thinking. He's thinking he'll ruin my relationship with Cal forever.

But I'm the one who will ruin Seth. By the time I'm done with him, everything he knew to be true will be shattered. Veritas Rex will never be the same again.

So I curl my fingers around Seth's neck and deliver a perfect kiss. I let Seth put his infested hands all over me. They run down my back and under my butt cheeks. Our lips part, and our tongues intertwine. I tell myself I don't enjoy any of it.

When we finally come up for air, I put my cuff on his chest, the position for the tightest blessing. "Seth, you've had a hard road. In so many ways it's difficult being you. But I know that you can do it. You have everything you need to achieve happiness."

"You think so?"

"I know so," I answer. The blessing always works.

Tell people what they want to hear.

"Blanca, you're different than I thought you would be." This time when Seth smiles at me, it's for real. And when he kisses me again, I can tell he means it.

Exactly like Cal wanted.

"You don't have to go back," Seth says later, his arms swathed around me as we sit on the bench. "Come home with me instead."

"Why would I do that?" I stare out at the city lights.

"Because he's old. Because he's bad news, and because you deserve better."

"He is not bad news," I say. "He's your dad."

"What's he doing with you, then?"

"I told you. Cal's lonely. He wants a daughter." I try to sound certain, but I can't quite keep the edge from my voice. The lonely part is right, but Cal doesn't want a daughter. He only wants Seth.

Seth pulls me onto his lap. "You shouldn't trust him." He flexes his arms and I have the weird sensation of feeling safe. Protected. "Come home with me instead."

I look into Seth's eyes, unsure if he's being sincere or not. *Nobody outside Tabula Rasa is truthful. Everyone is jealous of Vestals.*

"What do you want?" I ask.

"To keep you safe."

"I *am* safe."

"Not from him, you're not."

I smile, trying to lighten the mood. "You're the one I need to be careful of. If I listened to you, I couldn't be a Vestal anymore."

"So give it up," Seth says. "Be your own person. Own your own life."

"I have a contract. Remember? A thirty-two-million-dollar deal."

"That's exactly why it's dangerous for you! My dad thinks he owns you."

"No," I say. "That's how come I know he'll protect me. Cal won't let anything happen to me, not when I cost him so much."

"You don't know him."

"Maybe *you* don't. When's the last time you and your dad talked?"

"No idea. I try to avoid him at all costs."

"So how are you going to see me again?" I pause. "Or do you not want to?"

Seth looks at me, right in the eyes. "Of course I want to. Don't be ridiculous."

I tuck my head on his shoulder and fake a sigh.

Fatima would have played this scene differently. But I'm not Fatima. I'll never be the seductress, but my girl-next-door tricks work pretty well too.

All the McNeal Solar Enterprises board members have left by the time Seth and I return home. It's way past midnight. Cal waits on the threshold, pacing back and forth underneath the columns.

Seth rides the motorcycle all the way up the drive and then revs the engine before he cuts it right in front of his dad.

I haven't taken my helmet all the way off, and Cal is already yelling.

"Where were you, Blanca? I was so worried!"

I'd think, "Nice touch," but Cal's a horrible faker. This rage is for real.

"I'm sorry, Cal. I was with Seth."

"And you couldn't leave a note?"

A note? The concept honestly never occurred to me. It's not like I've ever left someplace before.

"And you," Cal says, turning his anger to Seth. "How could you? You know privacy means everything to a Vestal like Blanca."

Seth's about to say something, but I don't give him the chance. Ugliness isn't going to help. So I physically place myself between the two of them and try to broker peace.

"Nobody saw us," I say. "Seth wouldn't do that to me."

"Think again." Cal taps his wrist and pulls up a video screen.

And there I am, plastered all over the Web again. I'm turning into a real Net-rat.

VERITAS REX JOYRIDES WITH BLANCA, the tag reads. I'm captured at a red light, my arms around Seth, my platinum cuff clearly visible.

"What did you do?" Cal asks Seth. "Did you pay somebody to follow you?"

Seth starts to protest, but I don't give him the chance.

"You did this?" I say, turning to him. "You tricked me?"

"Blanca, no—"

"What kind of bastard are you?" I shove my helmet into his stomach and then hightail it for the house. There're about a dozen workers in the great hall, cleaning up after the party. I try not to run over a maid on my way to the stairs.

I slide the deadbolt behind me as soon as I get to my cloister.

Chapter Five

I've got this thing I do when somebody yells at me. I keep my eyes open but I try to look behind me, like I can see through the back of my head. I sit up straight and pull my shoulders down. Then I start counting. Usually by the time I get into the thousands, the worst is over.

The trouble with Cal, though, is that he's not yelling at me when probably he should. He's still royally pissed about me taking off with Seth last night. Cal saws away at his toast like he's attacking it, but when he talks to me, his voice is eerily calm.

"I was improvising," I say again. I must have said that a million times, but Cal still seems disappointed. "I thought you'd be happy."

"I was worried about you."

"But I was with your son."

"Exactly!"

"But the plan—"

"The *plan* was for you to go for a walk around the estate where I could keep track of you."

"I was improvising," I repeat. "You told me to improvise. I don't know what else to say. I'm sorry! You know I'd never disobey you on purpose. I'm not like that."

Cal looks beyond frustrated.

"You should have realized that going off the estate was a bad idea."

"But you said I needed to get Seth alone, and I did. You said hook him, and I did that too!"

"But at great risk to yourself." Cal wrinkles his forehead.

"I made him like me," I say. "You said to make Seth like me, and you said I could improvise."

"You risked your safety! I would never ask you to put yourself in harm's way. I don't want you to merely improvise, either. I want you to make positive choices about your own welfare. You've got good instincts."

I shake my head. Cal's being ridiculous. "Good instincts? The one time I try to improvise it gets all messed up!"

"But it didn't get messed up. Alan was able to find you in time. We still got the picture." Cal adds sugar to his coffee.

"Just barely," I say. "I made it hard for Alan, and I didn't think about what you'd say or how worried you'd be." The tears are coming now, my training at work.

Cal's voice softens. "We still got the picture."

"But I worried you. I made you upset! *I disobeyed*!"

"It's okay. People make mistakes. No matter what Seth says about me, I'm not a monster."

"Of course you aren't. But I've been horrible. I probably ruined everything. Seth might never come back again!"

"That's not going to happen."

"How do you know?" I ask.

Cal looks down at his wrist for a second. "Because Alan texted me. Seth is riding up the driveway right now."

There's barely enough time to settle this. I need Cal to know that I'm trustworthy. "Please, Cal. Please tell me what to do, and I'll do it."

Cal squeezes my hand. Then he leans over and wipes a tear off my cheek. "No, Blanca. You tell me. What should you have done last night?"

"Stayed home?"

Cal considers this. "Maybe," he says. "But what should you have done before you left the house? You tell me."

I'm totally blank for a second, but then I figure out the answer Cal wants. "I should have left a note."

"Exactly! If you go someplace, leave a note."

"So what's the plan now?" I ask. "Seth will be here any minute."

"Do whatever it takes to keep him coming back." Cal picks up his fork and digs into his scrambled eggs with gusto. "Keep him interested long enough that I finally get the chance to talk to him again. That's all I want. A conversation with my son where he really listens."

"Do whatever it takes." I can do that.

I won't let Cal down again.

You'd never know Seth once lived here by the manner he stands in the doorway of the breakfast room, like he's an armed intruder. The way Cal glares at him, he might as well be. It might be my imagination, but I think Cal just grabbed the butter knife. Seth holds his motorcycle helmet in front of him like it's a shield.

"Can I talk to you, Blanca?" Seth speaks without crossing the threshold.

"Talk to her, yes. Take her somewhere, no," Cal answers for me.

"I wasn't talking to you!" Seth says. "I was talking to Blanca."

I look away and contemplate the wall. "I'm not sure that's a good idea, Seth." I stare at the wainscoting. It helps that I've been crying. "I'm not sure I can trust you."

That's what finally gets Seth to leave the doorway and venture inside.

"It wasn't me. I promise! I didn't take that picture. I didn't pay somebody to take that picture. I wouldn't do that to you."

I turn back from the wall. "How do I know you're not lying?"

"Because I'm not a liar!" Seth practically explodes. "Tell her," Seth says, finally looking at his dad. "Tell Blanca I'm not a liar."

"He's not." Cal pours a cup of coffee from a thermal carafe and offers it to his son. "Sit down and join us."

Seth pulls up a chair to sit down, but he ignores the coffee and doesn't bother looking at his father. "Blanca, please," he says. "Spend the day with me. Give me a chance to explain."

Cal puts down the coffee. "What exactly do you want to do with Blanca?"

"What do *you* want to do with her?" Seth's chair scrapes across the floor with a *screech.*

"Nothing," Cal protests. "I merely want her to have a home here, as my daughter."

"Your daughter? Well then, I guess I should get to know your 'daughter' better."

Cal takes a deep breath before he answers. "If Blanca wants to spend time with you, fine. But only if you stay here at the manor. And no pictures!"

"I would never." Seth looks at me. "What do you say?"

I give the tiniest of nods. "Okay. I'll give you one more chance."

"Great. Nothing bad will happen; you'll see." Seth returns his glare toward Cal. "So what do you want me to do? Hang out with Blanca in my old room?"

"I don't care where you go," answers Cal, "so long as you stay right here."

"Is my room still there? Or did you screw that up too?"

Cal shrugs. "It's been five years. You can't expect me to leave your room untouched all that time. You don't live here anymore."

Seth clenches his fist like he could crush something. "Come on, Blanca." He pushes away from the table. "Let's go."

Before I follow Seth, I look at Cal. He has an expression I barely recognize. It's empty but hopeful, all at the same time. He gives me a little wave as I follow Seth out the door.

Once his dad is out of sight, Seth strides around the manor

like he does own the place—or at least used to be prince of the castle. He grabs my hand, and I have to race to keep up with him. We pass my cloister and keep going, all the way to the far end of the hall. Then we cross to another wing where I've rarely ventured.

Finally we come to a door flanked by two potted palm trees. Seth pauses for a few seconds before he tries the knob. When it swings inward, all we see is darkness.

But then Seth turns on the light, and we're both in for a surprise.

"That bastard didn't change anything!" Seth says, entering his old bedroom. He walks over to a chair by the window and pulls open the drapes. Light floods the room, illuminating every untouched bit.

What I notice first are the bookshelves full of old trophies: soccer statues, swimming medals, and framed certificates. There're also a bunch of photos: framed pictures of Seth and his mom, Seth and his dad, and the whole McNeal family together. Something else catches my eye.

"You won a blogger award?" I ask Seth. "Last year?"

Seth comes over to look. "Yeah." He runs his hand over his head, tugging at the dark hair. "The cheat must've framed the news release."

"And look at this." I point to the top of the desk. "Look at all of these clippings." Paper printouts cover the surface, some of them yellowed with age. "Your dad must have been following your career."

"My dad wouldn't do that." Seth shuffles through the papers.

"Huh. This one was when *Veritas Rex* hit the millionth-visitor mark. That was a while ago."

"Cal never gave up on you." I touch Seth's arm. "Maybe there's more to your dad than you know."

"No. There's not." Seth contemplates a picture of his mom for a long time. Then he walks away from me and crashes onto the bed.

I let him. Vestals know better than anyone when people need their space. Instead, I turn back to all the pictures of happier days. Seth looked so much like Sophia, except when he was little and had enormous teeth. She was exquisite. I can tell by the pictures how much she loved him.

Then, for some reason, I can't look anymore. There's something inside me that's sharp and hurting.

Seth's room is painted cardinal red. There're baseball pennants pinned to the walls, a guitar in the corner, and a model airplane hanging from a wire in the ceiling. I pull out the wooden desk chair and sit down, taking it all in.

"He ruined everything," Seth says. I'm not sure if he's talking to the wall or talking to me.

But I know that Seth is wrong. Because no matter what Cal did, or whatever he does in the future, the past stands as it is. All this will remain, even when every last stick of furniture disappears.

Seth had it all. He had a childhood that I've only read about in books. When I buried my head under the covers of my metal bunk bed so nobody in the Tabula Rasa dorms would hear me cry, Seth was here in this room, getting tucked in every night by a mom and dad who loved him. No matter what he thinks, Seth had a great childhood.

Little League, guitar lessons, smiling pictures. A mom who decorated his room, a dad who still cares about him. Why can't Seth see any of that? Why does he have to be such a jerk?

Cal wants Seth in his life for some reason, so that's what I'm going to accomplish. Cal said to do whatever it takes to keep Seth coming back. I'll do whatever it takes, all right.

In the meantime, I'm going to teach Seth a lesson.

Someone needs to cut this Virus down.

Controlling people is easier than you'd think, Barbelo Nemo wrote. *All you need to do is make somebody feel important. A little appreciation goes a long way. People love to talk about themselves. Speak their name softly, melodically.*

Then you're halfway there.

Next you make them think that what you want is what they want, and that it was their idea in the first place.

Appeal to their nobler motives. And when all else fails, smile.

That placid smile of Charming Corina's works in almost every situation. So I decide to play this by the book. Seth is so upset right now that he'll be easy to work with. "Seth," I whisper, lying down on the bed next him. "It's a big deal, you coming here. I bet that wasn't easy."

"No, it wasn't." Seth rolls over to look at me, so that we're nose to nose. "But it was worth it."

"Just to see me? But you're so busy. I bet you have a million things to do for *Veritas Rex*. I didn't understand how famous it was until Cal told me."

"My dad talked about me?"

"A little bit. I know he's proud of you." I run my hand down Seth's arm, and we link fingertips. "So what was it like growing up in McNeal Manor?"

"Ordinary," Seth answers.

Like I'm supposed to understand what "ordinary" means. But it's a good opportunity to keep Seth talking.

"From those pictures it seems like you had the perfect family," I say.

"Until he ruined it."

"But you're better than that," I whisper. "You're a man who moves on, who fights for the truth." I lean in for a kiss.

I never thought I'd be this involved with a Virus. Seth slides his hand down my back and pulls me snugly against his body. I let him, because that might be what it takes to hook him.

But first I need to get Seth talking. He needs to remember the good things about Cal and start thinking about making things right, all on his own.

I put some space between us by tracing one of his tattoos. "What's this one for?" I touch a Celtic knot.

"Family trip to Scotland when I was fifteen." Seth breathes hard. "I snuck out when my parents were at a pub. Boy, did my mom roar when I came back after midnight. You should have heard her." Seth smiles a bit, but then the happiness fades from his expression. "That was our last big trip together before her diagnosis."

I slide my gaze down his chest. Another tattoo peeks out from under Seth's shirt.

"What's this one?" I point to something that looks Egyptian. "Is that … is that an aardvark?" I'll never understand tattoos, ever. Blank skin makes me feel safe from bad decisions. Why would Seth want to spend the next eighty years with an aardvark?

But Seth's not embarrassed at all. He pulls his shirt off so I can see it better—or maybe to see *him* better. And I have to admit, Seth has a fine physique to display. "That's the Egyptian god Seth. He's always shown with the head of an animal."

"So you think you're a god, do you?" I say, teasing. I rub my hands across a wall of pectoral muscles and ignore the fluttering in my stomach.

"What do *you* think?"

My hands freeze. "I think you took a totally perfect body and ruined it with tattoos," I answer truthfully.

"Everyone gets tattoos, Blanca. Blank skin is really alternative."

"That's not true!" I say. "Your dad doesn't have any."

Seth hoots. "Whoa! Well that answers *that* question once and for all."

"What are you talking about?"

"My dad *does too* have a tattoo. But it's not someplace people can normally see. It's practically the only part of him that wasn't visible in that video."

I feel my cheeks burn. Cal's surreptitious tattoo is not something I want to know about.

"Don't you want to know what it is?"

"No," I say. "I'd rather not." Of course, as soon as I say that I immediately begin wondering. It's like something you wish you could un-know.

"My mom had the same one." Seth nibbles behind my ears, trying to pique my interest. When I lay my head on his chest and don't respond, he kisses my hair. "What do Vestals have against tattoos anyway?"

"They're inauthentic," I say. "They get in the way of who you really are. When people see you, they don't see *you* anymore. All they see are your tattoos."

"But my tattoos are exactly who I am. Every last one!"

"Truly?" I lift my head. "There aren't any you regret? Not even this one?" I tap an elaborate angel, right next to a sun, on his inside biceps.

"I got that one when my mom died," Seth murmurs. He wants me to feel pity, I know it. But I'm tougher than that.

"What about this one?" I point to a scribble on his abdomen. "Who's Tiffany?"

"First girl I ever, you know … " Seth grins. He rubs his hand down the pristine skin of my arm.

I smile like I think it's funny. "I hope you're not expecting to tattoo my name on your butt any time soon."

"Maybe not today, but the future is ripe with possibility." Seth leaves the unspoken question hanging in the air. What exactly are we doing here on this bed? Seth with his shirt off. Me willing to please. He slides his hands up my leg, and then rolls me over, crushing me with his weight. "Should I stop?"

"Whatever it takes," Cal told me. *"Hook him. Keep Seth coming back for more."*

So I say it, because I have to say it. Because I've gone Geisha.

"No. I want you to keep going."

And the sick thing is part of me does want him to keep going. The part of me that's one human being attracted to another, higher morals be damned. The part of me I could never let the Vestals see in a million years.

Seth stares into my eyes with his crazily tattooed face. He knows I'm telling the truth, but he doesn't know all of it.

"Blanca," Seth whispers hoarsely. "Blanca, I—"

But I don't get to hear what he was planning on saying next. Right then his fingers twitch. I can feel them on my thigh. They vibrate so hard it hurts.

"Sorry, but I need a minute," Seth says. "An important message came through. I'll be right back."

I watch him head through the door to the bathroom, hungry for tech.

That fluttering feeling evaporates like steam. There's something twisted about a guy who would leave me lying here in bed to go look at stuff online.

My white silk catsuit fits like a glove. I climb out of bed and slip on my boots. I bend over and shake out my brown hair. Then I run my fingers along my scalp to lift the roots.

Seth is still in the bathroom, and I knock gently on the door. "Are you decent?"

"Sure thing," he answers.

I swing the door open and find Seth sitting on the edge of the bathtub. The lion-headed snake hovers on the visual, floating right in front of the toilet. Seth types away at the air, a blur of fingers.

"What are you doing?" I ask, leaning against the sink.

"Nothing about you. Don't worry. Although, man, every other tabloid out there is talking about you. Whoever sold that picture from last night made a whole lot of money."

"We're like pandas," I explain.

"What?"

"Vestals are like pandas. That's what the teachers at Tabula Rasa used to say. Vestals are like pandas, movie stars, and Amish people all rolled into one. We're so rare that everyone wants to take our picture. That's why we have to be so careful."

"Pandas, huh?" Seth says. "I guess you *are* kind of cute. But I don't think that's why they took your picture last night."

"Why, then?" My heart pounds hard. Did Seth find out about Alan?

"There's a bounty on your head," Seth answers. "The other Viruses are totally pissed that I scooped them with that first shot. They're desperate to get some more."

A flicker of fright crosses over me before I can fight it. I pull my face to neutral but not before Seth sees the fear.

"Don't worry, Blanca. You're safe here." Seth reaches for me, and I sit down next to him on the bathtub. "My dad may be a huge jackass, but I'm pretty sure you're safe at McNeal Manor."

I rest my head on Seth's shoulder. "So why are you here in the bathroom?"

"I had to do some updates on *Veritas Rex*."

"About what?"

"Some tips about other things came in while we were … " Seth raises his eyebrows at me. "I'm blogging them in."

But I'm already pulling away. "You couldn't go one hour." I'm unable to keep the edge from my voice. "Not one."

"I could! Give me a sec, and I'll be right back."

"No!" I stand, and my heels slam the tile floor. "You couldn't spend one morning with me without sneaking off to the Internet. I don't know what I was thinking. A Virus like you could never understand what's important to me. I can't believe I've been falling for a tech-addict! This was definitely a mistake."

I'm gone before Seth pulls down his screen.

A mistake is right. Seth is every bit as selfish and disloyal as my textbooks said. A Vestal like me could never fall for a Virus like him. Hopefully I've captured Seth's interest enough that I can keep my promise to Cal. But right now I could use some air to cool down my tingling nervous system.

The trouble with being somebody who doesn't go anywhere is that when I do try to leave, I have no idea where I'm going. I'm not familiar with this wing of the manor, and I can't remember how to get out. All the potted houseplants look the same to me. One tapestry on the wall blends into the next. The red carpet is thick and unending. I run into dead ends with doors that I don't want to open.

Finally I find a small staircase. It goes up, but I follow it anyway. I hear footsteps behind me, but I keep climbing.

It's strange because I must have come to the only part of the mansion that's not scrupulously clean and heated. The staircase is claustrophobic. The coldness grows stronger with each step. When I get to the landing, there's a wooden door, cracked open.

This must be the attic Cal told me about a while ago. The one they had to dig around to find his chip-watch. It's almost as big as the whole wing below me. There's old furniture everywhere, covered with white cloths, and a bunch of boarded-up crates. Filtered light shines through the windows.

It's like walking through the buried memories of the house.

Under one sheet, I see a cello case; underneath another is the outline of a harp. There's an old dresser by a window with a rocking chair next to it. It's the perfect place to sit and gain some clarity. So I sit down to rest. I rock back and forth until I can no longer feel Seth. Until the memory of what almost happened is gone.

All this would be easier if Seth were ugly. If my body didn't betray me every time we touched.

I know better than to let Seth get under my skin even for one minute. I have a job to do. That's all. And I definitely don't care about anything. If Seth wants to be a tech addict, then fine. That's not my problem. It's not like I'm choosing any of this.

I concentrate hard on letting my mind go blank. I stare out the window, at the unfamiliar outside. I've never seen as much of the estate as I do now. The view from my cloister is the walled-in courtyard. But the grounds I see from the attic are green and flowering. There are orange trees and benches. Winding paths circle around the gardens. I also see the security cameras, which I know are still on.

In the far, far distance, I can barely see the billboards marking the entry to Silicon Valley. Somewhere out there my friends smile down at me, showing me what normal Vestals look like. Fatima … Beau … Ethan … Do they ever think of me?

Here, I am alone with my mission. I don't have anyone who understands what it's like to be me. I don't have anybody to witness my moments or experience them with me. Without the Brethren, I'm in solitary confinement.

"Sophia?" I hear somebody say from way behind.

I turn my head and look. Cal is standing next to the cello, and his face blanches like he's seen a ghost.

"Oh, forgive me, Blanca. I thought, I thought I—" But Cal can't finish his sentence. He sits down on a couch partially covered in a sheet and puts his head in his hands.

I go over and sit a few inches away.

"It never gets better," Cal mumbles. "It gets easier to deal with, but it never gets better."

"I'm sorry." I'm unsure if my words help. I don't know what it's like to lose a family member.

"I'm not the same person without Sophia. I'm different. I'm diminished," Cal whispers.

I nod like I understand what Cal means, though I don't.

Cal lifts his head. "Part of my life is going on fine, like nothing ever happened. And that makes me feel horrible! But the other parts of my life are total chaos. Like with Seth. And I haven't known what to do. I haven't known how to fix things."

"You're not alone anymore," I say. "You've got me. I'm on your side."

"Nobody's been on my side for so long. To hear you say that means everything." Cal takes out his handkerchief and blows his nose. "See that box up there in the corner?" He points to something gray and flashing up high. "That was one of the first power boxes McNeal Solar ever manufactured for home use. It's what launched our brand. Sometimes I come up here to see it working perfectly after all these years. It's the only thing I have left that's perfect."

The technology is suspicious, but I pretend to be impressed. "It's like a trophy almost. A reminder of success."

"Precisely. One little box powering a whole mansion. One powerful idea taking me from college graduate to self-made man." Sadness falls across Cal's face like a shadow. "But I got it wrong for so long. That box didn't make me important. It was the people in my life that mattered. Only I didn't see it until it was too late."

"Sophia and Seth," I offer.

"Yes, and I was a horrible father."

"What do you mean? This is a beautiful house. You gave them a wonderful life."

Cal shakes his head. "I was hardly ever there. I missed out on everything."

"You must have been there, Cal. At least some of the time."

"Some of the time, yes. But I was always in a rush. I never stopped to recognize that everything I wanted was right in front of me. My family."

When he says that last part, it hurts me for some reason. I've never had a family, and I never will. And I have to be okay with that.

"What happens after I get Seth back for you?" I ask. "What then?"

"What do you mean?"

I say it bravely. A statement of fact. "I know you don't want to adopt a daughter."

Cal's mouth opens but then closes again, like he's struggling to find the words. "No, I don't. Sophia always wanted a daughter, but I never thought about it."

That's what I suspected. The hurt continues.

"The irony!" Cal laughs. "Sophia always wanted a daughter, and now here you are, five years too late."

Cal thinks it's funny, so I fake chuckle with him.

But deep down and hidden, I ache. I've always wanted a mother. I bet Sophia would have been a good one.

Chapter Six

The flowers come the next day, a big bouquet of white roses. They're soft and yielding, like the inside of my elbow, the small of my back, and my creamy white skin that could have sold soap. If I had been normal.

"It appears you've got him," Cal says to me after breakfast, when he comes up to my cloister to survey the blooms.

"Yes." I crack the window because the fragrance is overpowering. "How much time do I have?"

"Seth just passed the front gate." Cal leans down to smell a rose. "Beautiful. I can't believe this is working."

"You can't?" I furrow my eyebrows. "But I told you I'd make him come back."

"I know. It's not that I don't have faith in you. But I've waited so long to see him … I'd almost given up hope. I'll explain to

Seth tonight. Okay?"

I nod.

"Whatever it takes, Blanca. Only please, get Seth to show up for dinner."

"Yes, Cal. Of course."

"Good."

Cal's gone by the time Seth knocks on my door. I don't open it on purpose.

"I'm an ass," Seth calls through the metal. "Can you forgive me?" When I don't respond, he tries again. "I'll give you my full attention today. I promise!" His voice is muffled by the lead-lined door.

I wait a full fifteen seconds. Then I slide the deadbolt, pull open the door, and find Seth holding yet another bouquet of white roses.

"No tech?" I take the flowers. "No *Veritas Rex*? No blogging? No texting? Just me?"

Seth nods. "Cross my heart. I promise." His dark eyes implore me to believe him. Nobody has ever looked at me with such longing. Something inside me zings back in response.

"Blanca," Seth says when I don't move an inch. "I know we just met, and … I mean … I thought this would only be a hookup or whatever. But the more I get to know you, the more I really like you. You understand what this place means." At this, Seth waves his arms around, indicating all McNeal Manor. "I haven't talked about my mom—or my dad—in forever."

I tilt my chin down and gaze up at him, like Ms. Corina taught me.

"Do you feel anything for me?" Seth asks. "Do you want to spend more time together, get to know one another?"

And I don't. A Vestal could never want a Virus. That's ridiculous.

I wasn't raised to allow lust to affect my decision-making either. It doesn't matter that Seth is swoon-worthy or that my breath catches when he's near me. It doesn't matter that something inside me wants to fix him. Get Seth help for his tech-addiction and show him a better way to live. Like he was my own personal reform project. He's an ass!

I have to focus. I have to finish this. I have to forget whatever stupid thing I might do or feel if I'm not careful.

I need him to stay for dinner. To complete my mission.

So I say "Yes!" and leap into Seth's arms, encircling my legs around his waist.

Seth barely closes the door behind him before he can't manage anything else but me.

"What do you want to do today?" Seth asks me, brushing a strand of hair behind my ear. He looks out of place here on my bed, lying on top of the velvet coverlet. Like a giant smudge on something pure and holy. But I let him trace his hands down my back, and it feels good. It almost feels like they belong there.

"What do *you* want to do?" I ask, so he'll think he's making the decision.

"Besides this? Hmm … Maybe I want to teach you to ride

my motorcycle. You seemed like you had a good time the other night."

"I did," I admit.

"So what do you say? Do you want to spend the day out in the sunshine?"

The sunshine? I've never done that before. Talk about reckless. I can only imagine what Headmaster Russell would do if he found out. But Cal wouldn't mind. "*Whatever it takes,*" he said.

Then for some reason I bury my face into Seth's neck. It feels good knowing that his arm is around me. It's peaceful, like I'm safe and protected. I'm so confused. I almost wish I could be with Seth without trying to control him. But then I'd be powerless and ineffective. So I lead with an old standby.

Get someone to agree with you by starting with a "Yes-Yes."

It's one of Barbelo's best techniques. Ask your target two questions you know they will say "yes" to, and then follow with what you really want.

"You want to teach me to ride?" I ask.

"Yes." Seth kisses my neck.

"You want to spend all day with me?"

"Yes," he says. "Of course."

"Okay. Let's do it. I'll learn here on the estate and then you can stay for dinner."

"What? Dinner? There's no way I'm—"

"I thought you wanted to spend all day with me!"

"Yes, but I—"

"I can't keep ditching your dad. If you want to see me, then you have to deal with him too. It won't work otherwise."

"But couldn't we—"

"No," I say. "We couldn't. That would be pushing it."

Seth rolls over on his back and blows out air. "Fine. It's a deal." Then he regards me slyly. "Make sure to wear leather."

I've never been out on the grounds in daylight before. It's hard to see in so much sunlight. I feel like my eyes are on fire. How do people deal with this? I guess I should have worn sunglasses.

Being outside also makes me feel super exposed. I know there's a ten-foot wall around the perimeter of the estate, I know there're security cameras, and I know Alan's watching the front gate, but still … All that blue sky above is intimidating. It takes me a bit to be able to focus on what Seth is saying.

"Okay, no shoelaces, ever! They could get caught on something. And always wear a helmet."

"Definitely," I answer. It's hard to imagine there ever being a time when I would take off joyriding on a motorcycle. I'm only going through with this lesson to get Seth to come to dinner.

"The left side of the bike is for gears; the right side is for breaking. Do you know about gears? Wait … Do you know how to drive a car?" Seth looks at me like I'm a potential idiot.

"Yes!" I snarl. I don't bother to tell Seth that my entire road experience involves driving around the underground parking lot of Tabula Rasa. I've never technically driven with other drivers on the road, but I'm exceptionally good at parking, and I understand old-fashioned maps.

Seth sounds relieved. "Okay, good. So the first thing you do is you turn the key, and then the fuel injection kicks on. Hear that?" The bike rumbles to life.

I nod, feigning interest.

"Then this light flashes, and that means the bike is ready to start. Here," Seth says. "Climb on in front of me."

I begin to straddle the bike.

"Wait!" Seth says, stopping me. "That was a test! Where's your helmet?"

Oh, right. The helmet. I pull it on, and the world gets a bit darker. Then I climb on the bike in front of Seth, and he puts his arms around me.

That's when things get interesting.

Because when I'm sitting there, in the front, it finally hits me. I see where Seth was going with this whole thing. If I learn to actually do this, I could go wherever I want. I could ride off into the sunset, and nobody could stop me. Not even Headmaster Russell. It's a power trip, sitting on this bike. It's the taste of freedom.

Of course, I don't want to go anywhere on my own. Obviously! I want to stay right here on the manor like Cal told me to. But the possibility? The knowledge that I could go somewhere if I had to? It's thrilling. That's worth doing this for.

"What's that again?" I ask Seth. He's saying something about the clutch.

"It's on the left handle here. Push down to first, then up to neutral. If you keep going up, you'll hit second, third, fourth, and fifth."

Fifth gear. I can't imagine going that fast on my own. I bet Beau doesn't get to go that fast when they shoot his truck commercials. They probably make him drive around in circles on the studio lot until they can get the right picture.

"The right hand has the accelerator." Seth puts my glove on the handle, and I feel the untapped power of the bike below.

"Kick the gearshift here," Seth says pointing down to my left foot. "Then there's your back brake over here on the right."

I'm listening, but I'm also ready to do this. I let the clutch out slowly and the bike starts to move.

"Good," Seth says. "If you let the clutch out too fast, the bike will stall. Smooth clutch control. That's what you want to shoot for."

I nod briefly and then I go for it. There's a lot of starting and stopping, and sometimes I screw up and the bike pops forward and Seth has to take the controls. But after an hour or two, I'm touring around the house so fast that Cal comes out on the balcony of his office to see what's up.

"What's going on out here?" he calls down. "For heaven's sake, Blanca? Is that you?"

I bring the bike to a stop and shut off the engine. Then I take off my helmet, and my hair falls down, sticky around my neck. "Yes," I shout. "It's me. But don't worry. We're not going anywhere."

"I'm not sure this is such a good idea," Cal says loudly. "I don't want you to get hurt."

"She won't get hurt!" Seth yells.

Cal's about to say something else, I can tell. Something

potentially not helpful to the situation. So I ask, "When's dinner? Seth's coming too."

For the briefest of seconds, Cal smiles. Then he bites his lip hard. "An hour," he says. "Dinner's in an hour. Have fun."

I shove my helmet back on with determination and twist the key. I'm absolutely going to have fun. I let out the clutch again, and we're off, all the way down the driveway to the gatehouse. Alan gives a little nod as we make a U-turn and speed back up to the mansion.

We're lying on the grass underneath one of the orange trees I saw from the attic window yesterday. The branches hang low with big balls of fruit, waiting to be tasted. Seth picks some for us and peels open the flesh. The oranges taste like sunshine, their sticky juice dripping down my chin until Seth licks it off.

"Stop that!" I laugh, pushing him back into the grass. I lay my head down on his chest and take a deep breath. I smell oranges, grass, leather, and Seth mixed together. I can feel Seth's finger-chips buzzing against my arm, but he ignores them. Then he flicks his wrist, and the blue turns off.

"Sorry about that." He runs his hands through my hair, and quivers of relaxation overtake me. "This day is all about you and me."

"You're not in tech-withdrawal yet?"

"I've been kind of distracted." Seth kisses me, and we roll across the grass a few times for fun.

And I try hard not to think about any of it. Because if I do, I'll start imagining crazy possibilities. Like maybe this day is changing my opinion of Seth. I'm having fun and enjoying the company of a Virus. Maybe he isn't the jerk I thought he was.

What if Seth is my only ticket to happiness?

I'm already helping Seth beat his tech-addiction. Would he take out his finger-chips for me? Seth wants me for real, and maybe I could want him too. Is it possible the comfort I feel sheltered in his arms is more than lust? Maybe after the blowout tonight Seth and I could be genuinely together.

Headmaster Russell doesn't have to know about Seth and neither do the other Vestals. I wouldn't have to tell anyone. I could be a Vestal, and I could be with Seth too. All I need is Cal's blessing, and he might actually give it.

I've always wanted to be wanted. I've always wanted a family. That was the hardest part about going Geisha. I never got the Vestal family that was promised to me. *"It's a lonely road,"* Ms. Lydia said.

All my childhood fantasies involved finding the perfect Vestal family after my Harvest. *Blanca,* I imagined my new Vestal-mom saying. *We hoped our corporation would bid on you.* Then my new Vestal boyfriend would lead me off into the sunset.

"What are you thinking about?" Seth asks me. "You look like you're a million miles away."

"I was thinking about you," I say. "I'm thinking about you and me together, being happy." At least, I think this is what happiness is.

"I'm happy too." Seth kisses the back of my neck. "I think you might be inspiring a new tattoo."

That's the last thing I want to hear! But the sick part inside me is willing to take it. I could put up with anything to stay here with Seth, coiled together in the grass.

I'm so busy looking at him and so busy feeling his hands on me that I don't realize what's happening.

I hear the gunshot in the distance, but it doesn't register. I hear somebody screaming, but I don't understand that it's Alan, back at the guard station, being shot.

I don't realize what's going on. Not until the flashes start. Not until I finally look up and see people everywhere, taking our picture.

It's the viral paparazzi, and they're here to ruin everything.

"Blanca, go!" Seth yells at me. He tosses me the keys and shoves my helmet into my arms. Then he's fighting every last Virus he can get his hands on.

But they're everywhere! They pour out of the bushes and climb the trees. Hands are up and flashes are in my face. Everywhere I look, there's another paparazzi.

"Go, Blanca! Go!" Seth shouts again. He knees a guy in the head and then kicks another Virus in the stomach. "Take the bike and go!"

For half a second I actually think about it. I could take that bike and ride away. I could protect myself and stay safe. *Stay private. Stay hidden.*

But I need to hide immediately. So I shove on my helmet

and crouch down low, like I'm a little ball of white. I put my arms around my knees and curl up into an egg. I close my eyes so I won't see the flashes reflect off my helmet. Nobody can see me now.

The Viruses holler at me. "How does it feel to go Geisha?"

"Does Calum McNeal know you're betraying him like this?"

"What do you look like under that helmet, girlie? Why don't you show us?"

"Asshole!" Seth yells, and then I hear the sounds of more fists.

"Get him!" somebody says. "Hold him down so we can get more pictures."

"How does it feel, Veritas Rex? How does it feel to be on the bottom?"

I open my eyes at that. And I see about a million guys holding Seth down, snapping away at him too. He's trying to shield his face, but he can't. But it's not merely the cameras that are the problem; they're actually hurting him, punching away until his face is bloody.

"Stop!" I shout. "Let him go!" I stand up tall and get their attention, exactly like they want. "I'll take off my helmet if you release him."

"What else will you take off, Vestal?" one of the men asks.

"No!" Seth screams, but his voice is muted by somebody's knee.

"Let him go, and I'll take off the helmet," I shout. "I'll start with that." I can hear Seth crying now. I can hear him screaming with rage. When I take off my helmet, his protests get louder.

"No, Blanca! Don't do it! Run!"

The vultures let him go. They're all too busy standing up and clicking away with their thumb-cameras, uploading me straight to the Web.

"Take off your shirt!" one of them yells.

Seth lunges at the guy, trying to strangle him. Then a bunch dog-pile Seth again.

So many people are yelling at me that I go on autopilot. *Do exactly what you're told.* I undo a button. Then one more. Then another. I would keep going except I hear footsteps coming from behind.

It's Cal running up the path, like he's on fire.

"Leave my kids alone!" Cal roars. He lunges at one of the men taking my picture and wrestles him to the ground. Then he pulls down another. "Fight back, Blanca! Don't let them hurt you! Fight back!"

So I do, because I'm really good at fighting, once I get going. I know exactly where to hit a guy too. I kick one of the men holding Seth right in the head.

"The police are on their way!" Cal bellows, and he's prying the bastards off too. "Get off my son! Leave my kids alone!"

The whole property swarms with cop cars. There are sirens and flashing lights everywhere, and the Viruses are rounded up one by one.

But I'm still fighting. I'm kicking every last Virus I can get my foot into. I don't stop until the cops pull them away.

And Cal is frantic, screaming at a police officer, begging for an ambulance. Because Seth isn't moving.

He's lying on the grass in a pool of blood.

Chapter Seven

Of course I can't go to the hospital with them. It's not safe for me there. And I can't get a message about how Seth is doing because I'm not connected. So I sit on the floor of the great hall and think about the worst. The hearth behind me is cold.

I remember the white roses from this morning. They mock me now. White roses are the symbol of death.

I also think about how somebody can do something nice and clueless all at the same time. Like trying to fight when you should run away. I don't know why Seth didn't run away. He should have jumped on his bike and escaped when he had the chance.

I thought all Viruses were selfish. But Seth risked his life to defend me. It doesn't make any sense. He's not the bastard I thought he was.

This is all my fault! I knew that Headmaster Russell would

get Seth back for taking my picture.

Vestals avenge all wrongs, especially when our honor is at stake.

At least, I think this was Headmaster Russell's doing. He knows people to call for every situation, even paparazzi thugs.

But maybe this wasn't coming from Tabula Rasa at all. I can easily see Headmaster Russell going after Seth, but he never would have told those people to take *my* picture.

Now that my stolen pictures are out there for the whole world to see, I've shamed the Brethren.

Vestals are a collective power. We are united by secrecy and code. Privacy is paramount.

There are some lines that Headmaster Russell won't cross.

So maybe this wasn't about Seth after all. Maybe this was about me being a Vestal. Maybe it was about Viruses hunting me down because I was top pick. Because I went Geisha. Or because they wanted to thrash Veritas Rex, one of the most popular Viruses of all time.

But no matter why it happened, I've failed Cal. Seth didn't come home for dinner after all. I failed, like the loser I am. Just like Headmaster Russell used to say about me during Discipline Hour. *"You're weak, Blanca. You need atonement."*

It's all my fault.

I don't know how I fall asleep, but I finally do, curled up on the marble floor. When I open my eyes, it's the middle of the night, and a cold draft wakes me.

Cal has come home, opening the front door and bringing the chill in with him. "Blanca," he's says. "What are you doing down here? Why aren't you in bed?"

I sit bolt upright and gasp for air. "Where's Seth?" I ask. "Is he … "

"Seth's okay." Cal sits down on the floor next to me. "It's all right."

"Where is he?"

"Back at the hospital, sleeping off the drugs. His nose is broken, and he has a couple of cracked ribs, but other than that, he'll be fine. He's coming home in the morning."

I don't think I've ever felt so much joy and relief at the same time. Then I look down at Cal's hands, and they're bandaged too.

"What about you, Cal? Are you okay?"

"Never better." Cal smiles. "I spent the past eight hours with my son."

"Did you talk to him?"

"Not yet." Cal sighs. "Later. When the drugs wear off."

"I'm sorry."

"For what?"

"For failing you."

"What do you mean?" Cal asks. "I'm the one who failed you. And Alan! I should have had bulletproof glass in the guard station. I should have—"

"Is Alan okay?"

"He's not going to come home any time soon, but he'll make it," Cal says.

"I'm sorry Seth didn't come home for dinner like you wanted."

"Is that it?" Cal puts his arm around me and hugs me gently. "Oh, my precious girl. You have nothing to be sorry for at all."

"But it's all my fault! If it wasn't for me, Seth could have gotten away."

"But why didn't *you* get away when you had the chance? I heard Seth tell you to run."

"They were everywhere!" I pull myself back to look at him. "I couldn't get to the house."

"But why didn't you get on the bike and go far, far away?"

"And leave the estate?" I ask, horrified.

Cal looks at me with equal horror. "Is that what this is about? You wouldn't leave the estate because I told you not to?"

I don't want to say it because I know he'll be mad. But I have to, because Cal asked me a question. "I always follow directions. I'm a Vestal."

"No," Cal says, his voice going deep. "No. I was wrong. I was wrong to have bought you."

I shake my head, but Cal keeps going.

"This whole thing was wrong!"

"No, it wasn't!" I protest. But Cal's not listening.

"I don't want you to follow my directions anymore," he says. "I want you to think for yourself, and I want you to make good choices for your own welfare."

"Stop. Just stop. You know I can't do that. You *know* that's not how this works. You're my purchaser. *You need to tell me what to do.*"

"No." Cal shakes his head. "No more directions. You've got good instincts, and you can think for yourself. That's my new request for you, for now and evermore."

"No, I can't. I'm sorry, Cal, but I can't." I say it again and again. I can't stop saying it, even when Cal pulls me to my feet and tells me to go to bed.

"Get some sleep now, and we'll talk about this in the morning."

But I can't move.

Cal considers me and my tears. "Look," he says. "I'll be honest. I don't know what to do with you now. But I don't want people to hurt you. I want you to have a real life. So we'll figure this all out in the morning, okay?"

I nod, like I agree. Then I suck back the tears like I've been taught. *Cry on cue. Stop crying. Tears are a tool.*

I wander up to my cloister in a daze, forgetting to bolt the door.

But I can't sleep. I'm a total wreck. It's like a switch has gone off inside me and I can't turn it back.

I'm sobbing. I'm raging. My old tricks don't work anymore.

When Seth comes into my room the next morning, his face bandaged and swollen, I'm still a mess. He kisses my wet cheeks and whispers in my ear. "Blanca, what's wrong? I'm okay. You're okay. They were only some pictures."

Seth thinks this is about the photographers. But it's not about pictures. It's about more than that. How the hell could Cal do this to me? How the freaking hell could he *do* this to me?

Vestals don't make decisions on our own. We always follow orders.

I need Cal to tell me what to do. That's the deal, and he knows it.

Cloistered with a Virus. I try not to think about what Headmaster Russell would say. Seth has his arms wrapped around me, even though his ribs must be killing him, as we lie together on the bed. The steady beat of his heart calls to my own racing pulse and challenges me to calm down.

"You're safe now," Seth says to me on repeat. "It's okay."

But it's not okay. It'll never be okay again. Not unless I can make Cal listen to reason.

"Shit, Blanca. You're still covered in blood. Didn't you shower last night? Maybe if you clean up you'll feel better."

I don't bother to answer.

Seth tries again. "I'm sorry I didn't protect you better. We have a deal. Remember? What you and I have together is private. It should never have been exposed."

"Is it all over the Web?" My words croak out of vocal chords raw from crying.

"Yeah. Everywhere but *Veritas Rex*." Seth shows me his bandaged hands. "I need new finger-chips. They got busted up in the fight."

"Maybe you don't need to get new finger-chips." I feel a brief surge of energy. A tiny glimmer of hope.

"No finger-chips? And what, be like my dad? With an antique on my wrist?"

"Why not?" I jerk away, and the absence of Seth's body leaves an emptiness I don't like. "You don't need to go back to *Veritas Rex*. I mean, do you want to be a Virus? Do you want to be like them?"

"I'm nothing like them!"

"Of course you are. You're just not as vicious."

"How can you say that?"

Anger invades me. "You took my picture. You destroyed my life."

"Destroyed your life?" Seth grabs his ribs and cringes.

I reach out to comfort him on instinct, but then pull my hands away. How could Cal leave me with Seth and tell me to think for myself? Being with a Virus is so awful it has its own page of tirades in the Vestal Code of Ethics.

"Well?" Seth glares at me.

We're interrupted by a knock at the door. I swing my legs over the bed and scoot away from Seth. "Come in," I say.

Cal enters the room and sweeps his eyes over the situation. "Am I interrupting something?"

"No," I answer.

"Yes," Seth growls. He gets up and walks over to the bouquet. Then he rips apart a rose petal by petal.

"Which is it?" Cal asks.

"Blanca thinks I've destroyed her life." Seth grunts.

"No," Cal says. "She doesn't."

Seth looks at his dad. "What do you know?"

"More than you think." Cal walks over to Seth and whispers something in his ear.

If I weren't so messed up, I'd think, *Shoot! I did it! These two are talking again!* It's hard to care about Cal and his stupid problems now, when he's trying to ruin my entire existence. So I sit on the bed and stare at my cuff, hating myself and my supposed free will.

"Blanca," Cal says at last, "you have visitors coming."

I barely look up. "Who?"

"Headmaster Russell and Ms. Lydia."

Now I'm really screwed.

"Did you call them?" I ask.

"No," Cal says. "I wouldn't do that."

"Then they must have seen the pictures!"

"Probably." Cal sits on the bed. His face is gray, like he didn't get any sleep last night.

Good. I hope he suffers.

"Are you up for visitors?" Cal asks me. "They just passed the front gate, but I'll send them away if you want me to."

"If I want you to?" The tears rush out again, and I can't stop them. I'm my own faucet of sorrow.

"What the hell's going on?" Seth asks.

Cal appears torn, helpless. And I of course, don't say anything. So Cal has to admit the truth himself. "I'm done with it," he says. "I ordered her to think for herself."

Seth laughs, like he thinks this is funny. "What are you talking about?" When we don't respond, he stops snorting. "You can't think for yourself?" he asks me.

"Not unless I tell her to," Cal says. "At least that's how they explained all this to me, that first day after the Harvest."

"But, Blanca, you—" Seth pauses. "You and me—" Seth takes a deep breath. Then he grabs his ribcage like that breath cost him.

And I know he's thinking about all of it. Me there at the precinct, where I supposedly released him according to my own initiative. Or that first night under the tree when we kissed beneath the stars. Or our morning together alone in his room. Or yesterday, eating oranges in the sunshine.

Seth whips around and points his finger right at Cal. "Did you tell her to do all of it? Did you make her pretend to like me?"

"I told her to release you from jail."

"Is that all?" Seth's voice is deadly.

"Almost," Cal answers. "I told Blanca to be friendly, to encourage you to come back home. That's it, Seth. I swear. I want Blanca to make her own decisions."

"Does she or doesn't she, Dad? Does Blanca make her own decisions or not?"

"No," Cal admits. "Not usually."

"It's better that way." I squeeze my eyes shut for a second. I can't stand having them look at me like I'm a freak show. I need to make them understand. "People make crappy decisions all the time. Then they plaster them over the Internet! Vestals are free from all that. We completely abstain."

"Abstain from technology, yeah, I get that. It's messed up, but I get it." Seth shakes his head. "But abstain from decision making?"

"I make lots of decisions," I protest. "Cal tells me what to do, and I decide how to do it."

"That's ridiculous," says Seth. He turns his derision on Cal. "I can't believe you'd go along with this."

"But it's not your dad's fault! It simply is how it is, and it's for the best. Please, Cal. Please don't make me see Headmaster Russell and Ms. Lydia without directions. They'll know!"

"You don't need directions," says Cal. "Be yourself, and you'll be fine."

I don't bother considering this. "Myself? *I am loyal. I am discrete. I follow the rules.* How can I be any of that if you don't tell me what to do?" I grab Cal's hands in mine and beg. "Please help me!" When that doesn't work, I get down on my knees and beg him again. "Please. Give me some directions."

Seth's gaze bounces back and forth between us. His attitude oozes revulsion. "You're both sick," he says. "I hope you know that."

Cal's expression is twisted in pain, but he comes through for me after all, like deep down I always hoped he would. I knew he'd be a good purchaser ever since that first night he told me his plans.

"Get up off the floor, Blanca." Cal squeezes my hands. "Take a quick shower and get ready. You'll follow my lead, okay? We'll tell your teachers everything is fine and then figure the rest out."

My tears start all over again. I knew I could count on Cal.

"Will you stay for this?" Cal asks Seth. "So Blanca doesn't have to face these people alone?"

I don't know what Seth is going to say. I don't think Cal knows either. Maybe Seth has to think about it, because he doesn't answer for a while. Then he says one simple word that proves once and for all he's loyal.

"Yes."

That bastard. That tech-addicted, ink-polluted bastard.

He just made me like him for real.

I'm showered, my face is scrubbed, I'm wearing a white dress, and I'm sitting between both of the McNeals. I'm pulling it together all right, exactly like Cal told me to.

And it's not like Headmaster Russell can do anything to me anyway, not with Ms. Lydia here. She appears graceful as always in a simple white dress. She's deceptively elegant, her power of persona cloaked in cotton.

Headmaster Russell is in full Vestal regalia, right down to his white leather boots. It's warm in McNeal Manor, and sweat beads his forehead.

"Does that Virus have to be here for this?" Headmaster Russell asks.

Seth opens his mouth, but Cal stops him. "This man has a very distinguished career."

"A career?" Headmaster Russell scoffs. "A scumbag like him?"

"Who are you calling a scumbag, asshole?" Seth retorts.

"He's not a scumbag, he's a viral blogger, and he also happens to be my son," Cal says. "I'm proud of what he's accomplished. *Veritas Rex* has broken ten top news stories in the past year alone. It has more followers than the president."

Headmaster Russell is about to pop.

Ms. Lydia stands up just in time. "You have a lovely home here, Mr. McNeal." Her heart-shaped face is the perfect type of tranquil. She's a reminder to me of all the ways I've screwed up.

"Thank you. My late wife oversaw the decorating."

Ms. Lydia doesn't balk, but Headmaster Russell does. He must know about the redhead.

"Let's get straight to the point, shall we?" says Ms. Lydia.

"Blanca, we'd like to ask you some questions."

My eyes flicker over to Cal, and he nods yes. Ms. Lydia notices and smiles.

Score one for me.

"Please go ahead," I say.

"Have you been following the Vestal Code of Ethics?" she asks me.

"Yes, Ms. Lydia. Of course, Ms. Lydia."

"Have you been safe-guarding your privacy?" Headmaster Russell asks next.

I don't know what to say. They know about yesterday. Why are they testing me?

"Frankly, Russell, I don't see how Blanca's privacy is any of your concern," Cal says, coming to my rescue.

Headmaster Russell blusters. "Not my concern? Vestal privacy is always my concern!"

"At Tabula Rasa, yes, but I've paid thirty-two million dollars to harvest Blanca's privacy. Her privacy is now my concern, not yours." Cal leans back in the sofa and takes a sip of tea.

Headmaster Russell isn't nearly so relaxed. "But certainly you don't want—"

"What I do or do not want is my private business. Yesterday was regrettable, but I'm beefing up my security team as we speak. For you to come here asking questions is intrusive." Cal sets down his teacup. "Honestly, I don't see what you are doing here at all."

Ms. Lydia smiles like this is social visit, although the room feels lethal. "We're here to assess the situation. We heard you were adopting Blanca as your daughter?"

"Yes," Cal answers, a little too quickly.

"Excellent." Ms. Lydia folds her French-tipped hands. "Unexpected but excellent. In that case, I'd like to ask if Blanca will be able to attend the Vestal corporate banquet next month."

"What banquet?" asks Seth.

Ms. Lydia's face freezes, like she can't believe she actually has to talk to a Virus. But once she says what she has to say, I can tell she relishes the effect it has on Seth. "Every three months we have a mixer to meet and mingle," she says. "Vestals only date other Vestals unless they're instructed to do otherwise by their purchaser."

Seth looks at his father, and Cal's face goes grim.

And I know, I just know. I'm never going to have another moment with Seth again. It's official. Even if Cal tells me to, Seth won't want to be with me anymore now that he knows his dad is pulling the strings. Now that Seth knows the truth.

Cal clears his throat. "Blanca's free to choose whomever she wishes."

I hate him for it.

Ms. Lydia glances in my direction and sees the hate. "Wonderful," she says. "It's so much easier this way. Lucky for Blanca, I've arranged the perfect Vestal match."

"Thank you, Ms. Lydia," I say, on automatic. "That's very kind of you, Ms. Lydia." But what I'm really thinking about is my perfect opposite. Seth's body stretched out next to me, completely trashed by chips and ink. Seth attacking those Viruses on my behalf, trying to protect me. Seth and his hundred white roses. Seth saying yes to helping me right now even though he has every reason to hate me ... but I have to stop thinking. I have to keep my face serene, like they want me to.

"I'm so happy you're happy," Ms. Lydia says to me. "The young man I've picked out for you has got a face that can sell soap, exactly like you. He's the perfect boy next door. You'll love him."

"Perfect," says Seth. "That sounds fucking perfect for Blanca."

"Seth!" says Cal sharply.

But I'm not rattled. I'm completely still, like Ms. Corina taught us back in charm class. And I don't say anything because I can't say anything. I can't say anything at all.

"We'll see Blanca next month then." Headmaster Russell stands up to go.

"Yes, Headmaster Russell. Of course, Headmaster Russell."

"Wonderful," says Ms. Lydia. "It's all settled. How about a blessing?"

She and Headmaster Russell lift up their cuffs. When my cuff hits my heart, it burns with cold.

"Blanca, Cal, and Seth, you've had a hard road. In so many ways it's difficult being you," Ms. Lydia begins, continuing the blessing to its conclusion. I notice that Cal looks discreetly away. But Seth? He stares at us like we're a freak show. Like he's ready to tear us apart.

As soon as our visitors leave, Seth turns on us. "What the hell is going on?" he demands. "What type of tricks are you pulling on me?"

"Seth," says Cal. "I—"

"No!" Seth shouts. "I'm tired of being jerked around by both of you. I can't believe you had Blanca do that! What type of monster are you?"

"I—" Cal tries again.

"Don't bother." Seth starts to stalk off.

"Wait!" I reach out and grab Seth's arm like I'm never going to let him go. "All your dad wanted me to do was make you listen. The rest of it was my fault for improvising." If I go back to the original plan, I'll still be fine. I can still fix this.

"Improvising?" Seth's face is all torn up. "You call that improvising?"

"What?" Cal asks. "Call what improvising?"

"Nothing." Seth sneers. "Nothing important. Nothing worth mentioning."

"Wait!" I run and throw my arms across the front door. I can still do this. I can make Seth listen, I know it. "Your dad has something to show you. Show him, Cal. Show Seth the truth."

"What's she talking about now?" Seth asks.

Cal looks sad, defeated almost. He knows what's coming next. But he types at his wrist anyway and the video emerges, there in the great hall. Cal blows it up large enough for all of us to see.

I can barely stand to watch. Cal shuts his eyes.

There's the same scene Seth showed me on *Veritas Rex*. The one that caused the riff, the one Seth posted online to publically humiliate his father. Cal in his bedroom with the naked woman under him. Only this scene is shot from above, from the surveillance cameras in the manor.

There's Cal and the redheaded woman. There's seventeen-year-old Seth surprising them both, and then running away. And then you see the woman sit up, totally distraught. The red wig falls off her head, and she's completely bald underneath. She's lying there naked, except for her golden pendant.

"It was Mom?" says Seth, his face blank. Then the rage comes back. "*You were screwing my mom? When she was dying?*"

"It wasn't like that." Cal furiously shuts off the image. "She was having a good day. She wanted—"

"Stop!" Seth covers his ears. "I don't want to hear it."

"You have to hear it, Seth." I put my hands on his tattooed arms and pull them down so he can listen.

"Your mother was so embarrassed." Cal stares down at his shoes. "I didn't want her to die being embarrassed in front of her own son."

"So you let me think the worst of you? You let me brand you a cheater?"

"I was going to tell you after she passed away," Cal says.

"After the funeral? But by then I had already posted it."

"Yes," says Cal.

They both stare at each other.

"The only good thing," Cal says, trying to get the words out, "is that it launched your career. Your mother would be so proud of you going viral. She would be so proud of *Veritas Rex*." Tears course down his face.

"You're lying," says Seth. "She'd be horribly ashamed. She'd hate knowing the world saw that video of her."

"Well, yes," says Cal. "That too. But she'd love you anyway. She'd still be proud of you and of what you've accomplished. Just like I am."

Seth crumbles. There's no other word for it. He absolutely crumbles. And then they're both hugging and crying, and there's no need for me anymore.

There's no need for me anymore.

And the force of that realization hits me like a stone. My work here is done. And I wait for it, because I know Cal's going to say it. He's going to say it again like the real rat bastard he is.

"Thank you, Blanca. Thank you so much, sweetheart. You've brought my son back to me!" Cal tries to hug me, but I slide away.

He continues talking. "You don't have to be a Vestal anymore. You can be your own person and think for yourself. I can release you from your pledge. *I release you*!"

See what I mean?

Cal thinks he can free me.

Chapter Eight

The only way I'll be happy is if Cal locks me in my cloister from the outside, but he refuses. So I deadbolt the door on my end, but it's not as good.

Whenever a student at Tabula Rasa was in ethical danger, Headmaster Russell would lock the offender in a sequestered cell. That way, the rest of us were safe from whatever trouble the perpetrator was causing. But it was also helpful for the wrongdoer. There, within his cloistered confinement, he could meditate on our values.

We are beacons of light. We are a sacred fire that won't burn out. We remind the world there is a better way to live.

When the internment was over, the released student emerged a model of perfect behavior, completely loyal to Tabula Rasa, and ready to rejoin the Brethren. But more than that, every returned individual radiated peaceful contentment. It was as if cloistering was a crucible that burned away every impurity.

Headmaster Russell isn't here to guard me, so I must be my own warden. I'll cloister myself until my purity is secure. I won't leave until Cal gives up this sick idea of releasing me from my contract.

But he won't.

"Think for yourself," Cal says through the door. "Do you want to be locked in here? You don't need me to tell you what to do."

He's such a bastard.

"Seth will be here any minute. Don't you want to see him?"

The wicked part of me *does* want to see Seth. That's another reason why I need to be locked in here. The only way I could ever hang out with a Virus again is if Cal tells me to. But he won't.

And then I have to deal with Seth too. "Blanca," he says. "It's me. Can I come in?" Seth's gravelly voice pulls at my heartstrings.

"Ask your father," I answer.

"He said to ask you."

I throw myself on my velvet coverlet and push away the memory of that safe feeling I had when Seth's arms wrapped around me in the sunshine. I muffle my sobs with a pillow.

"I can hear you." Seth scratches at the door. "Please let me in so we can talk."

I can't talk. I can't come out. I can't do anything until Cal sees how wrong he is and starts treating me right. If Cal releases me from my sacred Vestal calling, I'll be worthless.

Worthless!

"Can *I* tell you what to do?" Seth asks. "Will that work?"

"No!" I cry. "Don't be stupid."

"Well then, tell me how it works," says Seth, his voice stifled by the metal door. "I've never understood your Vestal shit."

"It's not shit!"

"Fine. Tell me your Vestal ways."

But what's the use? I'm not supposed to be talking to a Virus anyway.

"Blanca, you have a hard road. I can see that," Seth says through the door. "In so many ways it's difficult being you. But I know that you can do it. You have everything you need to achieve happiness."

There's silence for a moment. Then I get off the bed. I walk over to the door and crouch next to it, holding my cuff up to the metal.

"Can you hear me, Blanca?"

"Yes."

"Do you want to come out of there?"

"Yes," I say again.

"Then come."

"I can't," I explain. "Not unless your dad tells me to."

"Fuck it!" Seth pummels the door. "Forget all that crazy Vestal shit and come out of there already!"

"It's not shit," I say. "It's what I am. It's what I'll always be."

I was sealed for life.

Two weeks of cloistering. Two weeks of pacing my room, dusting the bookshelves, and pressing my face against the windowpanes, unable to see anything but the walled courtyard below. Two weeks of hoping Fatima, Beau, and Ethan didn't know about my disgraced situation. Two weeks of reciting my favorite verse from the Vestal Code of Ethics over and over again.

I am loyal. I am discrete. I follow the rules. I picture Fatima brushing her hair to the rhythm of Ms. Corina's voice at night in our dorm. "One hundred strokes, children," Charming Corina would tell us. Then her saccharine voice would call out, "*I am loyal. I am discrete. I follow the rules.*" Brush. Brush. Brush.

Beau told us that the boys did jumping jacks to the exact same mantra. "*I am loyal. I am discrete. I follow the rules.*" Jump. Jump. Jump.

It doesn't matter what Cal says to me. I'll always be loyal to my Brethren.

Now Cal is worried that I'm not getting any exercise. Of course he has every right not to want me to be fat, so when he brings me meal trays, I stop opening the door.

"Damn it, Blanca!" he yells after the second night of this routine. "Open the door!"

Directions, at last! I fling the door open, hopeful and starving.

Cal holds out a wooden tray piled high with roast turkey and mashed potatoes. "Are you going to eat this?"

"I don't know," I say. "Are you telling me to eat this?"

I look at him, and Cal is as angry as I've ever seen him. He is so angry that there are tears in his eyes.

"What do you think?" he asks. "Do you think you should eat this?"

I shut the door with a *click.*

"Blanca!" Cal pounds on the metal door. "Open the door and eat this food!"

I open it up again and sit down on the ground, right there by the tray. I cram the food in my mouth as fast as I can. The sudden rush of nourishment makes me queasy.

"Blanca. Sweetheart. Please." Cal sits down next to me on the floor. "Please don't do this anymore. You can't stay in there forever."

"Then tell me to leave." I wipe my face with a napkin.

"You need exercise. You need fresh air. You'll feel better if you go outside."

"Tell me to," I say. "Tell me to, and I will."

"No." Cal sighs. "I'm done with that."

"You're done with me then, because I can't live on my own."

Cal shakes his head. "You don't have to live on your own. Is that what you think?"

I push away my plate.

"You can live here as long as you want. For the rest of your life! You can be my daughter, Blanca, my real daughter. I'm sorry I didn't say that a long time ago. It's what Sophia would have wanted, and it's what I want too. You can make friends. You can go outside. You can do anything you want."

"Tell me to," I say. "Tell me to be your daughter."

"No. You have to choose for yourself."

"You know I can't do that!"

"Do you want to?" Cal wrinkles his forehead.

"Yes." I wipe my cheek on the edges of my sweater.

"Tell me what to do, and I'll do it. Tell me how to help you."

Tears run down Cal's nose.

"I *have* told you!" I yell. "But you won't listen."

"I'm trying," he says. "I'm trying to help you."

But he won't.

The next day, I wake up to the sound of hammering outside my bedroom window. Workers install a ladder into the courtyard.

So now every day I climb down the ladder and get some fresh air. I run around and around the courtyard in circles so I don't get fat. Because I know that someday Cal is going to want a Vestal again, and I've got to be ready.

I am loyal. I am discrete. I follow the rules. Run. Run. Run. *I am a beacon of light in a world that has forgotten what is important.* Run. Run. Run.

I am a Vestal.

No matter what Cal says.

I don't recognize myself anymore. Even though I'm wearing my standard-issue whites, I don't look like me. I don't know what's wrong or why this isn't working, but I know it's my fault.

It's been almost a month now, cloistered in my room. I've read all the books on my wall, and I've written about a thousand letters on my white desk, most of them to Fatima. But I never send any of them.

If other Vestals knew that Mr. McNeal released me, I'd be shunned. Headmaster Russell would probably take my cuff away. Once a Vestal is decuffed, they might as well be dead.

Four weeks of cloistering. At least, I think it's the fourth week. I should have created a calendar and crossed out the days because it's easy to lose track. I should have done that.

I should have done a lot of things.

I should have done a better job proving to Mr. McNeal what a perfect Vestal I am. I should have made him realize that he needs me in his life exactly as I am. One of the Brethren. Sealed for life. A blank slate for the genesis of anything.

I should have done better. I should have lived up to my platinum cuff. I should have embodied what it means to be top pick.

I should recite the Vestal Code of Ethics one hundred more times. That's more important than sleep.

Much more important.

Sleep isn't as important as being a Vestal.

I should know that.

Sometimes I climb down the ladder into my courtyard and look up at the sky. It's so blue and clear. I see clouds drift by and think about how clouds are like perfect Vestals. They're white and fluffy and higher than everyone else. *You're a little cloud floating in the sky above the whole world. And you're placid. Perfectly placid.* That's what I'm supposed to be. But now I'm down here in the dirt.

The Virus comes to the first-floor window and stares at me every day. I can see his fingers twitch when he sees me. He's itching to blog about me. I know it.

But I've never seen the Virus hold his palm up, so I guess he's honoring his promise. I don't think he's taken my picture. Yet.

I don't know how I got so confused by that Virus. He's not good-looking at all! He's tech-infested and covered in tattoos. I can't believe I let him touch me.

You can't ever trust a Virus. That's what Barbelo Nemo wrote, and he's always right.

When I run around in circles, I think about the Vestal Ms. Lydia arranged for me to date. The one who sells soap. I wonder who it was. I've tried to remember all the Vestals I know, but my brain isn't working right. The only thing I know for sure is that he and I would have been perfect together. We could have sold lots and lots of soap. I bet the whole world would have thought we were the perfect couple.

We would have been a beacon of light in a dark world. Everyone would have seen us and known that the people in front of you are what matters, not what's happening on your palm.

But I'll never get the chance to do that now.

Today I spend so much time in the courtyard looking at clouds that sleep finally overcomes me. The freezing rain wakes me up, and when I look in the first-story window, Mr. McNeal and the Virus are watching me.

But that's okay, because Mr. McNeal owns my privacy. He can watch whatever he wants. I just wish he wouldn't let his Virus watch too.

They're right there the two of them, and Mr. McNeal holds something up to the window. That's funny because he's never done anything like that before.

I walk to the glass and see that it's a sign.

It says GO BACK INSIDE.

So I do.

Water splashes down the ladder, but I hold on tight. I climb up to my room and drip water all over the carpet. I'm shivering, but that's okay. The lights blind me. I must have forgotten to turn them off. Was that this morning? Yesterday? I can't remember.

I hear pounding coming from the door, and it's Mr. McNeal and his Virus.

"Blanca," they shout. "Open the door."

I slide open the deadbolt, and they both rush in at once.

"She's freezing," says the Virus. "Get her something dry."

Mr. McNeal runs into the room with mirrors and comes out with a fluffy robe. He covers me up, and I finally stop shaking.

"You've got to do something, Dad," says the Virus. "Do what we talked about. See if it works."

Mr. McNeal sits me down on my bed.

"Blanca," he says. "Will you still be my Vestal?"

"Yes." Relief floods over me. "Of course I'll be your Vestal. I'll do whatever you tell me to for the next twenty-five years." My plan worked!

"Okay," he says. "I'll tell you what to do again, but you have to promise me one thing."

"Anything," I say.

"Don't *ever* put yourself in danger again. You need to stay safe."

"Yes, Mr. McNeal. Of course, Mr. McNeal."

Then they're both hugging me. I think somebody's crying, but I don't know who.

I should be whipped. I should be beaten. I should be kneeling in front of the Pool of Purity getting the thrashing of my life. That's the only way I'll ever be able to atone for my waywardness. If I were at Tabula Rasa, Headmaster Russell would keep me at Discipline Hour forever.

I slipped up today and said "Mr. McNeal" even though my purchaser told me explicitly to call him "Cal."

"Yes, Cal. Of course, Cal," I said immediately. But then he wrinkled his forehead and looked at me with pity.

So I went back to the hallway next to my cloister and sat by the door. *I'm not supposed to go into my rooms anymore until after dinner.* That's what Cal says. That's why I'm sitting here, overhearing him talking to the Virus, in the room below.

"I don't know what to do, Seth. She's not getting any better."

"Was she this bad when you first got her?"

"No," Cal says. "She seemed almost normal."

The Virus snorts. "How can a Vestal be normal?"

"I don't know anymore. But what I'm saying is when Blanca first arrived, she didn't appear to be *abnormal.* She was eager to hear my plan for her, to help me get you back, but that was it. Nothing else about her struck me as odd."

"Dad, there's nothing about Blanca that isn't odd."

"But she didn't seem that way at first! She used to be able to make her own decisions."

Is that what he thinks? Good. Ms. Lydia is a genius. Before

she put me in the car on the way to McNeal Manor, she gave me the best directions ever.

"Talk," she told me. *"Laugh at his jokes, converse, make polite conversation and occasionally supply your own ideas. That's probably what your purchaser wants to hear, so that's what you are to do."*

"Yes, Ms. Lydia. Of course, Ms. Lydia."

"Good. And if you ever get in a position where you don't know what to do, ask him. Clarifying questions are your friends. They always help, and they never look suspicious."

"Yes, Ms. Lydia. Of course, Ms. Lydia."

Ms. Lydia smiled at me. *"You'll do great, Blanca. Remember, follow my instructions until your purchaser gives you enough of his own."* Then she blessed me and sent me away.

If only she were here to tell me what to do now. Cal barely tells me anything.

"So what should I do, Seth?" Cal's still talking to the Virus, and they don't know I can hear. "I don't want her to trap herself in there again. Should I take away the lock on her door? Or perhaps remove the door completely?"

"No," says the Virus, for some reason defending me. "Don't take away the door. That would mean taking away the last ounce of privacy she has left. You've already done a pretty good job of that as it is."

"I didn't mean to hurt her," Cal sounds beaten.

"I know, Dad."

"Now I just want to help her."

"Me too," says the Virus. "So how do we do that?"

"I don't know." Cal clears his throat. "That woman Lydia

keeps calling me about letting Blanca go to that Vestal banquet she mentioned last month."

"Are you kidding? We should keep Blanca as far away from those people as possible."

"That was my first thought too," says Cal. "But then I wondered if maybe it would reinvigorate her."

"Reprogram, is more like it."

He's such an idiot. I've never seen a computer in my life. How could I reprogram one?

"Maybe she'll be happier if she spends some time with her own kind," Cal says. "Lydia wants to introduce her to a young man she thinks Blanca would like."

The boy who sells soap! My soul mate!

"I can't believe you're considering this," the Virus says, his voice rising. "None of those people should be trusted!"

"I'm not going to trust them, Seth, but I do want to hear what they have to say. Letting Blanca be around them for one night shouldn't damage her any more than she's already damaged."

I still can't believe he thinks I'm damaged. But Cal's right about one thing. Letting me go to the Vestal corporate banquet is the perfect decision. That will make everything better.

"That's the worst idea ever, Dad," the Virus says. "The only way it would be remotely okay is if you go too."

"To the Vestal banquet?" Cal asks.

"Yeah," says the Virus. "That way you can keep an eye on her."

"I'm not sure that's allowed. I don't think they let outsiders into a function like that."

"Make them," says the Virus. "Have Blanca call them up and say the only way she can come is if you go too."

There's silence for a moment. Cal must be considering.

I don't know what to think myself. There's probably no way Ms. Lydia would ever let Cal come, even though he doesn't have finger-chips anymore. I'm not sure I could convince her.

"Maybe ... " Cal says. "Maybe I could say that I can't let Blanca be introduced to this young Vestal Lydia wants her to meet unless I've met his whole family at the banquet."

"Yeah," says the Virus. "It's worth a shot."

There's more silence. My mind whirls. I'm already planning what I'll say to Ms. Lydia when I write her a letter later today. But then the wheels stop spinning, and I hear Cal say one more thing.

"I want Blanca to know that I'm sorry and that I only want what's best for her now."

"I know," says the Virus. "Hopefully she hears that message one way or another."

"She doesn't have anyone on her side," Cal continues. "Only me, and you too, if you still want to stick around."

I don't have anybody? Cal's so clueless! I've got a whole Brethren of Vestals behind me! I'm part of the most important society there is!

"I'll stick around," the Virus answers. "It's going to take both of us to help her."

"Great! It will be wonderful having you back at the manor. I'll ask Alan to arrange for movers to pack up your apartment."

"Whoa! Wait a second," exclaims the Virus. "I'm not moving

back home. Where'd you get that idea?"

"You said you'd stick around."

"Yeah, like stop by every day to see Blanca."

I clench my fists. There's no way I want to see the Virus that often.

"But I thought this was the opportunity for our second chance," says Cal, with disappointment.

"I'm not a kid anymore. I have my own life."

"I never should have given you that trust fund," Cal mutters.

"My trust fund? What does that have to do with anything?" Eavesdropping doesn't allow me to see his face, but I picture the Virus tugging at his unruly black hair.

"Everything!" Cal explodes. "If I hadn't given you your own bank account, you never would have moved out to begin with."

"Oh, I would have moved out, all right."

"Not until college. Your mother would be crushed you didn't get a degree."

"I didn't go to college. Big deal. I'm doing fine without a diploma."

"Yes, but someday … " Cal's voice trails off as he and the Virus move to another room beyond my hearing.

I take a deep breath and clear their argument from my head. I need to concentrate on more important things. Tonight I'll write that letter to Ms. Lydia, and soon I'll be at the Vestal corporate banquet dancing with my friends.

Chapter Nine

Barbelo Nemo has a brilliant understanding of human nature, as well as unlimited empathy. *Human beings want two things*, he wrote. *Relationships, and a feeling of importance. Vestals deserve both.*

That's why the Vestal banquets began.

In the early years, most corporations only owned one Vestal. It took years for companies to establish complete Vestal families, one Harvest at a time.

Vestals can't date non-Vestals; that would be ridiculous. How could you trust somebody? What if they took your picture and sold it to a Virus? An evil ex-boyfriend could ruin you forever. *The only person a Vestal can trust is another Vestal.*

So every three months Barbelo would call his followers home to Tabula Rasa. Even now, decades after Barbelo retreated, the

Vestal banquets continue four times a year.

All Vestals are invited, but whether you can come or not depends on your purchaser. Most companies readily agree.

Vestals dating is good for business because of synchronistic advertising.

Take Beau and Fatima for example. Every time Beau's company releases a photo of Beau driving Fatima around in a gigantic truck, Fatima is always pictured looking gorgeous. So her fashion house ends up getting publicity too. They then return the favor by running an ad showing Fatima strutting down the catwalk in a white version of their latest design with Beau sitting in the audience, so stunned by her beauty that he "accidentally" drops his truck keys, company logo and all.

America loves it. It doesn't matter if the Vestal relationships are real, arranged, or fake; the public doesn't care. All they want is gossip. Purchasers control the whole story, and they always leave the public begging for more.

It all comes back to supply and demand. Since so little of a Vestal's life is made public, there is high demand to exploit it.

I've never been to a Vestal banquet because only harvested Vestals are invited. But Fatima heard they're wild. *"The perfect place for hookups,"* she said. *"Secluded corners, dim light, and music so loud nobody knows what's really going on."*

In the middle of all that, my soul mate is waiting. Tonight I meet the boy who sells soap. My perfect match!

The only problem is Cal. Things are weird between us. Cal says he wants to be my father. And not in a creepy way like Ms. Lydia warned me about, but in a real way. Like I've read about in books.

Cal wants me to choose to be his daughter. He's not saying it, but I can see him thinking it every time I look at him. *Choose to be free, Blanca. Choose to make your own decisions.*

And I can't.

That doesn't mean I'm not proud of Cal. He's accomplished a lot, with my help. *I want you to bring Seth back into my life.* That's what Cal told me that first night at the manor. *One way or another.*

I would do anything for Cal too. That's how I got him invited to the Vestal banquet. I wrote to Ms. Lydia and explained that Cal directed me to secure him an invitation, and that I always deliver.

Ms. Lydia wrote back the next day. "Good girl," she said. "I'll bring you the invitations in person."

And somehow, when she did, Cal turned that into Ms. Lydia coming with us. In our car.

The backseat of the limo is roasting hot, even though the moon roof is open. Cal raps on the divider and asks Alan to turn the air system up to cool things off. My white satin pants are getting sticky. Ms. Lydia is probably overheated too, but she doesn't show it. She takes a deep breath, as if breathing is her own personal cooling system. Then she half-smiles again, and her heart-shaped face returns to a perfect mask of grace.

"Sorry, ladies." Cal tugs at his collar. "It's a great day for making solar power but a bad day for wearing a tux."

"I don't mind the heat," says Ms. Lydia, gracious as always. "Besides, I can already feel the air-conditioning working on overdrive." She points down to her ankle, and we can see the white silk of her dress flutter upward from the vent, exposing part of her leg.

"Nice view," says Cal.

Ms. Lydia looks at him sharply. But then her expression changes and becomes thoughtful. A few seconds too late, she laughs. It's a soft, silver laugh that sounds like she was saving it for a special occasion. It's a genuine laugh. I can tell. And I realize I've never heard Ms. Lydia laugh for real before. I don't think I've ever seen her authentic smile either, like the one she's wearing now.

"I'm so glad you said yes," Cal says to Ms. Lydia. "I didn't feel right about sending Blanca off to meet a young man that I had never met myself."

"Of course, Calum," says Ms. Lydia. "That's only prudent."

"And now," Cal continues, "I get the pleasure of not only escorting one but two beautiful ladies out tonight." His sun-lined face gazes at Ms. Lydia in awe.

If it weren't so totally ridiculous, I'd wonder if Cal was flirting with her.

Ms. Lydia flushes. "Usually I go to these things solo."

"Not tonight." Cal picks up her hand and kisses it.

Ms. Lydia blushes a deeper shade of red and pulls her hand away. Her face is prettier than ever. I wonder why I thought she was over forty.

"What do *you* think, Blanca?" Cal pats my knee. "Are you

excited to meet Soap-boy?" He uses that obnoxious nickname the Virus coined.

"His name is Trevor." Ms. Lydia giggles. "And Blanca's going to adore him."

Trevor? I remember Trevor! Ms. Lydia has never said his name before. But I know all about Trevor. He's a few years older than me and absolutely magnificent. Blond hair, blue eyes, and a smile that makes you melt. Back at Tabula Rasa he never gave me the time of day, probably because I was younger than him, but things will be different now.

"Okay, Trevor," Cal says. "Not Soap-boy. I'll try to keep that straight."

"Please do," says Ms. Lydia.

"But you remember, Blanca," Cal says, suddenly serious. "You get to choose, okay? You don't have to be with Trevor if you don't want to."

"Yes, Cal. Of course, Cal," I say, slipping up again. He hates it when I agree with him like that. But Cal doesn't correct me this time. He picks up my hand in his and holds on to it tight.

My alma mater is a fortress of secrecy and protection. Alan drives the limo down the ramp to the Tabula Rasa underground lot, and the whole car goes dark. Security won't let Alan past the gate, but when they see Ms. Lydia, they allow her, Cal, and me to walk into the compound on foot.

As soon as I step on Tabula Rasa ground, my eyes go wet. I'm flooded with feeling. It's been so hard to be special.

Everything I do. Everything I say. Out there in the real world I have to watch myself. I have been living my life through a filter. What will Cal think? What will the Virus think? It's exhausting.

Being a Vestal is something I'm proud of every second of my life. I don't want to hide who I am, but it's hard. I'm elite, but I don't want to appear elitist.

Now I'm home with my friends, and for one sweet evening, I can be unguarded.

Ms. Lydia takes us up the faculty elevator, the one you need a key to operate. I've only ridden in it once before, that time Ms. Lydia brought me to speak with Headmaster Russell about my stolen picture.

"I'm surprised you have elevators," Cal remarks. "I thought we'd be walking up stairs."

"We're not Amish!" says Ms. Lydia with a teasing smile.

"I hope not." Cal coughs. Here at Tabula Rasa, his tanned skin seems exotic. "Do purchasers usually come to these functions?"

"Not typically," Ms. Lydia replies. "But it's happened before."

I'm surprised at her answer. As far as I know, the only people allowed into Tabula Rasa are Vestals.

"What about your purchaser?" Cal asks her. "Does he ever come?"

The elevator slows to a halt, and the doors hiss open. Cal's timing is awful, and his question is even worse. Asking a Vestal private information is the biggest faux pas there is. But of course Cal wouldn't know that; he's not a Vestal.

Ms. Lydia's flirty smile is gone. She stands stiff and statue-like. When the elevator doors start to slide back shut, she lets them. It's only when we're closed off again that she answers.

"He used to come," she says simply. "But my contract is fulfilled. I come and go as I please."

There's nothing but silence for a minute, and nobody says anything.

Then Cal punches the button to open the elevator doors. "Good to know." He holds out both of his hands, one for each of us. That's how we walk into the banquet: all three of us together and connected.

●●●●⬤●●●●

I feel like I'm in a fishbowl of white. Every last Vestal at the banquet stares at us as we enter the room. But I don't know who's garnering the most attention: me, the new Geisha; Cal, the only outsider; or Ms. Lydia.

Headmaster Russell rushes over, and I start to sweat. Ms. Corina from charm and deportment is right by his side, glaring.

But I remember something important: Ms. Lydia is on my side. That's all that matters.

"Russell," Ms. Lydia says. "How nice to see you. You remember Mr. Calum McNeal."

"Yes, Ms. Lydia," Headmaster Russell says. "Mr. McNeal, how … unexpected."

Ms. Corina stands there like the Princess of Placid.

There will be words. I know it. "Blanca," says Ms. Lydia coolly, "I see your friends over there. Why don't you join them?"

When I turn and see Fatima, I feel my insides go numb. Will she want to see me? But Fatima runs toward me so fast that I almost don't have time to open my arms. We hug and jump up and down at the same time.

Ms. Lydia smiles at our reunion and leads the other adults away.

"Whoa there," says Beau, walking over. "Stop being a Blanca hog."

Fatima smiles and pulls away, leaving Beau room to pick me up and swing me around in an enormous bear hug. Then it's Ethan's turn.

"We haven't seen you in *forever*," says Fatima.

"We weren't sure if you'd be able to come," Ethan adds.

Fatima gives me another hug. "It's so good to see you. We've been worried."

"Incredibly worried." Ethan adjusts the button on his white blazer. "Nobody knows what's going on with you."

"You're all anybody talks about at the photo shoots," says Beau. "Nobody can believe you went Geisha."

I glance over to where Cal and Ms. Lydia are circling on the other side of the room. She holds his arm with both hands now, and they tilt their heads inward and laugh. Headmaster Russell and Charming Corina are gone.

"Is that your purchaser?" asks Fatima.

"Yes." I nod. "That's Cal."

"And he's with Ms. Lydia." Fatima raises her eyebrows. "Oh."

"Yes. I mean, no," I say quickly. "It's not like that."

Fatima, Beau, and Ethan stare at me, and I know that

curiosity about my situation is killing them. But none of them ask any questions. None of them pry into my personal business.

"Cal wants me to be his daughter."

"Wow!" says Beau. The way he says it makes me wonder if anyone believes me. Cal paying thirty-two million dollars for a daughter is a hard story to sell.

But I can't tell my friends what's really been going on. I can't tell them about crazy month or Cal trying to release me. Cal's given up on telling me to think for myself for the time being. But he's not giving me a lot to work with.

That's when I feel the sucker punch to my heart.

Because I thought tonight would be different. I thought with the Vestals, I could finally be myself. But I can't tell them the whole truth. I've exchanged one filter for another.

"I'm here to meet Soap-boy." I quickly correct myself. "I mean, I'm here to meet Trevor."

"Trevor?" Ethan asks. "You mean that Trevor over there?"

We all turn to look at the Vestal family entering the room. There's Trevor, and he's taller, blonder, and clearer-skinned than ever. He stands next to his Vestal-mom, who has ageless skin and gray hair. His Vestal-dad looks like he's about ready to step out of a shaving commercial. The entire Soap Family is stunning.

As soon as I see Trevor, I feel hope. Maybe with Trevor, things will be different. Maybe Trevor will make my whole world right.

"I guess that could have been your family too," says Fatima.

"What?" I ask.

"That's where you would've ended up, if you hadn't protected me from that picture," Fatima says quietly, almost apologetically.

Sensing the privacy of the moment, Beau and Ethan move away.

"You would have done the same for me," I say.

Fatima contemplates her golden cuff. "I don't know what I would have done."

My platinum cuff feels heavier than ever for some reason.

"I was *so* jealous," Fatima admits. "I always thought I'd be top pick instead of you. That's why I didn't say thank you."

"For what?"

"For protecting me. I'm sorry I was such a jealous idiot that I never thanked you for shielding me from that Virus. I'm sorry you had to go Geisha over it."

"But—" I say, trying to protest. I don't get the chance. Ms. Lydia and Cal are right there, waiting to introduce me to Trevor.

He's perfect for me. I know it the first time Trevor looks at me with his clear blue eyes. He's honest and kind and obedient and respectful, all rolled up in one. He's the perfect boy next door, and he smiles down at me like I'm the only girl in the room.

I could thank Ms. Lydia for a thousand years, and it would never be enough.

"Blanca," Trevor says.

I'm not sure if that's a question or statement, but I don't care. It's not like I'm going to be able to answer anyway, not with my tongue permanently attached to the roof of my mouth.

The woman standing next to Trevor speaks for me. "So this is Blanca," she says. Her skin is so smooth that the gray hair sets off her face like a frame.

"Yes, Lilith," says Ms. Lydia. "This is *Ms.* Blanca." She puts the emphasis on the Ms., and Lilith finches.

I take notice too, of course. Lilith is older than me, more experienced. I've followed her career ever since I was a little girl. I should be kowtowing to her, not the other way around. Why doesn't Ms. Lydia want that? But then I look down at Lilith's wrist and see gold, not platinum. For some reason, that loosens my tongue.

"It's nice to see you, Ms. Lilith," I say. "And you too, Trevor."

Trevor smiles back at me with a mouth full of perfectly straight, white teeth.

"And this is Blanca's purchaser, Mr. Calum McNeal," Ms. Lydia continues the introductions. Then she indicates the razor model behind Lilith. "And Richard, Trevor's father."

"It's a pleasure." Cal shakes everyone's hands. Then he looks at me and winks. "Richard and Lilith, I'm dying to hear about the soap industry. Let's give these two some privacy, and you can tell me all about your work."

The other Vestals try not to laugh.

Ms. Lydia actually does, that silvery laugh of hers that is so beautiful. "Calum!" she says as she leads him away. "You can't *give* privacy. You can only *protect* it. Once it's gone, it's gone."

And then it's me alone with Mr. Gorgeous, although we're in a room full of people.

"So, um," says Trevor. "You're Blanca."

"Yes," I say, "I'm Blanca. Do you remember me from school?"

"Um, no, not really. But Lilith, I mean … *my mom* said that you and I are going to be perfect together."

"Ms. Lydia said that too."

Trevor shoves his hands in his pockets and steals a glance at his mom.

"So," I say, "you're twenty?"

"That's what they tell me."

I struggle to think, but it's like my brain is made out of cardboard. "I've been a fan of your mom forever," I finally say. "I'll never forget that campaign she did for Citrus Sunshine when I was little." Then I start to hum the tune like a dork before I can stop myself.

But Trevor smiles and hums along with me. "Yes." He steals a glance at Lilith. "That was a good one."

I look at Lilith too. She glares at me like I'm a menace. But then she sees me looking at her and quickly turns around.

"Would you like to dance?" Trevor asks me. Without waiting for a response, he pulls me onto the floor. He binds his arms around me, and we float around the dance floor like we're clouds. Trevor's such a great dancer that for a second I forget about everything else. The Virus, the picture, the month locked in my room; it all spins away into oblivion.

"So you went Geisha?"

The question snaps me back into reality. "Yes. But it's not what you think. My purchaser and I, we're not … you know."

"Oh," says Trevor. "My mom said … Never mind. You and me? This could be for real?"

I feel my ears turn red. "If you want," I manage to get out.

"Cool." Trevor pulls me closer, and we both spin around.

We don't say much after that. I'm too busy thinking about how we're the perfect couple, and that it's a shame that Virus isn't here to see what a real relationship should look like.

I can't stay for the whole evening. I'm not exactly sure why. But right after dinner when the lights dim and the tables are being cleared away, Ms. Lydia suggests we leave. Cal immediately agrees.

It's been nothing but smiles and stolen glances between the two of them ever since we climbed into the limo.

"I appreciate you allowing me to be your escort tonight, Lydia," Cal says. "I realize now how courageous you had to be, to show up with an outsider like me."

"Don't mention it." Ms. Lydia blushes. "It was my pleasure."

"No, really," says Cal. "You're a remarkable woman, Lydia. Exactly like this young lady over here."

Cal elbows me in the ribs gently when he says that, and I flush too. He's sitting between Ms. Lydia and me in the back of the limo.

"I only have one complaint," Cal continues, and I can't tell if he's being serious or not. "Where was the food? I thought we were going to a banquet!"

Ms. Lydia giggles. "What are you talking about? There was plenty of food."

"Fish and vegetables *do not* count as plenty of food," says Cal. "I'm starving!"

"That's how Vestals eat," I say. I catch Ms. Lydia's glance, and we both start laughing.

"No wonder you people don't go out," Cal says. "Restaurants would be wasted on you."

"Fish and vegetables are good for you," insists Ms. Lydia. "That's what everybody should eat."

"Did somebody tell you that?" Cal asks.

Ms. Lydia's face freezes, and I feel a chill overcome the backseat. She recovers in a flash and changes the subject. "So, Blanca, what did you think of Trevor? You two were dancing all night."

"He's nice. But I had a horrible time remembering how to talk."

"Oh?" asks Ms. Lydia.

"Yes." My ears turn red.

Cal looks directly at Ms. Lydia. "I get tongue-tied by beauty too."

"Oh, Calum." Now Ms. Lydia's the one blushing.

Watching old people flirt is bizarre. But I'm happy for them, even though I feel out of place. So I do the only sensible thing possible: I rest my head on the wall of the car and pretend to fall asleep.

"Won't you let us drop you off at home?" Cal asks Ms. Lydia. "I hate to think of you out on the roads by yourself this late at night."

"Thank you, but no. I'll be fine."

"It would be no problem at all to take you to … " Cal leaves the sentence hanging, a question. A Vestal would know better than to press Ms. Lydia on where she lives, but Cal's not a Vestal.

"Thank you, Calum, but again. I'll be fine."

I give a snore. Not a that's-so-fake-I-can't-believe-it-snore, but a soft one, like I'm sound asleep.

"Poor girl," says Cal. "She's had a long night."

"Yes," says Ms. Lydia. "Blanca's so lucky to have you to watch out for her. I couldn't be happier with how things turned out. I wish I could spend more time with her."

"Then why don't you?" Cal says. "Come to dinner tomorrow night. Or the next night, or the one after that."

There's a few seconds of silence.

I try to calm myself, to keep my breathing regular so it still looks like I'm asleep.

"Well?" Cal waits for an answer. "I would love to see more of you. Would you consider that?"

"Yes," Ms. Lydia says, breathlessly. "I would."

I feel my eyes flutter, in spite of myself. Hopefully they still think I'm asleep. If I could fall asleep for real, I'd know exactly what to dream about.

I want to be like Ms. Lydia someday. I want to be a Vestal Geisha who has completed her contract. I want to be exactly like her. Ms. Lydia has her freedom and her cuff.

Ms. Lydia could have gone back to Tabula Rasa as a teacher, but instead she's our elected agent. Even Headmaster Russell fears her.

She's the most perfect Vestal I know.

The Virus waits for me at the door of my cloister. He leans against the door in a T-shirt and old jeans, his dark hair sticking up wildly all around his head. He clicks off his new finger-chips when he sees me approach, but I know he's been online.

"So you're back?" he asks.

A wave of heat rushes over me when I meet his eyes. "Yes." I take the key to my room out of my pocket and unlock the door.

The Virus follows me in. "Where's my dad?"

"Saying good-bye to Ms. Lydia." Then I turn to him and try not to smirk. "They really hit it off."

"What are you talking about?" asks the Virus.

"Nothing." I pull the mirrored doors half closed, so the Virus can't see me when I change into my nightclothes. But then on a whim, I open them again so he can see me when I head into the bathroom to brush my teeth. Through the mirror I see him lean forward and stare at my behind.

When I finally come out, he's sitting on the velvet ottoman in the center of my dressing room. He pats the seat in front of him. "You look pretty with your hair pulled back like that," he says to me, and for the slightest fraction of a second, I think it's a compliment. But then the Virus adds, "I bet you could have done a great job selling soap."

"Get out, Virus." I don't bother to sit. Why does he have to be so mean?

But the Virus doesn't move one muscle. "My name's not Virus. It's Seth."

I want him to leave. I want him to leave so bad that my fingers clench into fists and I'm ready to fight. But part of me wants to sit on that ottoman. To forget this animosity and remember the taste of his lips crushed against mine.

"Cal said—" I begin, but the Virus interrupts me.

"My dad said what about me? That you should call me Virus?"

"No," I admit. "He said to call you Seth."

"And what else did my dad say?"

I look at Seth lounging there, on my ottoman, in my room, saying every last thing he can to annoy me. He's ink-covered and tech-infested, and he's ruining my whole night! But Cal did say that I was supposed to talk to Seth.

"Cal said that I'm supposed to engage in ordinary conversation with you whenever the situation warrants talking."

"Well then," Seth says. "I have a situation that warrants conversing. Sit down, Soap-girl."

I take a seat on the edge of the ottoman as far away from him as possible and try to stay calm.

"What do you want, Seth?"

"Nothing." He taps his foot and his leg jitters. "I wanted to talk to you, that's all."

"We don't have anything to say."

"That's not true and you know it! Blanca, I thought—"

"You thought what?"

"I thought you liked me," says Seth, his face looking pained. "I thought you were falling for me as hard as I was falling for you."

"Well, you thought wrong." I only wish that were the truth. "Cal said I should do whatever I had to, so that's what I did."

"Whatever you *had* to?" Seth runs his hand through his hair so it's crazier than ever. Crazier in a good way. "Not *wanted* to?"

"A Vestal would never want a Virus," I say, willing it to be true. And I try not to remember. I try not to think about lying next to Seth with his arms around me, feeling his heart beat next to mine.

Seth sits there, breathing heavily, like he's fighting for some type of control.

I'm fighting for control too. There's something inside me, hurting.

"I wonder if you know," Seth finally says.

"Know what?"

"You're costing him." Seth says. "You're costing my dad everything."

"What are you talking about?"

"Your purchase price? Your crazy antics last month? They're pulling my dad away from his business."

"What?" I've never given McNeal Solar Enterprises much thought.

"So enough with this Vestal shit," Seth says loudly. "Keep your Ms. Lydia away from my dad so he can concentrate on his business. That company means everything to him."

"Seth." I reach out to his shoulder but he recoils from my touch. The missed contact burns. "I would never hurt your father. Never! Not on purpose, at least."

But Seth is already getting up to go. Right before he leaves, he turns and glares at me to get in one more jab.

"You and your Vestal crap are ruining everything!"

I sit on the ottoman, too upset to move. It takes me a while before I realize that I still haven't locked the deadbolt. But then I see that wall of mirrors and I remember something.

Seth may be wrong about practically everything, but he got one thing right. I've got a face that can sell soap.

Selling clean energy should be equally easy.

I'm going to be the face of McNeal Solar Enterprises and make things right.

Chapter Ten

Ms. Lydia's tempo is grueling. Right hook, left hook, right jab, kick. She puts me through my paces this morning, like she has every day she's been in town since the banquet. After Kenpō comes an hour of yoga. Then I'll run around my courtyard like a lab rat for an hour. Only now nobody can see me, because Ms. Lydia insisted that Cal put shutters on the *outside* of the first-floor windows. I don't know why that didn't occur to me during crazy-month, but it didn't. Now when I'm in the courtyard, I'm completely closed off.

Ms. Lydia thinks me being the face of McNeal Solar is the best idea ever, and she helped me talk Cal into it one day when we were swimming in the manor's indoor pool.

"But we don't do traditional advertisements," Cal said, wading into the shallow end. "We rely on trade conventions."

"Don't you want McNeal Solar to have a fresh, clean image?" Ms. Lydia sat perched on the edge of the pool wearing an ivory maillot.

"Well, yes, but—"

"And you want McNeal Solar to be seen as trustworthy, right?"

"Yes, of course! But—"

"Then you've got to use Blanca!" Ms. Lydia argued. "She's your best asset, and you haven't used her properly yet."

Cal winced. "I don't want to *use* Blanca. I only want her to be happy."

"Well, she'll never be happy. Not unless you give her a purpose. That's what Vestals live for." Ms. Lydia kicked the water with her dainty foot, making a small splash. "Vestals can sell anything. Give Blanca a chance, Calum. You'll be amazed."

Cal still wasn't convinced, so Ms. Lydia went at it from a different angle.

"Calum," she said, sliding into the water. "It would make me so happy too. It would give me the opportunity to be here all the time. I'll coach Blanca every step of the way. Please let *us* do this for you."

"Fine." Cal shrugged. "If this is what Blanca wants, I'll say yes."

"Yes! It's exactly what I want!" I bounded off the diving board and cannonballed into the water, splashing them both.

"I can't very well say no to both of you." Cal laughed.

And that was the moment it started. Ms. Lydia has become so tangled up with me and Cal and our lives together at the manor that it's become harder and harder to tell where one of our lives starts and the other's ends. She's always here, watching over me, keeping me safe.

"All this bread and butter!" she said at lunch one day. "You're not going in front of the camera just yet, Blanca."

Hence my new regime. It was a month before the first photo shoot.

Four hours a day of exercise and a strict fish-and-veggies diet. Cal's been complaining a lot about my new meal plan, but it always gets smoothed over.

Ms. Lydia's worked on Cal so hard that she practically leads him around on a leash.

"Calum, darling," she told him, entwining her arms around him after a particularly Spartan dinner. "We like to be healthy. Don't you want us to live a long time?"

Of course Cal couldn't argue with that. He was sneaking some whole-wheat bread into my diet when Ms. Lydia wasn't looking, but now she's here at the manor practically all the time.

"Doesn't it bother you, Calum, that there's no place to be in this whole house that's truly private?" I heard Ms. Lydia say to him one afternoon. "If there were some lead-lined walls, we could … "

As soon as I heard that, I made a beeline for my room. I try not to think about what they might be doing together while I'm in the courtyard, running around in circles. It's none of my business. But I'm ecstatic that Cal's happy.

And he is happy. Ridiculously so! I've never seen Cal smile so hard as he does when Ms. Lydia comes into a room. She's like sunshine on his heart.

The only bad thing is when the postal service comes with a letter for Ms. Lydia. Then she heads off for a couple of hours, or a couple of days. But she always comes back. When she does, Cal and I are both here waiting.

It's almost like we're our own Vestal family.

But I wish for Cal's sake that Seth wasn't such a troll. Since Ms. Lydia became part of things, Seth has pretty much stayed away. The one time Seth did show up for dinner, he and Ms. Lydia got into a huge fight over the proofs from my first photo shoot.

It was a picture of me wearing white yoga pants, doing the Scorpion pose in front of the newest McNeal Solar Enterprise factory. I was balancing on my forearms with my feet up in the air, hanging above my head. It was all very Zen. There was a warm glow over the whole picture and a caption that read MCNEAL SOLAR MAKES ALL THINGS POSSIBLE. ASK FOR MCNEAL SOLAR BY NAME, JUST LIKE BLANCA.

"I can't believe you're letting the Vestals worm their way into your business!" Seth said to Cal, like Ms. Lydia wasn't sitting right there at the table. We were eating grilled salmon and roasted Brussel sprouts.

"Don't be rude." Cal smiled apologetically at Ms. Lydia. "Vestals are experts at advertising."

Seth pushed a Brussel sprout around his plate with his fork. "What does yoga have to do with solar energy anyway? That's stupid!"

"It's not about yoga." Ms. Lydia sat up straighter. "It's about Blanca. She could be balancing a stack of dishes on her head, and it wouldn't matter. People will buy whatever she sells." Ms. Lydia was having a hard time staying placid. I could tell.

"That's crazy!" Seth turned to Cal. "What happened to giving Blanca her own life back?"

"This *is* my life," I said to Seth. "This is what I've always dreamed of. I'm going to be a traditional Vestal now."

Seth's voice dripped with disgust. "Everything always comes back to you and your weird Vestal shit."

"Seth!" Cal said sharply. "Please—"

"Don't bother." Seth dropped his fork. "I'm done."

That was a few weeks ago. We haven't seen Seth since.

I keep watching Cal, thinking he's going to be upset by this, but he's not showing the hurt yet. I know being apart from Seth must be killing him. Seth was the whole reason Cal harvested me in the first place! I guess Ms. Lydia and I must be doing a pretty good job of filling the part of Cal that was so lonely for family.

Right hook, left hook, right jab, kick. Ms. Lydia is right, like always. This workout is evil, but in a good way. Sweat drips down my forehead, and I don't bother to wipe it away.

"Higher, Blanca! Higher!" Ms. Lydia kicks along with me. Out here in the sunlight it's easier to tell how old she is. She and Cal are probably the same age. Maybe Ms. Lydia's even older.

"Okay," she finally says. "Let's get out the yoga mats."

When we're headfirst in Downward Dog, she starts talking about our plans for next week. "That print ad was merely the beginning, Blanca. People all over are calling up their local power company and asking for McNeal Solar by name. Calum can't believe it!"

I smile as I slide down to Plank. "I guess Seth leaking the photo on *Veritas Rex* backfired on him, huh?"

"Let's not talk about him. Viruses are beneath us."

We both slip into Cobra, and the stretch feels good.

"Already you've been a game changer." Ms. Lydia lifts her face to the sunshine. "Nobody ever thought of using a Vestal to advertise for energy before. Things are going to get bigger from now on. The commercial next week will take your image to a whole new level."

Ms. Lydia's probably right, like always. But the opportunity is fertile for humiliation.

"What if Trevor and I don't have any chemistry on camera?" I ask.

"Fake it." Ms. Lydia walks her feet up to the top of her yoga mat. She pauses for a minute and looks at me. "Lots of Vestals have their first public date on camera. It'll be fine. You'll see."

But I'm still pretty nervous. I'm not shooting one commercial next week, I'm shooting two. One for McNeal Solar with Trevor popping in at the end. The other will be Trevor's soap commercial with me in the final shot. Ms. Lydia has been arranging the deal for weeks.

By the next Vestal banquet, Trevor and I will be an established item.

There's a knock from above. Cal leans out my window over the ladder, trying to get our attention. "Lydia," he says, waving a white envelope and looking downcast. "You have a letter."

Ms. Lydia told Cal a while ago about her being the elected agent for Vestals, so Cal knows that Ms. Lydia has a busy job brokering the deals for Vestal photo shoots. But that doesn't stop the disappointment, for any of us, every time Ms. Lydia has to leave.

Ms. Lydia takes a deep breath and then rolls up her mat. "I'm sorry, but I have to go."

"For how long this time?" I ask. "What about the commercial shoot? Will you still be there?"

Ms. Lydia shrugs. "Maybe." She stares at the stone wall like she sees right through it.

"Ms. Lydia," I ask, my voice low and respectful. "Do you want—"

But she interrupts me midsentence. "It doesn't matter what I want." She chucks her yoga mat into the redwood storage box. "I learned that a long time ago."

"Blanca," Cal says that night over dinner, "I've got something to show you." Since Ms. Lydia is away, we sneak dinner rolls with our halibut.

Cal types on his watch, and a website pulls up, floating over the bowl of broccoli.

The Lighthouse, it says. Exposing the truth about Vestals one beacon of light at a time. Underneath is a supposed exposé on the Vestal blessing. Only instead of golden cuffs, they're demonstrating it with paper tubes.

Cal stares at me, examining every aspect of my reaction. But I'm as placid as ever.

"Why are you showing me this?" I try not to sound suspicious.

"Because I wondered if it might be what Lydia's been dealing with lately." Cal types something on his wrist and pulls another picture up. "And also because they've been blogging about you."

There's my print ad for McNeal Solar, but instead of the correct headline, it now says WHAT THE F--- DO VESTALS KNOW ABOUT ENERGY?

I feel horrible because it's the truth.

"What do you want me to do?" I ask. "Do you want me to cancel the commercial?"

"No, of course not." Cal observes me closely. "Should I leave this up? Do you want to read some more?"

"No!" I say a little too loudly. "I mean, no thank you." But before Cal taps on his watch to shut things down, I catch a glimpse of one more word: NEVADA. My mind goes back to my Harvest, when Headmaster Russell told the audience that I was born there.

"I have to say it," says Cal. "This website has a point. If you're going to represent McNeal Solar, you should at least know a little bit about how solar energy works."

I nod, despite the fact I have no idea where this is going. I'm still lost in Nevada.

"Good, I'm glad you agree," Cal says. "I'm going to instruct you in thermal engineering."

"Thermal what?"

"Don't worry. We'll start with physics first."

I have no idea what to say.

"One more thing," says Cal, as the server brings out the

contraband dessert. “Let’s not mention any of this to Lydia.”

My new education begins that night. Positive charges, negative charges, electrons running around circuits like little green men; my mind is already swimming. The books stacked on my desk are a tower of evil. None of this was covered in the Tabula Rasa curriculum. Headmaster Russell said the liberal arts were all we needed.

As it turns out, science is fascinating. Each lesson opens my mind to broader horizons. But I hope Ms. Lydia doesn’t find out about my new study plan. Or even worse, that I like it.

Chapter Eleven

I'm practically naked underneath the fluffy white bathrobe. I'm hardly wearing any makeup, only a bit of lip-gloss. The coffee cup in my hand is warm and steaming. Everyone watches as I bring it to my lips.

"From my first cup of coffee," I say.

Then flash forward to me at the gym, whacking a punching bag with my signature roundhouse kick. I'm wearing skintight white pants and a sports bra.

"To my trip to the gym," I say.

Now it's a boudoir shot. I'm leaning into a mirror and applying lipstick, wearing a white, strapless sundress.

"To preparing for a night out," I say.

Then it's me standing at a front door, holding a gigantic bouquet of red roses. Trevor leans against the doorjamb, with one arm around my waist.

"I rely on McNeal Solar Energy to heat things up," I say. "McNeal Solar makes all things possible." Then Trevor pulls me into the deepest, most perfect kiss ever.

Perfectly banal, that is.

On screen it looks absolutely beautiful. But in real life, it's just wet.

It's also awful because there are about thirty Vestal Rejects all around us filming the whole thing. I'm glad that there aren't random photographers taking my picture. But Rejects are creepy, especially the ones with tattoos. Headmaster Russell had solid reasons for expelling each and every one of them from Tabula Rasa.

That's probably why Lilith won't talk to the Rejects.

Trevor keeps looking at Lilith and tugging on his collar when he's supposed to be looking at me! The whole thing is weird. Why is his mom watching?

At least Ms. Lydia is pleased with how things turned out. "Beautiful, Blanca," she gushes. "Absolutely beautiful."

Of course I love hearing that from Ms. Lydia, but when the camera crew tries to chat with me, I stiffen up because I have no idea what to say.

The Rejects watch as the director pulls me aside to thank me personally. I recognize Jeremy as a Vestal dropout from six or seven years ago. He's one of the few students who left Tabula Rasa of his own accord. Now he's got piercings in his nose and tattoos on his neck. Jeremy directs all the Vestal commercials.

"You've helped a lot of people," Jeremy tells me. "That harvest price of yours is employing loads of workers. We're grateful."

I'm helping the Rejects? I had no idea! I thought it was the other way around. Ms. Lydia is a genius for organizing it this way.

Then there's Trevor's soap commercial. The camera crew got everything ready.

All I have to do is look pretty. I run down some steps from a fake apartment building, swing my leg behind Trevor on his white motorcycle, and then we drive off into the sunset.

Easy, right?

The problem is, Trevor can't figure out how to operate a motorcycle even if his life depended on it. After five hours of expert instruction, he still gets the left-hand clutch mixed up with the right-hand accelerator. He never remembers about starting the engine in neutral and has no idea how to upshift.

The Vestal Reject who's trying to teach him is about ready to scream.

"Look, Trevor," I finally say. I try not to compare him to Seth, but it's hard. "Riding a motorcycle isn't that difficult." I grab my helmet, climb on, and take the bike for a spin around the sound stage all by myself before anyone can stop me.

"Blanca!" Jeremy shouts, but I don't find that out until later. I can't hear anything underneath my helmet.

When I turn off the engine and park, everyone stares at me.

Lilith is ready to spit nails, but Trevor looks amazed, like he didn't know I could do something like that.

Leave it to Ms. Lydia to fix things. "Let's change course," Ms. Lydia tells Jeremy. "You can't see anything under those helmets anyway. Let's have Trevor *lean* on the bike, and Blanca run down to kiss him."

So that's what we do. The commercial becomes Trevor getting cleaned up in the shower, and then me running down to meet him. Trevor's leans next to the motorcycle he's too clueless to ride.

Then comes our date.

The sound stage is set up to look like a restaurant. Trevor and I sit at a table with a red-checkered cloth and a candle stuck in an old wine bottle. There are enormous plates of spaghetti in front of us and a basket of garlic bread.

"Don't really eat that!" Ms. Lydia cautions, even though she knows I know better.

"Act natural," Jeremy adds. "Forget the cameras are here."

But it's hard to forget. Especially with Lilith glowering at us across the room, her face smoother than ever. Something about the corners of her eyes makes her look different than she did so many years ago in the Citrus Sunshine commercial. They must be loading Lilith up with anti-wrinkle cream. It's ironing out her face to perfection.

"So," says Trevor. "Our first real date."

"Yes," I say. "This is awesome."

I'm such a liar. This is awful! What are we supposed to talk about? Maybe I could say, "Hey, Trevor, did you know what a bad kisser you are?" Let's get *that* conversation on camera.

Jeremy gestures for us to do something, so Trevor grabs my hand. His own is slimy with sweat.

But he whispers something honest, something that makes me like him all over again. "This is awkward," he says. "I'm not normally such a turd."

"You're not?" I giggle. There're multiple flashes as the cameras catch my response.

"If there weren't all these people ..."

"Exactly," I whisper. "And your Vestal-mom over there, looking pissed."

Trevor's face darkens at that. I must have said something wrong.

"I'm sorry," I say. "I didn't mean to offend you."

"No. That's okay. Things are ... complicated."

"'Vestal families are always complicated.'" I quote Barbelo Nemo.

"Yes," agrees Trevor. "'But we have everything we need to achieve happiness.'"

"Exactly." Then I look over at Lilith again and do a double-take. She reminds me of somebody I know, and not only from the Citrus Sunshine ad. But before I can ask Trevor about it, he leans in to kiss me.

"Bingo," says Jeremy. "That's a wrap."

My videos are everywhere. On the drive to Cal's office today, we see an enormous glowing billboard of me holding the roses and Trevor leaning in to kiss me. I'm finally up there with all my friends! I'm a real Vestal now, and it's all thanks to Ms. Lydia convincing Cal on my behalf.

Cal slides the privacy divider so Alan can't hear our conversation, and then leans back into the plush upholstery of the limo. "Thanks for coming with me today. I didn't want to leave you at home to fend for yourself with all the remodeling going on."

He means the workmen crawling over the house, lining Cal's room with lead. Ms. Lydia has taken off for the week on business. But she'll be moving in when the work is complete. She also promised to be here in time for the next Vestal banquet.

"Ms. Lydia says your office is lovely," I say.

"It is," Cal says. "Sophia decorated it. Then I had it lined with lead a month ago, once I … started seeing Lydia."

I'd cover my ears and start singing if I could forget hearing that last part. I don't want to spend any time at all wondering what Cal and Ms. Lydia do behind closed doors. But I understand Ms. Lydia wanting to take every precaution to ensure her privacy and not be accidentally uploaded to the net.

"I only wish that Seth wasn't being so difficult." Cal peers down at his chip-watch. "He hasn't messaged me in a couple of weeks."

"Maybe he needs some time."

"Maybe," Cal says. "I wish that he could understand that I'm really happy. For the first time in a long time, I'm *really* happy. And I want him to be a part of it. But every time I try to talk to Seth, we start fighting about his apartment or college or Lydia."

"I'm sorry

"Will you do me a favor?"

"Yes, Cal. Of—I mean yes."

"This isn't an order; it's a request. Would you go to Seth's apartment and give him a message for me? Alan could drive you."

"A message?"

"Yes. Make Seth listen. Make him understand that I'm in a

good place right now, but that I miss him."

I look down at my engineering books. They're weighing me down but are fascinating. I was hoping to read more of them today.

"What about my studies?" I ask. *Clarifying questions are my friends.* Cal told me to learn about science too.

"I don't want to interfere with that," Cal says. "You've got a real head for engineering. I had no idea you'd learn all of this so quickly."

It's true. I've been dreaming of solar circuits.

"In fact, I've been meaning to talk to you, Blanca. Have you ever thought about going to college?"

"What? How would I do that?"

"You could become an engineer for real, or anything else for that matter. You could make friends, you could—"

"Are you telling me to?"

"No," answers Cal quietly. "I'm only asking you if you've thought about it."

"There's no way it would be possible. Not without having to go public." Ms. Lydia leaves for a few hours and already Cal is going nuts.

"What about online classes? Correspondence courses?"

"Not unless you tell me to." I pause. "Will you?"

"No," Cal says. "I'm done with that. But I'm asking you, *as a favor*, to go to Seth's apartment after lunch today and see if he will listen to reason. Could you? Please?"

"Of course," I say. "I'll do anything you want."

Cal grimaces when I say that, and then he stares out the window.

Chapter Twelve

I always knew Seth was a pig. Seeing his apartment proves it. There are half-eaten pizzas, boxes of donuts, and empty liters of soda everywhere. It's like junk food came here to die.

And don't get me started on the connections. Seth clicks screens down right and left. Even in the bedroom, where his unmade bed is a tangle of sheets, there are video screens on every wall.

"If I had known you were coming, I would have cleaned up a bit," Seth says.

If I didn't know him better, I would think he was embarrassed. "Fair is fair, Virus. You've barged in on me before."

"I thought we agreed you'd call me Seth." He slides some dirty socks off the couch so I can sit down.

"Oh right. I forgot." When I sit down on the couch, my hands go straight into a melted bowl of ice cream.

I pretty much freak out.

"I've been stained!" Rocky road drips down my arm, ruining my white shirt. I glare at Seth's smirk.

"Um, let me show you to the bathroom," Seth offers. There's an awkward moment where he holds out his hand to help me get up, and I refuse to touch him. There's been enough touching already.

Ten seconds in Seth's bathroom and I already know a million more things about him than I would have liked. Most importantly, Seth doesn't have any soap. So I come out with my hands held up and still dripping.

"Any soap?"

"Sure," says Seth. "In the cabinet."

I root my feet to the floor.

"What's the matter now, princess?"

"I can't open your cabinets," I say. "That would be an Invasion."

"A what?"

"An Invasion." I try to stay calm. But it's tough when you're talking to a Virus. "If I look in your cabinets, it would be an Invasion of Privacy."

"Again with the Vestal shit," Seth mutters. He scoots past me into the bathroom and I follow behind. It's tight quarters in here. "I don't see what the big deal is." He opens the cupboard and gets out some soap and a fresh towel. Then he stands there, watching as I wash up.

"It's a huge deal," I say. We're standing so close I can smell him. At least he smells clean. Exactly like I remember.

"Oh yeah?" Seth says. "Why is that?"

I nod at the medicinal shampoo in the shower. "You have dandruff." Then I look at the floor and counter. "A girl was here, maybe a while ago by the looks of that hairpin on the floor, and you leave weird notes next to your shaving brush. That's way more about your life than I ever wanted to know."

"I don't have dandruff," Seth says, his voice getting louder. "No comment on the female visitor, and you can blame my mom for the notes under the shaving brush. That's just a thing we used to do." His chest moves up and down rapidly like his blood is pounding hard. He always gets worked up when he talks about his mom.

I remember that too.

I turn away and dry my hands off on the towel, trying to stay in the present and forget all of the rest. "My shirt's ruined. I look like I'm wearing brown."

"I'll get you a clean one." Seth comes back a minute later with a crisp white oxford. It smells like detergent but also like him.

I wait for Seth to leave the bathroom before I strip off my T-shirt and button up the broadcloth.

When I return to the living room, it's slightly cleaner, like Seth raced around picking up trash the few minutes I was alone in the bathroom. I head back toward the couch, but Seth stops me.

"Don't sit there! Here," he says, pointing to a chair. "Sit here. There's better light." Then he clicks on the lamp next to my chair and another one on the wall behind him.

"I'm here to deliver a message from your dad," I say, sitting down. "Cal wants to see you again. He's upset about how things turned out. He doesn't want Ms. Lydia to come between you."

Seth runs his hands through his dark hair, and it sticks up in spikes. "The thing is," he says. "Maybe I could be cool with this. But Lydia being a Vestal weirds me out." He leans forward and gazes at me intently. "Maybe I could be more comfortable with the situation if you tell me more about her."

"Sure." I try to think what I could say that would make Seth understand how wonderful Ms. Lydia is without giving too much up. "She's brilliant. She can talk about anything."

Seth hangs on every word. "Tell me more," he says.

Something about the way he's suddenly being so polite makes me suspicious. "We still have our deal, right? What's said between you and me is private?"

"Yes, Blanca. Of course, Blanca."

He's such an ass. I don't trust him one bit.

"Look." I rub my platinum cuff for support. "The bottom line is that your dad is super happy, and it's all because of Ms. Lydia. The only thing missing from his life right now is you. Won't you give it a chance?"

"A chance? You want me to watch my dad make a fool of himself?"

"What are you talking about?"

Seth grits his teeth. "Do you know what Lydia's story is? Where does she live? Who purchased her? What do you really know about her?"

"That's none of my business."

"And it doesn't bother you?" Seth presses on. "It doesn't make you mad that Lydia's probably going off to another guy who purchased her and then coming home to my dad? I thought you cared about him."

"I do care about Cal!" I protest. "And that's not how it is. You've got it all wrong." I'm so angry at how Seth is slandering Ms. Lydia that my words spill out before I can stop them. "Ms. Lydia's giving your dad *all* her free time. She's giving him her choice. She's choosing to be with him! That's more important than anything else."

"That's so messed up I can't believe you're saying that."

"It's not messed up!"

"It is too!" Seth says. "Look, how do you know that Lydia's purchaser isn't *telling* her to like my dad?"

"Because her contract is—" I start to say. But I stop myself in time.

"Her contract is what?"

"Nothing." I can't tell Seth that Ms. Lydia no longer answers to her purchaser. Her business is private. I shouldn't trust Seth at all. Not one bit!

"I know you know something," Seth says.

"No. I mean, no, I don't. I'm only guessing. It's none of my business."

"Admit it. It's possible that somebody's pulling Lydia's strings."

But I don't admit it because I know it's not true. Ms. Lydia's contract is up. She's with Cal because she wants to be with him. She's the most perfect Vestal there is. She's everything I want to be.

"I would never let anybody hurt your dad," I say with sincerity.

"Look, Blanca. I'm never going to be okay with my dad and Lydia being together unless you can tell me some more information about her."

"That's not going to happen!"

"Then I guess we're done here."

"No. We're not."

"How do you figure?" Seth rubs the back of his neck.

"Because your dad told me to make you listen. He said to make you understand."

"And you do everything my dad tells you to?" Seth asks.

Seth's mocking me again, and it hurts. I look down at my platinum cuff and try to remember my long-ago lessons from Ms. Corina. First I relax my forehead, then my cheeks, then my smile, until finally I straighten my spine like it's being lifted from above, and I'm placid. I'm perfectly placid.

"I'll come back tomorrow," I say. "I'm going to make you understand."

"I'll never understand."

"Maybe so," I say. "But Ms. Lydia's moving in with us anyway."

Set's face goes white, the tattoos sitting on his skin like liquid ink. "What?"

"The workers are there right now, lining your dad's rooms with lead."

Seth doesn't say anything. He stands there, stunned. And deep inside, I find the urge to reach out and comfort him. To wrap myself around him in a hug. But I don't have the courage.

"See you tomorrow," I finally say.

I'm not sure if he hears me.

Cal waits for me in his office. He purses his lips when he sees my new shirt. "What happened?"

"Ice cream." I shrug. "I'm sorry, Cal, but I couldn't make Seth listen to reason. I'm going back tomorrow to try again."

Cal raises his eyebrows. "I see. Well, here's something for you in the meantime." He shows me the miniature solar cells he's brought in for me to play with. They're hooked up to an old-fashioned calculator that's broken.

"This is your new task for today. Figure out how this works." Cal smiles, encouraging me with his faith in my capability. Then he leaves for some meetings.

The tiny solar circuit is like a little mystery. I look at it from every angle before I open up my textbooks. Then I take the circuit apart, tinkering until it works.

There's something about the circuit that reminds me of a cloister. A cloister has to be completely secure so your privacy doesn't escape. All the windows and doors are locked. It's the same thing with the circuit. One little opening and the electrons run free.

When Cal comes to get me at the end of the day, I'm standing next to the window. "Well?" he says. "Let's see what you accomplished."

I hold the calculator to the light, and the solar cells charge after a few seconds. The little calculator fires right up, flashing numbers and ready for work.

"This is only the beginning," Cal tells me. "If you can do this, then you can do anything."

And I smile because I know he is right.

I can do anything if Cal tells me to.

The next day Seth's apartment is considerably cleaner. He must have spent the last twenty-four hours covering the whole place in bleach. Lights are on everywhere, and one of the windows is open, letting in some fresh air. It even looks like Seth brushed his hair.

"It's a nice place you've got here," I say, "once you finally cleaned it up."

Seth shrugs. "I decided to give the maid a call."

I throw down my jacket on an armchair and make a turn around the room, fingering the bookshelves like I'm examining his knickknacks. Really, I'm looking for hidden cameras, just in case. I've been thinking about Seth turning on all those lights yesterday and hoping it wasn't some sort of nefarious move.

"We still have a deal, right?" I try to sound friendly. "You promised to keep our conversations private?"

"Of course, Blanca." Seth grins. "Don't you trust me?"

"About as much as you trust me." I sit on the edge of the couch. Maybe I'm being paranoid.

"In my defense, you did try to trick me. That night, under the tree, in my room, the rest of it … " Seth comes to the couch and sits next to me. "You really messed with me. For a couple of days there I thought … But then it turns out you were under directions from my dad."

I shouldn't feel guilty, but I do. Because maybe I did like Seth—for a few minutes, at least. But there's no way I'm admitting that I ever liked a Virus.

"I'm sorry." It takes a lot to say that.

"To be clear," Seth says, "my dad didn't tell you to mess with me now, right?"

"No," I say, instantly defensive. "But he wants you to understand. Cal's happy, and he wants you to be part of that."

"Maybe I could be … Maybe if you told me a little more about the Vestals, I'd understand."

"Okay." If Seth thinks he can trick me, he's got another thing coming. I know what I'm allowed to say.

I give Seth my best, most innocent girl-next-door smile. I can sell soap, I can sell clean energy, and I can sell Seth the cleaned-up version of Vestal history. I'll just leave out the part about the dissenters. That's harder to explain. "The Vestals were founded fifty years ago by a man named Barbelo Nemo, who lost people he loved in the Brain Cancer Epidemic."

"Was Barbelo Nemo his real name?" Seth interrupts.

"Yes, of course it was. Why would you ask that?"

"No reason. I'm naturally inquisitive. What does Barbelo Nemo look like?"

"He has long white hair, a beard, and glasses."

"So he basically looks like Santa?"

"Stop being an ass!" I snap. Then I fight not to seem annoyed. Vestal history is pure, and I need to do it justice.

"Sorry," says Seth, and his apology seems genuine. "Have you ever met Barbelo?"

"No. He stays private now. Barbelo has retreated to his estate, but nobody knows where that is. Nobody has seen him in the past twenty years, but Headmaster Russell receives messages from him almost daily."

"How?" Seth asks.

"What do you mean?"

"How does Russell get messages from Barbelo, if neither of them are connected?"

What an idiot! "Um, the postal service? Ever heard of that?"

"The mail? You mean like snail mail?"

"Yes."

"Nobody but the government uses snail mail anymore."

"Well, Vestals use the postal service too."

"But," Seth protests, "you'd have to have a special permit. You'd need to be a politician or somebody to still get the USPS. It went bankrupt years ago. Now it's only for VIPs."

"Exactly," I answer.

Seth pauses a second, letting that sink in. Then he asks, "So how did it all start? Why were the Vestals founded to begin with?"

"Barbelo began the order with the children of his friends who had died. He vowed to protect them. He vowed to keep them safe from all the things that had consumed his loved ones. He was brilliant because he saw that technology and cancer were one and the same. Some people were dying of brain cancer and some people weren't, but everyone was suffering the same fate in the end. *Technology was driving people apart and tearing them away from the physical presence of the people they loved.*"

I've got my cuff against my heart, and I don't remember putting it there.

"That's why the Vestals were founded, Seth. We are living reminders to the rest of the world that there is a better way to live."

"And you buy that?" Seth asks. "You believe that a bunch of people who died would name Barbelo—if that's his real name—as the guardian to their kids?"

"Of course," I say. "That's what happened. Everyone knows that."

"Only Vestals would say that," argues Seth. "Normal people would ask more questions. They'd want to see evidence."

"I *am* normal." I get up, ready to leave, but Seth stops me.

"Wait," he says. "Explain the Harvest to me."

"That's easy," I say. "The world was fed up! People and companies were sick and tired of celebrities hawking products one day and being on the front page of tabloids the next. Nobody could trust anybody. It was bad for business. That's why companies started harvesting Vestals instead. We're completely trustworthy and consumers know that."

"*And* you can't be scanned."

"Yes." I smile. Seth's finally getting it! "Nobody can look up our past history of transgressions at the scan of a fingertip. There're no dumb pictures of us as teenagers following us around. Vestals are virtually blank, and that makes us special."

"Special is right," Seth says. But he doesn't say it like it's a compliment.

"So you see?" I continue, ignoring the slam. "Ms. Lydia and I, we're completely trustworthy, like the rest of the Vestals. That's why—"

"Why what?"

"Nothing," I say. I was about to tell Seth about the Vestal Archives, but I stopped myself before the slip.

"I want to trust you," Seth says. "But I'm worried about you too."

"Why?"

"I'm scared for you. Do you know what my mom said the definition of a god was?" When I don't move a muscle, Seth answers for me. "Somebody you're willing to bet your life on."

"I don't think Barbelo's a god," I say quickly. "I'm sorry if I gave you that impression."

"You have, and you don't even realize it. That's the scariest part of all."

"Well, now you're being ridiculous."

"I am not. You're so hell-bent on following Barbelo Nemo and believing that whatever he says is right, that you've lost all sense of self."

"How can you say that?" My back tenses.

"Because you don't make your own rules. You don't think your own thoughts!"

"That's not true!"

"Is it?" Seth asks. "Here's another question: what do you like to do, Blanca? What do you like to do for fun?" Seth looks at me closely. His dark eyes pierce me so hard that I have to fight the urge to look away.

"What type of question is that?" I stall for time. Nobody's ever asked me that before.

"I'm proving a point. What do you like to do in your free time?"

"I like to read," I answer. "I write letters. I do yoga. I go running. Normal stuff like that."

"Those are all things they tell you to do," Seth says.

I start to protest, but he stops me.

"If you could do anything … If you had one perfect day to yourself, what would it be?" Seth stares at me so hard that all of a sudden I feel like I can't breathe.

"That's private," I finally say, getting up to go.

"Then I'll see you tomorrow," says Seth, still sitting on the couch. "You haven't made me listen to reason yet."

I don't bother to argue. The sooner I can get to the cloister in my car, the better.

We kiss in the rain. My white dress clings to me and becomes transparent, but the way my breasts are crushed into Trevor, I'm completely covered. He's got his arms around me, pulling me up to my toes. The water pours down his back, hitting every angle of his muscled shoulders. It's another perfect date caught on camera for our companies to market.

It's too bad Trevor's mother is watching. Lilith shoots daggers my way every time I turn around. She makes the camera crew of Vestal Rejects seem friendly.

Then Lilith glares at me one more time, and I finally get it. I can't believe it took me so long to figure the situation out.

That woman isn't Lilith at all!

At least, she's not the Lilith I remember from the Citrus Sunshine commercial. I think she's actually Sarah, who used to come to my kindergarten class. Lilith and Sarah are dead ringers for each other.

"Am I doing better this time?" Trevor whispers, interrupting my thoughts. The stage techs adjust the rain machine, and a gentle mist envelopes us.

"Much better." I lean into him. But when my ear is pressed against solid shoulder, I think harder.

Sarah's been going gray since ninth grade. Now she's making women all across the world believe that she's Lilith, and that wrinkle cream will make them look as young as her. And how is anyone going to ever find out the truth about Sarah being twenty-five? They're not! Sarah has no virtual fingerprint. She's a blank slate, like me.

But the real question is, what happened to the previous Lilith? Why did they need to replace her?

"I could get used to this," Trevor murmurs into my hair. "You're so perfect," he says before he kisses me again.

And I love him for saying that. Even though I know it's not true. But with Trevor, it feels like it could be true, no matter who his crazy Vestal-mom is.

We shot a picnic-in-the-park scene this morning, and he fed

me chocolate-covered strawberries. Then a scene at the pet store with all the puppies. This has been the best day of filming ever.

Things are about a thousand times better with Trevor than they were last time. He's really loosened up. It's like he knows all the right words to say. The only time it's awkward is when Lilith/Sarah is around.

I wish that Ms. Lydia could be here. She'd know what to do.

Trevor pulls me in for one more kiss. "You're adorable," he says. "Am I making you happy?"

"Yes," I answer. "More than happy.

"Good," Trevor says. "You'll come to the Vestal banquet next week, right?"

"Yes! If it's okay with Cal."

"Do you think you can convince him?" Trevor asks. "If you tell Ms. Lydia how great things are between us, will that help?"

"Probably," I say. "I'll figure something out."

"Excellent, Blanca. I know you can do it." Then he kisses me again as the cameras flash.

It's late by the time I stop by Seth's apartment. I knock on the divider and ask Alan to text Cal to tell him what's up. *When you go someplace, leave a note.* I'm trying one last time to complete my mission.

"I thought you blew me off," Seth says, after I come inside.

"I keep my promises to your dad," I say. "He still wants you to listen."

Seth flicks his thumb, and a silvery-gray photo shoots up of Trevor and me just hours before in the rain. Seth points to it with his other hand. "Is this real, Blanca?"

"What do you mean? Of course it's real! That's me, isn't it?"

"Do you actually like this guy? Are you kissing Soap-boy for real or because my dad told you to?"

"That's not what it's like! Your dad would never tell me to do that."

"So it's real then?" Seth asks again.

"Yes," I say. "Definitely."

"For Soap-boy too?" Seth holds up his palm right in front of my face so I can stare at Trevor and me. "How do you know that somebody isn't telling Soap-boy to make you like him?"

"I can tell when somebody is kissing me for real."

"Can you?" Seth's eyes flash. "Because I couldn't."

"Well that's because—" I start to say. But then I stop myself.

"Because what?"

"Never mind."

"I bet you couldn't tell," Seth says. He's close enough now that I can smell his shampoo. "I bet if I kissed you right now, you wouldn't know if it was for real or if I was faking it."

"Don't be ridiculous. Of course I could tell." But I don't move away.

"Prove it." Seth cups my face in his hands and presses our lips together. Before I know what I'm doing, I'm kissing him back. His arms go around me, and my arms reach for his neck. We're all tangled up in a mess of heat.

"Real or fake?" Seth asks, finally pulling apart.

I want to be honest, and that terrifies me. It feels like my filters are slipping away. Seth already knows so much. Would it hurt to tell him a little more?

That's the dangerous part about Seth. He makes me forget everything that's truly important. All I feel is chaos. For a half second I think about doing something stupid and telling him the truth about what I'm feeling. I mean, what I felt.

"Seth, I—"

From somewhere in the corner of the room, a buzzer sounds. Lights flash and a silvery screen pulls down from the ceiling.

"What's that?" I shield my face from the tech on instinct.

"It's okay." Seth gently pulls down my hands. "It's only a rival site. All that means is that *The Lighthouse* has another post." He keeps his arms around me, and I feel his fingers press into the small of my back.

"The site that bashes Vestals?" I ask, trying not to view the screen. That means that I have to turn inward, toward Seth.

"You've heard of it?" Seth clicks a hand toward the visual, making it larger.

"I'd better be going." I step away.

"Wait!" Seth tries to hold on. "Do you still have that white bike?" Seth points to pirated video from my photo shoot.

There I am, tooling around on Trevor's motorcycle for the whole world to see! One of the Vestal Rejects on the camera crew must have betrayed me and uploaded the footage online. Jeremy better fire the culprit immediately.

"No," I say. "That was for a photo shoot. So what?"

"So," says Seth. "Maybe that's something you might like to

do sometime, for fun."

"That's not going to happen."

Seth nods back at the screen and then looks at me. "Well, what about Nevada?" he asks. "What do you know about that?"

"What?"

Seth points to the text floating in the air. I turn away, not reading it, although the headline is already seared in my mind.

"I don't know anything about that," I say. "I don't know if Barbelo lives in Nevada or not."

I can't get out of there fast enough.

Chapter Thirteen

When I was growing up at Tabula Rasa, every last minute of my day was orchestrated for me. I'd wake up in my cloistered dorm and wait in the long lines to brush my teeth. All of us girls would spy on each other in the mirrors, trying to see whose teeth were becoming crooked. They'd let you get braces, but it was better if you had naturally straight teeth.

Then we'd eat some gluten-free porridge for breakfast with a hardboiled egg. The kids who complained or were noncompliant were kicked out faster than you could say, "Please sir, can I have some more?"

Classwork was always my favorite part. Grammar, rhetoric, logic, music—I soaked up learning but was never showy about it. I understood early on that it was better to lie low.

I also learned not to get too attached to anyone.

I had this one friend named Amy all the way until I was ten years old. One day we were whispering goodnight to each other across our bunks, and the next morning, Amy was gone.

I held back the tears for weeks.

Amy was sent home for an online transgression. Her mom posted a baby picture of her along with a message that said "Happy birthday to my ten-year-old at Tabula Rasa!" Who knows why the lady was so stupid. Maybe she wanted her little girl home.

The point is, I didn't bother becoming close friends with anyone for a long time, until one day when I was thirteen and some of my hair fell out.

It was right before bedtime, and Fatima and I were the only two left in the bathroom, brushing our teeth. I leaned over the sink to spit when I noticed a chunk of brown hair had fallen into the basin.

"Shoot!" I whispered hoarsely. "Shoot! Shoot! Shoot!"

"What's the matter?" Fatima's words were garbled by her toothbrush. Even at thirteen, she filled her black nightshirt in a way that would have made the boys go nuts if they could have seen.

"My hair!" I cried. "Look at my hair!"

Fatima came over and examined my head closely. "You can't see the bald spot yet, not if your hair is brushed back. But this isn't good."

She didn't need to say that last part for me to know the truth. If I lost my hair, I'd lose my looks. If I lost my looks, I'd be sent home. Nobody wants to go home to parents who didn't want you in the first place.

"Lights out in two minutes!" Ms. Corina called from down the hall.

Placid, Fatima mouthed at me. *Don't let her know.*

"Girls?" Ms. Corina asked, coming into the bathroom. "Why aren't you in bed?" Right as she approached us, Fatima slid over. She walled off the sink so my hair in the basin wouldn't show.

"'Special attention to oral hygiene is a must,'" Fatima quoted.

"Of course," Ms. Corina said, squinting at us. "But it's bedtime now, so get a move on."

"Yes, Ms. Corina," we both answered at once.

Later on, when we were walking down the hallway to our dormitory, I started to cry. "What am I going to do?" I whispered, more to myself than Fatima. Fatima had never paid any attention to me before that night. But she stunned me.

"Don't worry," she told me. "We'll figure it out."

I don't know why she decided to help me. Maybe it was because Fatima was always looking for an excuse to break the rules. She was a rebel, but she also has a big heart.

A couple of days later, I was headed toward Latin class with my hair carefully pulled back in a ponytail so the bald patches wouldn't show. Fatima came out of nowhere and grabbed my arm, pulling me into a supply closet.

"Here." She shoved a bottle of pills into my hand. "Iron tablets, for anemia."

"Where did you get these? What are you talking about?"

"Anemia." Fatima flipped back her own dark tresses. "I asked around, and it's really common here because we don't eat red meat. Have you felt faint?"

I nodded.

"Dizzy?"

"Yes," I said. "That too. But how do you know for sure? I can't take random pills somebody gives me."

"I worked hard to get those for you!"

"What did you do?" This was getting sketchier and sketchier.

"I can't tell you. I called in a favor." Fatima bit her lip.

I looked down at the orange bottle. "325 mg ferrous sulfate."

"If these don't help after three months, then there's nothing I can do for you," Fatima said. "You might have alopecia … but hopefully it's low iron."

"Look." I hesitated. "I can't take these. Not without talking to a doctor. But I appreciate this. You've given me courage to deal with this, so thank you."

"What are you going to do?"

"I'll go to Headmaster Russell. I'll ask to see the doctor."

"But what if you get kicked out?" Fatima's eyebrows flew up.

"What if I die? What if these aren't actually vitamins? What then?"

"They're iron tablets," Fatima whispered. "I promise."

"I believe you," I said. "I believe *you* believe these are iron tablets. And thank you. But I can't sneak around. It would drive me crazy."

"Sometimes crazy is a good thing." Fatima smiled.

Things ended up being better than all right. After that moment, Fatima and I became best friends.

Things with Headmaster Russell weren't so easy. He was awful when he found out about my hair. But the doctor said it *was* a vitamin deficiency, not permanent hair loss. Iron, zinc, and B12. They hopped me full of vitamins the size of horse tablets. A few months later, my hair grew in thicker than ever.

So when Fatima knocks on the metal door of my room tonight an hour before the Vestal banquet, I let her into my cloister immediately. It's the first time she's ever come to McNeal Manor, and I'm thrilled to see her, although I have no idea why she's here.

Is this a special surprise? Did Ms. Lydia arrange this? Does Fatima get to ride to the banquet with us for some reason?

But then Fatima takes off her white traveling cloak, and I see that she's covered in color.

That's when things get weird.

"Nice place you've got here." Fatima runs her hand over my desk like everything is normal. Her butt models those blue jeans in a way that makes you notice the label.

"Fatima," I say. "What's going on? Where did you get those clothes?"

"Not all of my friends are Vestals," she answers calmly, as if everything's all right. But I know better. I can see Fatima's breath go in an out like a jackrabbit's. I've never seen her so scared before. "Don't you get tired of wearing all white?"

I let the question slide. If Fatima wants to wear a red sweater, then that's none of my business. But I have to ask her the most important question. The one I can't ignore. "Does your company know you're here?"

Fatima gazes out my window. "Nope."

I take a few moments to let my own heart slow. "What's

going on?" I step beside her at the windowpanes.

"I wanted to see where you live. I wanted to—" But Fatima can't finish her sentence before her voice starts breaking.

"What's the matter?"

"I'm pregnant!" Fatima crosses the room and sinks onto my bed. Before my eyes, she crumples into tears.

I don't know what to say because I can't tell if Fatima is crying with joy or sorrow. But then she pushes herself up on her elbows and smiles.

"It's a miracle. The operation must have reversed itself! I'm going to have a baby!"

"How is that possible?" I sit on the bed next to her.

"I don't know. I've never understood things like that."

"Whose baby is it?" It's a foolish question, because I already suspect the answer.

"Beau's, silly. It's our *baby*."

"But wasn't Beau sterilized too?"

"Supposedly," Fatima says. "But I don't know if I can believe anything they tell me ever again."

"Fatima," I whisper, afraid for her. She's totally losing her mind. "If Headmaster Russell finds out, or Ms. Lydia—"

"They'll kill it," Fatima interrupts me. "That's why I came to you. You're the only one who can help."

"Why me?" But I know the answer to that one too. I'm the only one who's different. I'm the only one who went Geisha.

"Will you see if your purchaser can help?"

I look at Fatima, sitting there in her new clothes. She's covered in color and ruined now, on the inside and out. Fatima already doesn't look like the Vestal sister I knew. But I hold my cuff up to her heart anyway.

"Fatima, you have a hard road. In so many ways it's difficult being you. But I know that you can do it. You have everything you need to achieve happiness."

"Thank you." Fatima throws her arms around me, and we both weep together. And I know that I'll do anything to help her.

That's why I go get Cal.

That's why I screw everything up.

He's holding his toothbrush when he opens the door. I've never been in Cal's rooms before, and I don't care to be there now. It feels wrong to invade his privacy.

I smell the fresh paint covering the newly installed lead walls. Ms. Lydia's white traveling cloak is lying on the bed. I hear the shower running in the background.

"I need your help," I whisper. I've never asked Cal for anything before.

He doesn't even put down his toothbrush. He nods his head and follows.

When we get to my cloister my rooms are empty. "Fatima." I knock on the open door. "We're here."

Fatima emerges from the corner, behind one of the drapes. She looks younger than usual, and scared.

"What's going on?" Cal sets his toothbrush down on my desk.

"Fatima's operation didn't work," I explain.

"What are you talking about?"

"I'm pregnant," says Fatima, coming to sit on my bed.

"I still don't understand," says Cal. "Are you talking about an abortion?"

"No!" Fatima cries, and her eyes go wild. "That's what they'll do to me if they find out."

I feel awful. Fatima has already said too much. I sense the danger seep through the room like it's Discipline Hour and Headmaster Russell is approaching my desk with the whip.

Cal speaks slowly, like he's still trying to understand. "So what do you mean about the operation?"

But Fatima doesn't say anything. She's too afraid.

Cal looks at me directly. His face is more lined than I had ever realized. "Tell me, Blanca," he says to me. "Tell me what you mean."

"Vestals can't get pregnant," I say quickly. If I say it fast enough, maybe he'll understand. Maybe he'll know, like I know, that Barbelo knows what's best. "It's for our own good. That's why they fix us when we turn fourteen."

Cal stands there, taking it all in. Then he steps closer to me and cups my face in his hands. "That is horrible, Blanca. That is evil and wrong. *Never for one second do I want you to believe that what they did to you is okay.*"

All I can do is nod. I have to believe because Cal told me to, even though I know that he's wrong and Barbelo's right. *Our founder is always right.*

Cal releases me and walks over to Fatima, putting his hand on her shoulders. "I know someplace you can go. There's someone

I can call." Cal grips his forehead. "But Lydia! We can't let Lydia know about any of this. Go to my room, Blanca," he says. "Go distract Lydia. Keep her there. Do whatever you have to do to keep her there as long as possible. Improvise! Be cunning! I know you can do it." Then he enfolds me in a hug and kisses my cheek.

I am at the door, ready to leave, when Cal stops me.

"One more thing," he says. "You are never, ever to tell Lydia about any of this. Do you understand?"

I nod, but I feel guilty. Chemistry lessons, dinner rolls, accidentally kissing Seth and liking it—there are so many things I'm keeping from Ms. Lydia at this point, I'll just add Fatima and her unborn baby to the list.

"Calum, is that you, darling?" Ms. Lydia opens the door wearing a silk kimono, her face freshly done up. "Oh. Hello, Blanca."

"Cal said to come ask you," I say. "I asked him what I should do with my hair tonight, and he said to come and let you decide."

Ms. Lydia sighs. "Your hair? Really, that does seem like a decision you could have made on your own." But she steps back, inviting me into the rooms.

"I was thinking of cutting it."

"Cutting it? Don't be ridiculous. What would Trevor say?"

"Well that's another thing I wanted to talk to you about." I stand there immobile, trying not to observe my surroundings. The pictures of Seth as a young boy framed on the wall, the bronze Don Quixote statue standing sentential on the desk, the solar calculator that I fixed the other day, lying next to it; I'm learning too much already.

But Ms. Lydia doesn't seem to mind the intrusion. Maybe this isn't an Invasion after all. She pulls me into the dressing room and sits me down on a velvet bench. I see Cal's shaving brush on the counter next to her perfume.

"Let's talk about your hair first, shall we? That's the simplest issue to solve." Ms. Lydia brushes my hair. As she does, the old memory calls from my psyche. *I am loyal. I am discrete. I follow the rules.* Brush. Brush. Brush. She makes long strokes from crown to tips. "You've always had the most beautiful hair," says Ms. Lydia, "ever since you were a baby."

"You knew me when I was a baby?"

"Yes," says Ms. Lydia, brushing away. "Tabula Rasa was different in the early years. Less structured. I used to help out in the nursery." She pins my hair around the crown, coiling it into a roll. "We didn't have thirty-two-million-dollar Harvests back then, making life easy."

I know a compliment when I hear one. It makes me bold.

"Did you know that I come from Nevada?" I ask.

Ms. Lydia pauses mid-pin. "Nevada," she says carefully. "What makes you think that?"

"That's what Headmaster Russell said about me at the Harvest. He said I was from Nevada."

Ms. Lydia rolls her eyes. "Russell will say anything to rile bidders up. That's one of his strong suits."

"So I'm not from Nevada?"

Ms. Lydia opens her mouth to answer, but then she stops.

Finally she says, “Honestly, I have no idea.”

“So you don’t know who my parents are?”

Ms. Lydia doesn’t say anything. She shakes her head.

I bet she’s disappointed in me for asking. So I fix things right away. “It doesn’t matter where I’m from. The only thing that matters is that I’m a Vestal.”

“That’s exactly right,” says Ms. Lydia. My hair is done, and she puts our faces close together, looking at our reflections in the mirror. “And now we can be together forever. Are you happy that I’ve come here?”

“Yes.” I beam a smile. “It’s almost like you’re my Vestal-mom. Like we’re a real Vestal family.”

“Darling, I’m so happy to hear that!” Ms. Lydia takes my hands in hers. “You know, I’ve told my purchaser about you.”

It’s the first tidbit of information Ms. Lydia has ever shared with me about her situation.

“You have? You still see him?”

“Yes,” says Ms. Lydia. “He loves hearing about you. He knows how hard it has been on me all these years to never have a traditional Vestal family.”

“That’s the problem with going Geisha, isn’t it?”

Ms. Lydia nods. “Yes. But now I’ve got you, and I can do whatever is necessary to stay close to you and make you my daughter.”

It’s a golden ray of happiness, hearing that Ms. Lydia is choosing me as her Vestal-daughter. It’s almost like she’s choosing me over everybody else.

But it’s that last thought that makes me wonder. Ms. Lydia

wants to be with Cal too, right?

"About your hair," Ms. Lydia continues. "I don't think you should cut it. I wore my hair long like this when I was your age too. Now tell me about Trevor."

"Trevor?" I ask. Everything swirls around in my mind, and I can't think straight. Cal has been so happy since Ms. Lydia joined our lives. She's not tricking him, is she? No, that's just that bastard Seth putting ideas in my head.

"Was your last date with Trevor more successful? I'm sorry I couldn't be there."

"Yes, Ms. Lydia. It was. Trevor made me think everything was perfect."

"That's a funny way to put it. Wasn't it perfect?"

"No." I look down at my cuff. "Sarah kept staring at us."

"Sarah?" Ms. Lydia quickly puts down the hairbrush. "We don't mention that name anymore."

"So, I've gathered," I say. "Why didn't you tell me about Sarah being Lilith?"

"Tell you? I thought you knew. You've known Sarah for a long time."

"But what happened to the real Ms. Lilith?"

"Sarah *is* the real Lilith. She's completely legitimate."

"That's not what I mean," I protest. "What happened to Ms. Lilith number one? Where'd she go?"

Ms. Lydia glances across the room at the freshly painted walls. Her lips press together and form a thin line. "Her work was done," she says simply. "Lilith was needed elsewhere."

"Was her contract up?"

"Really, that's none of your concern."

"None of whose concern?" Cal asks, suddenly coming in. He's got his toothbrush in his hand, like he was out for a stroll.

"Nothing, darling." Ms. Lydia smiles and tilts her head to let Cal kiss her cheek.

It doesn't matter that Ms. Lydia didn't tell me the whole truth. It doesn't matter that she kept the details from me. Seth is wrong about Ms. Lydia, I know it. *You can't ever trust a Virus.* That's what Barbelo wrote, and he's always right.

I think I was wrong about Cal too. I always thought he was a horrible actor. I thought he wore his heart on his sleeve. But you'd never know now that he helped rescue Fatima. He seems calmer and happier than ever. Every time he looks at Ms. Lydia, he smiles harder and harder.

And she eats it up.

I get up to go. Right before I close the door behind me, I hear Cal say, "Lydia, my love, do we need to go to this banquet tonight? Let's send Blanca on her own and enjoy some time to ourselves."

I never hear Ms. Lydia's answer. But an hour later when Alan drives me away to my second Vestal banquet, I am the sole passenger.

Chapter Fourteen

"You're the only one I want to do this with," Ethan says to me. "I've been waiting forever." Ethan's showing me something private.

We are hidden behind a ficus tree in the corner of the room at the Vestal banquet. The music and dancers swirl around us a few feet away. But tucked where we are, nobody can see us. We are completely hidden.

The first time I went to a Vestal banquet, Ms. Lydia made us leave early. Now I know why. After dinner, the lights dim and the music cranks up. The whole room becomes dark and shadowy. It's exactly like Fatima said it would be: the perfect place to hook up. Probably Ms. Lydia didn't want Cal to see all of that.

Before dinner, I spent the whole banquet dancing with Trevor. But then we got separated somehow, and Ethan grabbed my hand. The music was so loud that he put his mouth right next to my ear. "I have to show you something," he hissed. "It's important." Then he pulled me away into a secluded corner.

Ethan's left his glasses at home, but he has his white suspenders on. It's his signature look. He slouches against the wall so that he doesn't tower over me like a scarecrow. "Can you see anything?" Ethan holds up his wrists.

I look at his palm, his fingertips, and the top of his hand. "No, nothing."

"Exactly. They're brilliant."

"What are you talking about?" I shouldn't be here in the corner with Ethan. Trevor will come back soon. "What's brilliant?"

"The new invis-chips," Ethan says. "They're so small you can't see them with the naked eye."

"You've got finger-chips?" I say, a little too loudly.

"Shhh!" Ethan puts his finger on my lips. "It's a secret."

"But your vows! What if Headmaster Russell finds out?"

"He's not going to find out." Ethan flexes his hand. "They're nearly invisible, remember?"

I pick up his hand and look at it more closely. I don't see anything until tiny blue pinpoints catch my eye.

Ethan's connected.

"Have you been online?"

"Yes, and it's the best thing ever."

"What?" My neck is so tight it feels like it could snap.

"We were lied to. The Internet isn't evil. It provides instantaneous knowledge. It helps us connect with people all over the planet. There's a whole world that we're missing."

"But we're supposed to miss it," I say. "That's how we stay safe."

Ethan shakes his head. "It's how they control us."

That's when I realize how dangerous Ethan's become. How I shouldn't even be talking to him. I turn to go, and he stops me.

"There's this website called *The Lighthouse*."

I don't say anything. There's no reason for Ethan to know that I have any idea what he's talking about.

"Your Ms. Lydia?" Ethan says. "She's —"

He's stopped by a rustle of leaves. I push Ethan into a darker, safer part of the corner just in time. Our space has been invaded by a lip-locked couple.

It's Trevor and Sarah.

Trevor's hands are under Sarah's skirt, lifting it up. "Lil," he says, moaning.

She undoes his pants with nimble fingers.

Ethan mouths *Vestal-cest* to me in the semidarkness. As if I hadn't already figured that out for myself. Then he starts holding up his hand. He's connected, and he's corrupted.

"No." I push Ethan's hand away. "Don't film that."

"But he's tricking you," Ethan whispers. "They're using you as their cover."

And it really hurts to know the truth. But posting it online for the world to see isn't the answer.

Ethan used to know that. Technology has alienated him already.

Beau catches us slipping from behind the ficus tree. He gives Ethan the thumbs-up, jumping to the wrong conclusion.

"You're a popular lady tonight, Blanca," Beau says. He spits his words out fast and grins ear to ear. "How about a dance?" At my nod, Beau takes me in his arms and spins me away.

Once we're out there on the darkened dance floor, Beau's smile freezes like it's plastered on his face. Then he whispers between his teeth. "Have you seen Fatima?"

So that's what this is about.

"She's safe," I whisper back, trying to smile, like him. "I don't know where she is, but she's safe. You don't need to worry."

"Don't worry? This is all my fault!"

"Of course it isn't."

"Then whose fault is it?"

"Nobody's," I answer. "It's just the way it is." I'm not sure if that's the truth or not.

I can feel Beau's blood beat fast as I hold onto his shoulder. I can smell him sweat. His smile is turning false.

"Neutral," I remind him. "Placid, calm, not easily upset. Remember what Ms. Corina used to say."

There's nothing better than neutral. Staying poised could get you through anything. Keep your face placid and everything will be okay. Because if somebody does know what you're thinking, then you've already lost a little bit of your privacy that will never come back.

"Headmaster Russell already cornered me tonight, asking me about why Fatima's not here. What am I going to do?" Beau knits his forehead into a mass of wrinkles.

"I don't know."

"How will this work?"

"I don't know," I say again. "*But you have everything you need to achieve happiness.*"

"I don't, Blanca. Not without Fatima. Not without my child."

We don't get the chance to say anything else because the music stops. Beau spins me around in a final twirl, and there's Trevor, waiting to cut in.

"How're you doing, beautiful?" Trevor asks me as the music starts up. He's sticky under his white shirt and smells like cheap body spray.

"I've been better." I fight to stay calm.

Trevor isn't listening to me. He navigates our way through the dancers and steals glances at Sarah.

I look too.

She's over by the water table talking to Headmaster Russell. The conversation appears animated. Sarah knocks over some water glasses on purpose and tries to stalk away. Headmaster Russell grabs her arm and then glares right at us.

I feel Trevor's muscles stiffen. He pauses, missing a beat, but keeps dancing. "Blanca, you're beautiful," Trevor says, not meeting my eyes. "Blanca, you're perfect. I could dance with you all night."

I don't want to dance with Trevor all night! In fact, I strongly consider rearranging that Soap-boy face of his until the only thing he can sell is Band-Aids. But I smile up at him anyway until Headmaster Russell lets Sarah go.

"Where's Ms. Lydia?" Trevor asks, like everything is fine. "Did you get the chance to talk to her?"

"I most certainly did."

"Did you tell her how things are going? Did you tell her how much I want to be with you?"

"Yes." I'm smarter than this. Trevor's trying to control me. I see that now. He's giving me the full force of his Soap-boy smile.

But Cal said I could choose about Trevor. He said I didn't have to be with Trevor if I didn't want to.

So when Trevor starts in again about how pretty I am and how I'm such a great dancer, I make my decision. "Stop," I say. "Please."

"What?"

"I'm going to do you a favor," I say. "I'll tell Ms. Lydia that you're the best boyfriend ever, only I'm not interested."

"I don't understand." Trevor looks into my eyes at last.

"I'll tell her it's my fault," I whisper. "I know about the Vestal-cest."

Trevor's usual clear skin floods with color and becomes splotchy. "How'd you find out?"

"It doesn't matter. But why'd you make me your target?"

"I had to." Trevor slumps his shoulders. "I was under directions."

"From who? Your company, or Ms. Lydia?"

"Do you even have to ask?" Trevor says. "She wants you to be happy. For some reason, you've really captured Ms. Lydia's attention."

"I'll tell her I'm happy, all right." I stick out my chin. Happier on my own, alone with the truth.

I'm beginning to sound like Seth.

The manor is quiet when I arrive home. There's no Cal, no Ms. Lydia, and no Seth waiting to pounce.

I don't know why I'm disappointed.

I thought at least Ms. Lydia would be there waiting up for me, to see how the banquet went. To hear Trevor talk, Ms. Lydia cares about me a lot.

But Ms. Lydia's not there tonight, and she's not there the next morning either. When I ask Cal about it at breakfast, he says Ms. Lydia was summoned.

"I have travel plans too," he says. "I've some business to attend to that might take a few days. Will you be okay here on your own? Do you want me to call Seth?"

"No, thank you. I'll be fine."

"I know it." Cal winks. "You've got good instincts, and you can think for yourself."

"That's not what I meant!"

"But it could be." Cal smiles. "It could be."

Chapter Fifteen

Sometimes people do things that are so wicked they don't want anybody to know about their transgressions. Their secrets need ultimate protection. That's where the Vestals come in. Our Archives are top-notch and so exclusive that only a select number of the most powerful people in the world know about them. We store wills, documents, passwords, and formulas. VIPs trust us because they know Vestals will never betray them online. Archive business is conducted strictly by word of mouth and priority mail.

The Archives have been part of Vestal legacy ever since our inception. Barbelo began the Archives with the last specimen of the HIV virus in existence. Even today, countries argue about where that sample is hidden. Nobody knows the truth except the Vestals and the secret holders we protect.

So when Headmaster Russell shows up at the manor and tells me that Ms. Lydia is in danger, I believe him, although I don't want to. Headmaster Russell knows what he's talking about because he's the master of secrets.

"Fatima disappeared three days ago," Headmaster Russell says to me. We stand in the great hall, in a pool of colored light from the stained glass windows. "Now Beau is gone too."

"Beau's missing?" Maybe that's where Cal went. I haven't seen Cal since yesterday, right after breakfast.

"Beau's gone, and my sources say that Ms. Lydia might be disappearing next." Headmaster Russell glares at me sternly, the way he used to with the paddle in hand. "It's imperative you tell me where Lydia is."

"I don't know." It's the truth. But that doesn't stop my skin from going clammy.

"You're lying!" Headmaster Russell snaps his fingers. "Tell me, Blanca. Tell me what you're hiding."

I swallow back bile. Goose bumps prickle down my legs and tears blur my vision.

Headmaster Russell practically growls. "What's been going on here?"

"That's private," says a voice from behind me.

It's Seth. He's standing in the corner, next to the tapestry of the McNeal family crest. His palm is up, filming the whole scene.

"I believe my father was clear the last time you were here," Seth says. "Thirty-two-million dollars means you don't interfere with Blanca ever again. What she knows or doesn't know is none of your concern."

Headmaster Russell grits his teeth. "Put your hand down, Virus. This is a private conversation."

"Not anymore it isn't." Seth's other hand types into the air. He turns his palm over, and I see my silvery image pop up on the floating screen.

Seth uploaded me to *Veritas Rex*.

"You bastard!" I cry. "You promised!"

Headmaster Russell blanches. "Is that public?"

"He's put us on *Veritas Rex*!"

Headmaster Russell gathers himself. I can tell by watching his jaw tighten that he's plotting. He's thinking about what he'll do to Seth. And I'm very afraid because I'm not sure Seth understands the enormity of what he's done and what he's risked.

"That was a very foolish move, young man," Headmaster Russell says.

But Seth snaps his fingers. "Time to go, Russell."

Headmaster Russell's face darkens until he looks the meanest I've ever seen him. Before he leaves, he turns to me and looks me right in the eye. "Lydia's in danger. Don't say I didn't warn you." Then he's gone in a swirl of white cloak.

"You tricked me!" I shout at Seth, when Headmaster Russell is gone.

"I protected you." Seth types at the air, shutting down the video.

"You betrayed me."

"Blanca, I—"

"Don't. Just don't." I turn to run—flee, is more like it—when Seth grabs my arm.

"I brought you a present." He smiles hopefully. "It's in the driveway."

"I don't want anything from a Virus!" For a half second, I think about kicking him again, right in the crotch. But this time I know how to hurt him harder.

"I'm never leaving my cloister again," I say. "At least *there* I'll be safe."

"Blanca, wait!" Seth yells after me. "It's a motorcycle!" he shouts. "Your very own ride!"

But I don't look back. I only keep running.

A cloister is supposed to keep you secure. It's supposed to keep predators out and the most private part of you safe, hidden away. But my problem is that a little piece of me is now tied up with Ms. Lydia, and another piece with Cal. I couldn't stay in my cloister forever, not when they're still not home. Not when Ms. Lydia is in danger.

Headmaster Russell wouldn't have come to McNeal Manor unless it was dire. And now he can't come back because Seth scared him away!

If I were in danger, Ms. Lydia would look for me in a heartbeat. I know she would. But at least she would know where to look.

I don't know the first place to start

So that's why I accepted Seth's gift after all. That's why I'm out here in the night, tearing up the pavement on this motorcycle.

The streetlights are bright, and the traffic is gnarly. At every red light somebody tries to scan me to see if I'm a fake Vestal or not. When I turn out unreadable, they take my picture.

I'm not totally reckless. When I suited up in white leather, I made sure my platinum cuff was covered. I also studied the old-fashioned map of Silicon Valley I found in Cal's office and left a note for Cal under his shaving kit. `Going to see Ethan. Please keep this private.`

There's Ethan's building now, towering above me. I'd recognize that emblem anywhere. His company is the king of chips, the biggest player in Silicon Valley. If anyone can help me find Ms. Lydia, it's Ethan.

I'd ask Cal, but Cal's not here. And Cal would want me to make sure Ms. Lydia's safe.

Ethan's the only one left I can trust. I know he's corrupted, but I don't think he'll betray me.

I coast down the ramp to the security station, and then come to a safe stop. But I don't take my helmet off. "I'm here to see Ethan the Vestal," I say, my voice barely audible.

The security guard tries to scan me too. But I'm not any old girl in white.

"Let me see your cuff," he growls.

I expose my platinum wrist, and he opens the gate.

It takes one lap around the underground parking lot before the white elevator door opens. When it does, I cut the engine and put up the kickstand.

"Fatima?" Ethan asks, as he steps out of the elevator.

I don't give Ethan a chance to realize his mistake. I push him back inside the elevator and press the button for the door to close. By now Ethan can see my slim figure and realize there's no way I'm Fatima.

"Wrong guess," I say. I pull off my helmet, and my brown hair tumbles down.

Ethan's jaw drops. "Blanca," he finally says, punching the button for his own private suite. "It's really you." Then he pulls me toward him in a crushing hug, the type of embrace that pushes the borders of friendship to the very limit. I peel myself away. I don't want Ethan to get the wrong idea about why I've come.

When the elevator doors open, Ethan leads me into his apartment. It's pristine white, from the thick shag carpet to the modular furniture with chrome finishes. Ethan flicks his hand and the lights turn on, bathing the whole apartment in bright neon. Then he tries again, and the lights dim, except for one spot by a couch overlooking the thirtieth-story view.

"Nice place." I follow Ethan over to the enormous couch. The furniture fits him, like his fake glasses, suspenders, and new ability to go online.

Now that I'm in his apartment, I know I made the right decision coming to Ethan for help. *You can always trust a Vestal.* Graduation was six months ago, but it's like no time has passed between us at all. Ethan won't betray me. He won't try to trick me either.

"Why'd you think I was Fatima?" I ask.

"Because she's missing. It's all over the Net."

"Fatima *and* Beau are missing."

"What?" Ethan asks. "Beau's missing too?"

"Yes," I answer. "Headmaster Russell told me. Didn't you see our conversation on *Veritas Rex*?"

"No. There's nothing about you up there. But there're lots of pictures of you on *The Lighthouse*. That's how I knew somebody was coming." Ethan clicks on his hand and a tiny video of me on my motorcycle shoots out of his palm screen. "Nobody can tell it was you, though. Even I wasn't sure."

On the Net again! This situation was becoming more dangerous by the minute.

"Ethan." My tone is urgent. "We need a plan. How can we help Fatima? How can we find Beau?"

"I don't know." Ethan scratches his head. "I've been searching for Fatima all day, but there's no trace of her online. Only some junk her fashion house puts up." He flicks his fingers, and pictures of Fatima wearing diamonds and white lace pop up.

I glue my eyes to the screen. "I want to see all of it."

"Really?" Ethan asks, surprised. He shakes his hand so that the screen appears larger.

I scoot closer. Whenever Cal or Seth showed me something online, I felt hesitant, afraid to really see. But with Ethan, it's okay to be curious. He'll let me explore as much as I want, and he won't judge me either.

"Show me more," I whisper.

"I'd love to show you more," Ethan murmurs. "I've been waiting for you to say that for a long time." He grabs a blanket from the corner of the couch and pulls it over our laps.

We're snuggled there, the two of us, and I feel warm and safe. But I know what I'm about to do is dirty.

With his free hand, Ethan scrolls through the screen, and I finally see what *The Lighthouse* is all about.

Fatima's disappearance is a top story, but there's nothing about Fatima being pregnant. Most of the site is dedicated to Vestal history. Barbelo's early writings are there, plus news feeds going back five decades. There are property records from Tabula Rasa and tax records from every Harvest. It's like somebody has been researching us forever.

"They know about the Archives," says Ethan, pulling up the video. "A former senator spilled everything. But nobody believes him! Other bloggers are saying *The Lighthouse* is making things up."

"Why don't they believe the senator?"

"Because politicians are coming forward and icing him out, saying he's crazy." Ethan answers. He points to the headlines, so I can see the names.

"But those are all people who use the Archives too!" I remember a lot of them. Senior year at Tabula Rasa is spent on Archive duty, at least part of the time.

"That's not the worst part" Ethan crinkles his eyebrows and he pulls up another page. "Amy's come forward with a tell-all."

"Amy?" I don't bother to pretend. Ethan knows about how Amy and I used to be best friends. So when I see her face on the screen, I don't try to hide it. I let my anger show through.

"She's told all about us, Blanca, including Headmaster Russell and his logical consequences."

But I don't need Ethan to explain. I can read the story for myself right there. FORMER VESTAL CLAIMS HEADMASTER WHIPPED

STUDENTS ON A REGULAR BASIS.

"Amy left when she was ten." I curl my fist so tight the nails pierce skin. "How much can she know?"

"Enough that her parents have asked for police protection. They're afraid she'll go missing too."

"I don't understand. How long has this website been running?"

"It's new." Ethan scrolls through more pages. "It started about a month or two after our graduation. It's giving *Veritas Rex* some competition."

Seth. The name explodes in my brain, but I don't dare to speak the word aloud. "Show me *Veritas Rex*."

"That's where things get interesting." Ethan flicks his hand. Seth's lion-headed cobra bursts onto the screen. But there's nothing about my conversation with Headmaster Russell from today.

That Virus tricked me! He didn't upload me to *Veritas Rex* after all. But what's up there instead is worse.

It's a grainy, black-and-white picture from an old-fashioned newspaper. There's a little girl from almost fifty years ago. She's got a heart-shaped face.

"It's Ms. Lydia!" I reach out to touch the picture. My hand falls through the virtual screen, distorting the image.

"She was one of the original Vestals," Ethan says. "She's ancient."

"That's not possible—" I start to say, but then I stop myself. Sometimes I've thought Ms. Lydia was forty, or perhaps older than Cal. At other times she seemed much younger, like she was in her thirties. I really have no idea how old she is. But then I think harder. Her contract was for twenty-five years, and she was harvested at eighteen. That means Ms. Lydia is at least forty-three.

"Do you realize what this means?" Ethan takes off his fake eyeglasses.

"No," I whisper, confused.

"It means Ms. Lydia knows Barbelo!"

"But how did Seth—I mean, how did *Veritas Rex* find that out?"

"Who's Seth?" asks Ethan.

"Nobody important." I examine my cuff. "Just my purchaser's son."

"Oh," says Ethan. He puts his glasses back on.

That's when I get it, clear as day. Headmaster Russell's right, like always. Ms. Lydia is in danger. She's been in danger all along. And it's my fault!

Seth's been pumping me for information about the Vestals so he could plaster it all over the Internet! Was Cal in on this too?

It wouldn't be the first time I was bait.

"Do you understand now?" Ethan asks me. "We've been lied to our whole lives."

"What do you mean?" I shiver underneath the blanket.

"The Internet isn't evil. It doesn't rip relationships apart." Ethan pages back over to the picture of Amy. "Look. With one click, you could reconnect with your old friend."

Amy's blue eyes gaze at me with their familiar warmth. I blink and look away. "But the Internet is addicting. It tears users apart from the people they love."

"It doesn't have to." Ethan pulls up one more shimmering image of Amy. This one shows her surrounded by her mom, dad, and a panting golden retriever. "Finger-chips make things better if we don't become obsessed. That's what they should have taught us in school."

Chapter Sixteen

McNeal Manor has never looked more imposing. It's backlit by moonlight and looms in front of me, like the whole mansion anticipates my arrival. But there's only one person I want to see, and Ms. Lydia isn't home.

Cal, however, is.

"Blanca," he says to me as soon as I enter the foyer, like he's been waiting for me too. "Where were you?"

"At Ethan's." I set down my helmet. "Didn't you get my note?"

"A note?"

"Under your shaving kit?" I prompt.

"No. There wasn't a note." Then Cal gasps. "Unless … Let's check again. I'm positive there was nothing." He grabs my elbow and pulls me along.

I've never seen Cal like this before, so brusque and demanding.

It's making me fearful as I follow him up the stairs and through the halls in silence, trying to figure out what's going on. Cal doesn't say anything either, not until the metal door of his room shuts behind us.

It's dark and quiet, like we've happened upon the sleeping stillness of the entire house. Cal turns to me in the half-light and says harshly, "Headmaster Russell is never to come here again. Do you understand me, Blanca? Don't trust Headmaster Russell! *He's dangerous!*"

"Yes, Cal." I stop myself before "of course." But how did Cal know about Headmaster Russell coming today? Seth didn't post the video, after all.

Cal pulls me into the bathroom. He picks up his shaving kit and shakes it out in front of me. "Do you see?" he asks me. "Nothing!"

I don't know what Cal wants. "I swear," I say. "I left a note folded up in a square and put it right there."

Cal looks at me hard. At first I think he's examining me, trying to discern if I'm lying or not. But then I realize he needs me to listen.

"Lydia must have gotten to your note first."

"I don't understand." I jerk back. "Ms. Lydia wouldn't do that. She wouldn't read something that was private."

"Not like some people," says a voice from the doorway. Ms. Lydia steps forward, emerging from the shadows.

She's wearing color.

And she's holding a gun.

"You thought you could trick me, Calum? You thought you could share our private conversations with that Virus son of yours? Well, the joke's on you." Ms. Lydia aims her weapon straight at Cal, like she knows what she's doing. Then she throws some rope to me. "Tie him up, Blanca."

Is this a trick? Ms. Lydia knows I can't do that to my purchaser! I take orders from Cal, not her.

"Well?" Ms. Lydia snaps her fingers. "What are you waiting for?"

But I don't move.

Cal looks scared. His sun-worn face grows old in the bathroom light. But he also looks brave. "Blanca." His voice is steady. "Remember your promise. Keep yourself safe."

Tears roll down my cheeks. I'm so confused I don't know what's happening anymore. I take the rope to where Cal stands, and he puts his hands behind him. I tie up his wrists, like Headmaster Russell used to do to us during Discipline Hour.

Then, before I lash the final knot, I feel Cal grab my fingertips. He slips something into my hand that Ms. Lydia can't see.

It's his chip-watch.

I tuck it up my sleeve just in time.

Ms. Lydia's coming toward him, about to knock Cal out cold with her platinum cuff. But right before she does, Cal manages to speak to me, one last time. His brown eyes have never appeared so kind. "Blanca, remember you are loved."

"Good girl, Blanca," Lydia says to me across Cal's slumped-over body. "Now I need to tell you something."

"What?" There's nothing Lydia can say that will make me listen, not after what just happened. She doesn't deserve my respect.

Lydia holsters her gun underneath her jacket. From an inside pocket, she pulls out a picture, folded in two. "This is what you need to know." She hands the picture to me.

I don't want to take the photograph, but I do. When I open it, I see it's the same picture I saw on *Veritas Rex*, only this picture is in color.

And Lydia's version is complete.

There before me is her childhood visage, her face a perfect little heart. Standing next to her is a young man, maybe in his thirties. He's got long brown hair and glasses.

"That's Barbelo," Lydia says. "He wants to meet you."

"Meet me?" I ask. But that's not what I want to say. I want to ask her what the hell is going on. How could she do that to Cal?

"Now go to your cloister and grab what you need." Lydia slips the photograph back in her pocket. "We leave for Nevada tonight. I'm taking you to Plemora."

If Lydia really is taking me to Plemora, then that will make everything all right. If I get to meet Barbelo, then he'll make everything okay.

Can I trust what Lydia is saying?

I could follow her directions right now and still be safe. I could run to my cloister and lock myself inside, like I told Seth I was going to do forever. I could stay in there and never come out.

That would mean leaving Cal unguarded with Lydia, and I won't do that. I don't know what Lydia would do to Cal alone here with her gun.

But if Lydia thinks I'm disobeying her, then we're both done for.

I tilt my head and look up at her with soft eyes, the perfect look of submission Ms. Corina taught me years ago. "Can't I take some of your clothes, Ms. Lydia? I don't want to ever leave you again. Headmaster Russell made me think you were in danger!" I make my chin quiver.

"Oh, baby." Lydia hugs me across Cal's lopsided body. "Don't listen to anything that buffoon has to say. Grab my suitcase and let's go."

That's what we do. When we close the doors to Cal's cloister, Lydia locks him in there for good. I have to follow her, even though I have no idea if Cal is still alive. So I try not to think about him. I try not to think about Cal kissing my cheek or teaching me about science. I try not to think about how worried he was the night I went out riding or how he flew across the ground, attacking those Viruses and yelling at them to leave his kids alone. I try not to think about what Cal said to me just now, maybe the last words I'll ever hear him say. *Blanca. Remember you are loved.*

I wish there was a way to fix this. I wish somebody would tell me what to do. But the only person I can count on right now is me.

That's how I know I'm screwed.

Keep yourself safe. Leave a note. Don't trust Headmaster Russell. Those are the instructions Cal has ingrained in me. Those and the last direction he gave, *Remember you are loved.*

But I'm in Lydia's car right now leaving Silicon Valley, and I have no idea if I'll ever come back. All the road signs point to Nevada.

"Don't lean too close to the windows," Lydia cautions, as she shifts gears.

"Yes, Ms. Lydia. Of course, Ms. Lydia." I pull back and align my body to the seat. From the corner of my eye, I can still see the billboards: Trevor and me kissing in the rain. Sarah and her wrinkle cream. The dozens of other Vestals I know selling things money can't buy.

Then we pass a newsboard.

THE VESTAL ETHAN FOUND DEAD, HANDS SEVERED!

A chill comes across me, and I feel my palms go sweaty. I turn to Lydia, not wanting to utter the words, but needing to know the truth. "Is Ethan dead?"

Lydia keeps her eyes on the road. "Yes. Barbelo's been monitoring him for months."

"Why?"

"Ethan corrupted himself. He sealed his fate as soon as he got those chips."

That's not true, and I know it. Ethan sealed his fate as soon as he got his golden cuff. I look down at my own wrist and wish I could tear the platinum right off.

Lydia flicks on the turn signal before changing lanes. "Once you enter the public world, you can never go back. Ethan opened himself up to chaos when he got those chips. Barebelo said it was my duty to cleanse him."

Lydia killed Ethan? Something inside me breaks. My heart crushes my lungs, and my stomach feels sick. A dark thought occurs to me. "People might think it's me," I say, "because I was riding my motorcycle."

"That, and the security guard footage." Lydia smiles like it's her own private joke.

"I have to go back, Ms. Lydia! I have to let people know it wasn't me."

"Already taken care of it. Open up the glove box." Lydia glances at me sideways.

The glove box opens with a *thud.* Inside is a video camera smashed to bits, along with a security box.

"Nobody's going to know you were there unless we allow them to," Lydia says.

"Good." I fight for the muscles in my face to relax. "I knew I could count on you."

"But why'd you go over there in the first place?"

I don't have to lie. I tell the truth straight out. "I was worried about you. Headmaster Russell said you were in danger. I thought maybe Ethan would know where you were."

"Why Ethan?" Lydia asks me. "Did you know about the finger-chip?

Shoot! Is this another trick?

"Ethan showed me," I answer. I just don't say when. Instead I look at her, and I think about Cal. I remember the blood pouring from Cal's temple where Lydia hit him with her cuff. I remember locking him behind us in the lead room. "I was worried about you," I say to Lydia, letting the tears finally come. "I would have done anything to help you."

"Oh, baby." Lydia reaches out for my hand and squeezes it. "It's going to be okay. We're together now."

"Are you still my Vestal-mom?"

Lydia doesn't say anything. She only nods her head. If I didn't know any better, I'd think the tears streaming down her face were for real.

But I bet Lydia is the master of crying on cue.

Keep yourself safe. Leave a note. Don't trust Headmaster Russell. Remember you are loved. I repeat Cal's instructions to myself over and over again like a new mantra. Maybe he was really trying to protect me all along. Now I'll never know.

I wish I could go back and have more courage. I wish I could go back and choose me. I wish I could have been Cal's daughter for real. Not just his Vestal.

But all I have left of Cal is his chip-watch.

A lot of good it does me now. Lydia's car is completely cloistered. Wherever she's taking me will probably be cloistered too. Even if I could connect to the outside world, I wouldn't know how. And who would I call?

Seth. I would call Seth. I can still feel his heart beat right next to mine if I remember hard enough.

"Finally, a gas station." Lydia pulls the car up to a pump. "I'll fill up before we head over the mountains. Stay here."

Keep yourself safe. Leave a note. Don't trust Headmaster Russell. Remember you are loved.

"I have to go to the bathroom." I unbuckle my seatbelt.

There's a sharp intake of breath. "That's not a good idea."

"I can't hold it anymore."

"Fine." Lydia sighs. "Let me fill up the tank and then I'll escort you."

As soon as she leaves the car, I take out the chip-watch. If I can get out of this cloistered car, maybe I can use it to call for help. I struggle to figure the watch out, but I'm not sure it's on. Then I hear Lydia coming back! I pocket the watch right before she opens her door.

"Put on my scarf." She tosses me something red and wooly.

"But—"

"Just do it. We don't want to arouse suspicion." Lydia opens my door, and I scramble out, the red scarf bound around my neck like a noose. Together we walk to the back of the station where the restrooms are. She unlocks the door with a key dangling from a wooden chain. "You've got two minutes, darling. I'll be right here."

As soon as the door clicks behind me, I flush the toilet. Then when the water's still running, I tap the watch and pull up the screen. "Message Seth," I say softly. But nothing comes up. "Call Seth," I say, trying again, desperate to see that inked black snake.

"Dad?" Seth's voice sounds from my wrist.

"No, it's me, Blanca." I whisper.

"Blanca? Are you okay? Where are you?"

"You've got to get Cal," I say quickly. "Lydia hurt him. He's in his rooms."

"I'm on my way! Where are you?"

"I don't know," I say. "She's taken me, Seth. We're going to Nevada. I think she might have—"

But I don't get to say anything else. Lydia's behind me with the cold tip of the gun in my back.

"Drop it, Blanca."

I don't want to, so I don't. She pushes the gun barrel deeper into my skin, and I reconsider. I undo the strap and hand the chip-watch over.

"Blanca? Blanca?" Seth calls to me frantically over the connection.

Lydia drops the watch into the toilet, silencing it forever.

"That was special," I somehow whisper. "Cal gave it to me."

"Really?" Lydia puts her gun away. "You can keep your little trinket if you want. It won't work now." She rolls her eyes when I reach into the toilet to fish out the chip-watch. "Why were you calling him anyway?" Lydia asks as we walk to the car. "You can't ever trust a Virus. You know better than that."

I do know better than that. Now I know the truth.

Keep myself safe.

Leave a note.

Don't trust Headmaster Russell.

Remember that I am loved.

So that's what I'm going to do. I'm giving myself those directions now and forevermore.

Chapter Seventeen

Long, winding roads leading nowhere. Broken-down cars, ramshackle cabins, and the occasional shuttered store—we've driven all night through the abandoned unknown. I'm not asking any questions either. It's like I'm back at Tabula Rasa during Discipline Hour, ready to parrot whatever is required.

Only on the inside, I've changed. Hopefully Lydia doesn't know that.

"We're almost there, Blanca." Lydia pulls down the visor. The sun is coming up, shooting us right in the eyes with bright, golden light. "We're almost at Plemora."

"Yes, Ms. Lydia. We're almost there."

"You're going to love it. Plemora's so quiet and peaceful."

"Yes, Ms. Lydia. I'm going to love it."

"Barbelo's curious about you. He was my purchaser, you

know, if you haven't already guessed that."

"No, Ms. Lydia. I didn't guess." Barbelo was Lydia's purchaser? Eight hours ago I thought he could solve everything. Now I'm not so sure.

"I don't know what he'll want you to call him. We'll have to wait and see." Lydia pulls the car to the side of the road, where there's nothing but dirt stretching to the horizon. "Got to change into my whites," she says, and she pops the trunk. She takes the keys with her when she climbs out of the car.

When she comes back a few minutes later, I realize there's something sick inside me.

Seeing Lydia back in her Vestal whites makes me feel better. It calms me down.

What the hell is wrong with me?

"Are you ready to go home?" she asks.

And I do want to go home, but not to Nevada. "Yes, Ms. Lydia. Of course, Ms. Lydia. This is my dream come true," I answer as Lydia drives us farther down the road. She smiles at me like this is the best vacation ever. Finally, the car stops.

"Excellent, darling. We're here." Lydia gets out of the car, but I stay put.

We're parked in front of an enormous metal gate at least ten feet tall. It's padlocked multiple times. Lydia takes out keys and deftly unlocks each chain. She pushes the gate inward so that our car can pass.

That's how I enter the compound, peacefully, in the passenger seat.

All the while knowing it's the most dangerous cloister of all.

The first things I notice are the chickens, defecating everywhere on the porch. The sunlight is white-hot now, and it reflects off the adobe walls. I hold up my hands to filter my eyes, which means I don't get a good look at the front door. All I can see is that it's rounded at the top, like a Roman arch.

But inside the villa, it's cool and dark. My eyes dilate, adjusting to the light. There are plants everywhere, turning the interior into a lush greenhouse. Vines creep upward to the ceiling where skylights filter the heat.

"Come, Blanca. He's waiting." Lydia speaks softly, almost reverently. I fight the urge to kick off my shoes.

We cross the Spanish tiles through another doorway into an atrium. Here the garden is wilder than ever, at least at first glance. A veritable jungle is before me, bathed in the light of a single oculus at the center of the glass dome. The air is thick with humidity. I breathe in, and my lungs fill with moisture.

As Lydia leads me through the vegetation, I realize it's not wild after all. Everything is proportioned, controlled, and cultivated. The jungle builds up in terraces. Planters and lattices pull everything together. Fruit trees are clipped into espaliers. Tomatoes are grafted upward. This garden is both verdant and measured.

At the far corner, I see the gardener pruning a fig tree. He wears a white linen tunic and drawstring pants. A straw hat covers his long white hair. The gardener hears our footsteps and turns around. It is then that I see his beard and glasses.

At long last I meet Barbelo Nemo.

"And so," he says, putting down his pruning shears. "It's my little Vestal. Welcome to Plemora." He reaches out his hand and grasps my shoulder. "Blanca, you have had a hard road. In so many ways it's difficult being you. But I know that you can do it. You're here at Plemora now, and you have everything you need to achieve happiness."

I try to feel nothing. But it's hard, especially when he blesses me. Icicles prick down my spine. "Thank you very much." I'm overcome with the strange feeling of having met him before.

And it's more than that. It's more than just a feeling. Because when I look underneath his glasses, I see that Barbelo Nemo has green eyes flecked with gold.

Just like mine.

I've never been here before, but I know what to do. I know what's expected of me. Headmaster Russell trained me well. Old habits come back to me easily, like pulling on an old pair of shoes. They're comfortable and damaged at the same time. Maybe they're even dangerous.

"Did you know I could cook?" That's what Barbelo's asking me, here at the dinner table.

"No, sir. I did not, sir. This is excellent, sir." I take another bite of tilapia, poached in water and seasoned with lemon juice.

"Not only that, but everything on this table was raised right here at Plemora. We're completely self-sustaining." Barbelo digs into his tossed salad with gusto.

"The fish too," offers Lydia. "Barbelo breeds them right here in the garden."

"A three-hundred-gallon tank," he says, "with its own geodesic dome. Tilapia live on algae."

I finish chewing and wipe my lips with the linen napkin. "Yes, sir. That's amazing, sir." Fish and vegetables. Cal would have words about food like this.

But I shouldn't be thinking about Cal or Seth. I need to stay present. I need to focus, so I can stay safe, like they would want me to.

"I've been watching you for a long time." Barbelo taps his fork against his plate to dislodge a bone. "You might say I've followed your career."

I shouldn't feel chills, but I do.

"You have a very clean soul, Blanca. I've always admired that about you."

"Thank you sir," I say automatically. And I'm trying to concentrate. I'm trying to figure it out.

"You're so rule-abiding," Barbelo says. "You've always been so obedient until now."

Something's coming. I know it.

Barbelo takes a long sip of water. He puts down the glass exactly one inch away from his plate. "The trouble is, you've been running wild. I think you should remain cloistered until you can clear your head."

"Yes, sir. Of course, sir." I try to stop my insides from decomposing into mush.

"Blanca has an excellent character," Lydia tells Barbelo. For some reason she's arguing on my behalf. "Blanca always does what she's told."

"Not always." Barbelo's voice is cold. He takes off his glasses and polishes them with a handkerchief.

I wonder which time he's talking about: my online transgression with Ethan or trying to call Seth on the chip-watch?

"Ethan was a corrupting influence that has been dealt with." Lydia swallows hard. "I still think Blanca's trustworthy."

"Well, it doesn't matter what you think, my dear, now does it?" Barbelo reaches for a toothpick.

"No, Barbelo. Of course not, Barbelo." Lydia folds her napkin into a tidy triangle.

"That's a good girl." Barbelo reaches over to squeeze Lydia's hand, and she beams with pleasure. "A week of cloistering will do Blanca some good."

"Yes, Barbelo. Of course, Barbelo." Lydia doesn't look at me.

"Besides, Lydia," Barbelo says, pushing himself away from the table, "you've been gone a long time. I have needs that you need to take care of."

The last time I was cloistered for this long, I went crazy. I can't let that happen again.

At least at McNeal Manor I had more space. Here at the villa, I'm alone in a tiny cell. There's a cot, a nightstand, and a tiny bathroom. High up above me is a skylight full of the never-ending sunlight.

I think Lydia might be trying to help me. She brought me a yoga mat my first day and a hairbrush the next. But Barbelo must have found out, because since then, there's been nothing. She no longer brings me my tray of food. Barbelo unlocks the door in the middle of the night and slides the tray in on the floor.

I can't let myself go crazy. Not like last time. So I've been trying to think. I've been trying to dig deep within myself to come up with answers. I need to figure out the genesis of how I got here. That's the only way I'll escape.

Lydia told Barbelo that I have the perfect character. But that's not true. My character isn't perfect. It's nonexistent.

If you take off my platinum cuff, then there's nothing left of me. In that long-ago conversation with Seth, I couldn't tell him what I liked to do for fun.

The truth is, I have no idea.

So I revert back to the old ways. An hour of Kenpō. An hour of yoga. Running around my little cell like I'm a trapped animal. Only there isn't any room to run, so I jog in place instead.

But the harder I run, the more I know. Even with the old routines, I'm still different. And maybe the part of me that's always been is still here—the part of me that fights to survive.

Lock me in a box, and I'll fight to get out.

Because that's who I am at my very core. That's my character. I've finally figured it out.

I'm a survivor.

No matter what shitty hand life deals me, I keep going.

I've got good instincts, like Cal told me. And my instincts are telling me loud and clear that I can do this.

I can think for myself.

There's another thing about me that's important. It's really important to know this. I'm smart. I'm a fast learner. Even Cal said so. He said he'd never seen anybody with such a scientific mind.

It's been six days in this cloister, and I'm keeping track. I don't have anything to write with, but I'm marking the time with my hairbrush. I know it sounds funny, but each day I bend down one more wire bristle. *I am loyal. I am discrete.* That's how I keep track of the days.

Barbelo said I'd only be here one week. But you can never trust a Vestal. You can't.

He shouldn't trust me either. Because today I had an epiphany. I was lying on my bed looking up into the skylight. The sunshine made me feel safe and warm and happy, like the great hall at McNeal Manor. And I remembered Cal saying, "It's a great day for making solar power." It's a great day.

I've got a scientific mind. Cal said so. Solar circuits are like little cloisters. Close off the doors and the electrons won't run free. Close me off in my cloister, and I'll fight to get out.

So I take out Cal's chip-watch, and I turn it over and look at the sun. Lydia thinks it busted when it fell in the water. She's right, but she's also wrong. Just the power is wrong. Just the battery.

It's a great day to make solar power. It's a great day to rip little bristles out of hairbrushes. It's a great day to take things apart and see how they work. See if I can fix them. It's a great day to bring broken things to life. It's a great day.

It's a great day.

It's a great day.

Sophia McNeal speaks to me. I see her now about two inches tall hovering above the chip-watch. I can't connect to the outside world, but I can access the watch's memory. It's Cal's own private archive of secrets, and I'm conducting the ultimate Invasion.

"I won't be with you much longer," Sophia says. She's sitting down in her hospital bed, a scarf around her head. "But, sweetheart, remember. Remember always that I love you. You are loved."

That's what Cal said to me too. Almost. That's probably what Seth would have said as well, if I had given him the chance. Maybe even Ethan, if Lydia had allowed it.

It's day eight of my captivity. I was hopeful yesterday that Barbelo would let me out. He didn't.

But I'm a survivor, I've got good instincts, and I can think for myself.

And I'm okay. Because now I can go into the little bathroom and lock the door behind me. McNeal Solar makes all things possible. I can bring Cal's watch to life and see all his favorite messages, played right here before me. I can see evidence of love and joy in every saved thought.

Seth as a teenager, calling home to say he'll be late. Sophia calling Cal at work to ask how his day is going. Seth calling Cal a few months ago, asking him to put their argument aside and work together on a special project. I wonder what that was about?

When I'm done listening to the messages, I turn the watch over and look at the sun etched into the back. Seth has one exactly like it tattooed on his arm. I smile because I've finally figured out a family secret. I bet that's a tattoo the whole McNeal family shares. A sun.

I can stay in here a long time, and I can keep going. Because I've been thinking a lot about my perfect day. If Seth ever asks me again, I'll know exactly what to tell him.

I want to go outside.

I want to go for a ride on my new motorcycle. Thank you very much for that!

I want to go to a restaurant and eat a hamburger.

I want to kiss Seth and tell him it's for real.

I want to give Cal back his watch.

It takes me ten days to figure out what Barbelo wants. Today when he opens my door at four a.m., I am waiting for him, fully dressed and sitting on the end of my bed.

"Hello, sir," I say. "What can I do for you today?" I am prepared for all possible answers, except for the one he gives.

"You can call me Father." Barbelo narrows his eyes at me, challenging me to disobey.

"Yes, Father. Of course, Father."

A moment passes in the semidarkness. "Well, perhaps you're ready to come out after all," he says at last.

"Yes, Father. Of course, Father."

"I've been waiting for you to be ready, Blanca. You're a prize. Did you know that? A real prize."

He's lying to me. I know it. He's buttering me up to control me.

"You're very kind, Father."

"Good, very good. Then why don't we eat breakfast in the atrium this morning? You can pick up your tray and follow me." Barbelo turns to go, leaving my door open.

His back is to me.

I could kick him. I could strangle him with the pillowcase I've ripped into strips.

But would that be patricide, or not? Would I be killing my very own father? That's why he's a sneaky bastard. That's why you should never trust a Vestal.

I can't kill him, not until I know whether or not he really is my father.

Not until I know the truth.

Chapter Eighteen

Generosity is a fallacy. It's a figment of the imagination. I've never known anyone to be generous in my entire life. When somebody gives you something, it's usually because they want something in return.

Take Fatima, for example. She's willing to risk her life for her unborn child, but she wants a baby. Fatima still wants something in return. And Beau? He wants Fatima. And Cal wants Seth, and Seth wants the truth, and I want to be free from all of it.

So when Barbelo says to me at that first breakfast, "You're a prize, Blanca. Did you know that? A real prize," I wait for it. Barbelo's lying to me, I know it. He's softening me up to control me. Sooner or later, I'll hear what he wants.

"You're very kind, Father."

"The world can be confusing, but I can be generous."

"You're the only one I can trust, Father." I curl my toes so the rest of me won't squirm.

"I'm glad you see that because you've been wayward. I know about your online transgressions with Ethan. I know about your relations with that Virus. That's why you had to be cleansed. A week in your cloister was a good way to start." Barbelo pours me another cup of green tea.

It wasn't a week; it was ten days. I know that. *I'm a survivor, I've got good instincts, and I can think for myself.* Barbelo doesn't understand who he's dealing with.

The first rays of morning sun pour through the oculus now, and I get a better look at my surroundings. The rooms span outward from the central courtyard. I don't see any windows, only skylights. I don't need to be at tech wizard to know this place is cloistered up tight.

"Yes, Father. Thank you, Father." I take a sip of my tea. It's boiling hot and burns my tongue. I pray that it isn't drugged.

"Are you wondering why I asked you to call me Father?"

"No, Father. Not unless you tell me to."

Barbelo considers this, and then smiles. "Yes," he says. "That's a very nice answer." He watches me eat my figs. "You know, I've helped a lot of people like you."

"Yes, Father. You've helped many people, sir."

Barbelo gazes at me intently, with his green eyes just like mine. "Technology is a cancer of the soul," he says. "It's like a weed growing in the garden, stealing light from the living things that matter."

"Yes, Father."

"One little weed can do so much damage."

"Yes, Father. So much damage."

"That's why Vestals are essential. We are a beacon of light. We show people there is a better, simpler way to live. People all over the world know that we can help. They look to us for guidance. Don't you want to help? They crave our wisdom." Barbelo's eyes bore through me. He thinks his words are having an effect.

And for a moment, just a moment, I remember what it was like to believe him. The strength of his persona is a drug I've been hooked on my whole life. But I'm fighting to stay clean. *I'm a survivor, I've got good instincts, and I can think for myself.*

"I think Lydia is right about you, Blanca. You're a good girl after all. You could make a great leader."

"A leader, sir?" So this is it. He *does* want something from me.

Barbelo nods. "I need eyes and ears on the ground back at Tabula Rasa. Lydia won't be able to do that anymore. Not now that she's dealt with your purchaser."

Dealt with my purchaser? Is Cal … dead? But I don't let myself think. I don't let myself feel. I fight to stay calm. It takes everything I have to nod and take another sip of tea.

"First we need to make sure your soul is truly cleansed. Don't you agree?" He's watching me, seeing how his threat affects me. Dangling my cloister in front of me like an axe.

"Yes, sir." I say. Placid. I'm completely placid. I've been taught well.

"Would you like to be my right hand? Russell can be so obstinate sometimes. He needs to be reminded about who's in charge."

"Yes, Father. Of course, Father." And I imagine what that would be like, to hold power over Headmaster Russell. I'd really be top pick then, like Lydia.

"Excellent." Barbelo wipes his face with a cloth napkin. "I knew you'd see it my way. People always do because I'm always right." Barbelo smiles. He thinks he's won. He thinks I'll be the new Lydia.

But I'm nothing at all like Lydia. Not anymore. *I'm a survivor, I've got good instincts, and I can think for myself.*

I don't see Lydia until several hours later when I'm scrubbing the tile floors of the east wing. She approaches on quiet footfalls and bends down right next to my bucket.

"Blanca, sweetie?" she whispers. "I'm so happy to see you."

I put down my brush and let my eyes go dead. "Yes, Ms. Lydia. Of course, Ms. Lydia."

"Blanca? He's released you out now. It's going to be okay. Do what he says. Okay? Just do what he says." Lydia turns her head and checks behind her. Her hair is twisted in a roll. She looks tan in her white tank top, sophisticated and vulnerable at the same time. "I didn't tell him about the watch," she whispers. Then she kisses my cheek and whispers one more thing in my ear. "I told him I shot Cal. Barbelo thinks I left Cal for dead. But he's not."

"Lydia?" Barbelo calls.

I watch her as she walks away, and I wonder what trick they are playing on me now.

Murder isn't the only way out. I could also escape through the front door if I had the keys. But I'm not sure where they are. Lydia has them, I know it. But I hardly ever see her except at dinner. So I'm biding my time.

I'm a survivor, I've got good instincts, and I can think for myself.

Barbelo likes to spend his days in the atrium garden or in his office answering mail. He gets a lot of mail. Every day Lydia brings him a new stack of letters from the mailbox outside of the compound.

A few days after I'm released from my cloister, I'm outside in the hallway washing the floor when I see Lydia come into Barbelo's office with her delivery. I spy on them, through the crack in the doorway.

"You're a good girl, Lydia," Barbelo says when she drops the basket of mail on his desk. "I'm sorry you have to be cooped up with an old buzzard like me instead of delivering these in person."

"There's no place I'd rather be." Lydia drapes her arms around his neck. She tries to kiss him on the cheek, but he shrugs her off. Lydia straightens and reaches for a brown envelope. "This one's from the prime minister." She inspects the postmark.

"I've been expecting it. I'll need to contact Russell right away. Did the letter from the sheik arrive yet?"

"No, not yet." Lydia drops the envelope.

"Damn. I'll have to write that CEO and tell him it'll be another million dollars to make that problem go away. Everything we need is in the Archives."

There's a slight rustle of papers before they close the door.

It doesn't make any sense at all. The only thing I know for

sure is that I was wrong. Headmaster Russell isn't the master of secrets; Barbelo is. He's not retired; he's orchestrating it all. Lydia is his conductor, At least, she used to be. Headmaster Russell is only one of many instruments.

We are all Barbelo's instruments. We have all been played.

A few days later, I'm invited inside Barbelo's office to wash the floors. I've spent the whole week washing floors in the villa. I've cleaned out almost every room.

"See that?" Barbelo asks me when he invites me into his office. There's a row of filing cabinets longer than the Archives at Tabula Rasa. "Those files are all mine. Nobody tells me what to do because I know so much." He puts his hand on my back. "Someday soon I'll need your help. I can't send letters forever."

I don't know what he's talking about, but I remember back to the manor. I think about all of the letters Lydia got, calling her away. I always thought she was coming home to her purchaser, but maybe not. Maybe it was Barbelo sending her away to do his bidding.

"Important people trust us." Barbelo stands up and walks back to his desk. "Vestals are incorruptible." He peers at me over the rim of his glasses. "We're unreadable, and we can go anywhere."

I'm everywhere too. Barbelo lets me clean all over the villa. That's my job. I'm the new cleaning lady. "I always like a girl around to make this place shine," he says.

That's what happened to Lilith. Barbelo liked her face in the Citrus Sunshine campaign and decided to bring her home to Plemora for himself.

At least, I think that's what happened. I found the white headband Lilith used to wear in the commercial tucked behind some cleaner in the broom closet. When Lydia saw me holding it, she snatched it away like it was evidence.

All I know for sure is that I spend every day making this villa sparkle. I've also cleaned Barbelo's cell, which is totally ordinary. Lydia's room is right next door and is every bit as basic but does include a closet.

There're plenty of locked closets, but there's only one room in this whole place that I haven't been in yet. I can smell its stench coming from under the floor.

That's where we're standing today, the three of us.

"Don't make her do it, Barbelo," Lydia pleads. "Please don't send her in there."

Barbelo snaps his fingers. "That's enough, Lydia. It's time Blanca sees our guest. I think she's ready."

"She's not ready. She'll never be ready." Lydia steps in front of me, protecting me from the unknown.

That's when Barbelo slaps her across the face.

"Blanca, get your bucket," he says.

So I grab my supplies. And when Barbelo opens the door, the smell becomes overwhelming. It's the stench of rot, shit, and despair all rolled into one.

Somewhere inside the little room, someone or something is moaning. When my eyes finally dilate, I see a creature, huddled underneath the cot.

It's Beau.

"Do you know why he's here?" Barbelo asks me from the doorway.

"No, sir. I don't."

"Because Beau tried to run. He thought he could follow that whore of his. But Lydia found him first, and we'll find Fatima too. She can't hide forever. Not when we've got her lover boy as our hostage."

"That's brilliant," I lie.

"Of course it is," Barbelo says. "Now clean this place out. I'll be right here watching."

"Yes, Father. Of course, Father." It hurts me, knowing that Beau is hearing me call Barbelo Father.

But I'm not sure if Beau can hear me. All six feet of him is crouched into the fetal position, and his eyes are wild. As I scrub away the filth, he stares at me without recognition.

At least I can make his prison clean.

I think Lydia's trying to protect me. She slips me extra food when Barbelo's not looking. She brings me books. After the blessing ceremony last night, she brushed a strand of hair off my face and behind my ear. I wonder if she was thinking about the manor, and about that time she brushed my hair. *I am loyal. I am …*

I wonder if she wishes we could go back home.

Maybe Lydia can't leave anymore, after what happened with

Ethan. Maybe this is it for her, and she thinks that we're going to be our own weird family. But you can't trade a McNeal for a Vestal; it doesn't work like that.

I've lived my whole life knowing that my parents didn't want me. They castrated my virtual identity for the chance of a better life. But that payout was for them, not me. So if Barbelo Nemo really is my father, what difference does that make? Either way my dad is an asshole.

I would like to know about my mother though. The closest thing I've ever had to a mom is Lydia, and that was pretty much messed up from the start.

But Lydia still might be my best hope. She might be Beau's salvation too. That's what my instincts tell me. Because I could fight Barbelo or I could fight Lydia, but I probably couldn't fight them both. Not when Lydia has a gun. Not when Beau's in no position to fight.

So today when Barbelo is in the garden, I approach Lydia. She's in her cloister on her yoga mat, but the door is open. I'm supposed to be washing dishes.

"We have to help Beau," I kneel next to her mat.

Lydia's in Lotus position. She opens one eyelid and peers at me. "That's not possible."

"I have to help Beau," I say again. "I'm going to do something, with or without you."

Now I've got her attention.

"No way," Lydia says quickly, opening both eyes now. "You can't do that. He'll lock you up again."

"Not if you don't tell him." I put both of my hands on

her shoulders and give her my most intense smile ever. "You're inspirational. I've looked up to you ever since the first time we met. You always make the best decisions. You always protect the weak. You're the most courageous Vestal I know."

But the truth is Lydia looks scared. Even with me telling her exactly what she wants to hear, she doesn't say anything. Or maybe the problem is that I'm not telling Lydia what she wants to hear after all.

"Please, Ms. Lydia. We have to do this. It will be like a mother/daughter adventure."

"After lunch," Lydia whispers with tears in her eyes. "I'll unlock the door for you at one o'clock, but you won't have much time."

We don't have much time now either. Our conversation is interrupted by the sound of footsteps approaching.

I slide into Downward Dog, like a yoga genius. Lydia and I both Salute the Sun. When Barbelo walks in, the two of us are doing yoga together.

Like the old days, back at the manor.

Tiny sips of water, little bits of fruit, gentle words and cooing; coaxing Beau out from underneath his cot is like helping an injured bird. He is startled and shaky. When I reach out to touch his hand, he pulls it back.

"Beau, it's me," I whisper. "I'm here to help you."

Beau stares at me without recognition. He's been cloistered too long.

I feel like a traitor for trying, but I say the blessing, in case it will help. "Beau, you have a hard road. In so many ways it's difficult being you. But I know that you can do it. You have everything you need to achieve happiness." I hold my wrist out to him so he can see my cuff.

Beau doesn't respond for a few moments. But then he reaches out his own cuff, and the blessing is complete.

"Blanca!" he says harshly, as if his vocal chords have been damaged.

"You need to eat," I say. "Come out so I can give you some food."

He's skeletal. As soon as Beau crawls out from under the bed, I see how much he's truly suffered. I don't recognize him. His hair is matted around his face like he's grown wild.

"Eat," I say. "Eat your fill and get stronger."

Beau waits a few seconds, suspicious, and then he tears into the food with both hands.

I take the linen napkin and wipe away the plum juice dripping down Beau's chin. He scarfs down the food so fast I worry he'll choke. "I'm going to be back, Beau. I'll get us out of here. So you have to be ready. Do you understand me? You have to be prepared."

"Fatima?" Beau says, suddenly remembering. "How is Fatima?"

"She's okay," I say, hoping it's the truth. Cal will keep Fatima safe, if he's still alive. "You need to get stronger so that when we escape, we can go back to her."

"But what about Barbelo?" Beau asks. "He says that—"

"It doesn't matter what Barbelo says," I say softly. "He's not the boss of you."

"Then who is? Who?"

"Nobody's the boss of us," I answer. "That's why you need to get better. So you can take care of yourself. We both need to be strong so we can both leave."

I'm a survivor, I've got good instincts, and I can think for myself.

Beau takes deep breaths, gasping for air, like he's breathing for the first time. "Blanca, I … " But he can't finish his sentence.

"I need to go now, but I'll return tomorrow." I enclose Beau in my arms and rest his head on my shoulder. "I'll take care of you. I promise."

Beau doesn't say anything. But he hugs me back.

Right before I open the door to leave, I pause. "Remember, Beau," I say, turning to look at him. "Remember that you are loved."

Chapter Nineteen

Opening a door is easy. Opening a mind is hard. That's the only excuse I can give for what happens today at the villa. It's the only excuse I have for my own deadly stupidity.

It starts when the well won't work, and there's no water to clean up the breakfast dishes.

"The generator must be out." Barbelo throws his dirty gardening gloves on the clean kitchen counter. "Damn it, Lydia! Turn off the sink before the pipes break."

"Yes, Barbelo," she says. "Of course, Barbelo."

But Lydia's not quick enough. Barbelo knocks her in the jaw with his fist. She sits down at the kitchen table, holding her chin, not saying anything until he leaves.

I get some ice from the freezer and wrap it in a little cloth. Then I press it gently to Lydia's face.

"Why do you let him do that?" I ask her. "Why?"

Lydia doesn't answer. She rocks back and forth in her seat, holding the compress to her chin.

"Back in California, you were so powerful." I picture her standing up to Headmaster Russell. "What happens here, when you get to Nevada?"

"I'm sorry, Blanca," Lydia says. "I'm sorry. You don't know. All the years. My sister." Lydia isn't making sense. She's rambles. Then she reaches in her pocket and takes out the key. "This is a good time," she says. "I saved some figs for him in the bowl over there." I think she means for me to go see Beau.

"Keep the ice on that," I advise.

Lydia nods and rises from the chair, one joint at a time. I follow her out of the kitchen.

It's been five days now of helping Beau get better. He's in his right mind again and gaining some weight. Each day he's growing stronger. I know it.

And I'm getting stronger too. I'm as strong as I've ever been. *I'm a survivor, I've got good instincts, and I can think for myself.*

I feel the heat press into me as we walk down the hallway to Beau's cell. Whatever stopped the well from pumping must also have affected the cooling system.

The temperature is becoming unbearable.

Lydia unlocks the door for me and then sits down on the tiles, her back against the wall. She's still holding the ice on her chin. I kiss her on the forehead to say thank you, and a tear rolls down her cheek.

"You're here again." Beau smiles as I enter his cell.

"Of course. I said I would keep coming. Didn't you believe me?"

"You also said we would escape." Beau eyes the food plate and twitches.

"We *will* escape." I hand him the tray. "I promise."

"Do you have a plan yet?"

"Almost. I need to figure out how to get keys for all of the locks."

Beau nods, understanding me. "There're a lot of locks," he says.

But it's not only that. It's something else too. I've been ready to fight Barbelo for a long time. But I'm still not sure what to do about Lydia. I don't know if I could attack her. I don't know if I still want to.

I'd rather Lydia come with us. I'd rather she *choose* to come with us. If she does want to come, then that's how we can get out. That's how we undo the locks.

I've had enough of being locked up.

"I'll come back for you," I say. "I promise." I'm not sure if Beau believes me or not.

By the time Barbelo returns from the outside, I'm already in the hallway, scrubbing down Spanish tile. That's when I see my mistake. That's when I realize how stupid I've been.

When Barbelo walks through the front door, I realize that the door isn't even locked. It's been unlocked, perhaps this whole time.

The only thing keeping me in this villa is me.

The air is thick with heat. The cooling system has definitely stopped working, probably a couple of hours ago. Down here on the ground it's still cool. The Spanish tiles feel cold against my legs as I scrub the floor with a bristle brush. Barbelo stands in front of me, holding a metal wrench. He looks ready to swing at any moment.

But I'm ready.

"Damn heat," he says. "Damn fucking technology."

I scrub the floor so hard the wooden brush scrapes my palm. I'm worried about Beau locked up in his cell. The heat is oppressive.

Lydia comes into the hallway, without her ice. "What's wrong, Barbelo?"

"The solar system's busted." Barbelo wipes his forehead with a rag. Drops of sweat hit my face.

"I can fix it." I set down my brush.

Barbelo stares at me with eagle eyes. "You?" he asks. "What do you know?"

"Please, sir," I say. "Don't be mad, but my purchaser made me learn all about solar energy systems."

Lydia glances at me quickly, surprised by this.

I wipe my hands on my drawstring pants. "I can fix that solar generator. I'm positive."

Barbelo rubs his chin, considering. "What the hell," he finally says. "It's either that or I have to go into town."

"I could go to town," offers Lydia. I can tell she doesn't want me to leave.

"And get arrested? No, let's have Blanca climb up there and see what she can do."

"Yes, Father. I'll try, Father," I say. The chip-watch is in my pocket. As soon as I walk through that oak door, I'll be connected to the outside world.

Hopefully somebody out there is waiting for me, looking for my signal.

With clarity comes responsibility. With knowledge comes action. Up here on the ladder on top of the villa, I see what's wrong immediately.

This solar cell system is archaic and easy to decipher. One of the cells is broken, causing a break in the circuit. Slide in a replacement panel, and Beau won't be in danger from the heat any longer.

"Well?" Barbelo calls up to me from the ground.

I walk to the edge of the roof. "I can fix this, sir. Do you have an extra panel?"

"I think there's one in the shed. I'll go look."

This is my chance, my golden opportunity. I scramble back up the roof and away from Barbelo's view. I take out the chip-watch and click it to ready.

"Call Seth," I say clearly. But there isn't any answer. There's only a beeping sound and a robotic voice telling me to leave a message. I'm not even sure *how* to leave a message. Shoot! More beeping!

"This is Blanca," I say. "I'm being held captive in rural Nevada by Barbelo Nemo and Lydia. They've got Beau too. They're responsible for Ethan's death." I pause, trying to think of what to say next. What if this is my last chance to talk to them? "Cal and Seth, I'm sorry," I whisper urgently. "I'm sorry I was so messed up. I'm trying to come home. I'm—"

I don't get the chance to say anything else. All I hear is more beeping. What the hell does that mean? So I try something different.

"*Veritas Rex*," I say clearly. "I want *Veritas Rex*!" I stand up straighter, trying to get a better signal, and the lion-headed cobra springs up from the chip-watch. When I see the few inches of silvery screen, my heart stops.

There's a picture of Cal, Seth, and me!

It was the night of that party, the one where I met all the McNeal Solar people. One of those board members must have snapped my picture after all. There I am in my white dress with a McNeal on each side.

MISSING, the headline reads. BLANCA MCNEAL. Then underneath that is a message for me, it says—

But there's no time to read more. I hear footsteps on the ladder. I look frantically at the buttons. I'm trying to turn off the visual, but I can't remember how it works. Everything seems foreign. Then before I get the chance to fix things, it's too late.

Barbelo stands in front of me, holding the solar cell.

"So," he says. "You thought you could trick me."

"No," I answer. "Of course not."

"Technology is never the answer, Blanca. You used to know that. Sometimes the simplest ways are best." Then he sideswipes my leg, tripping me before I know what's happening.

Before I get the chance to fight back.

I slide down the roof, struggling to stop my fall. But I can't. Solar cells and roof tiles spin around me, evading my every grasp. The adobe walls whip before me, and then there's nothing. Nothing but white-hot pain.

I see the dirt first. My vision has doubled, but I can still make out the dust. I feel the dirt smeared across my face. If I concentrate hard enough, maybe I won't feel the searing pain, splintering into my side. I can barely move my arm, and I think my leg is broken.

"Blanca," Barbelo calls. "Come out where I can see you."

I hear him coming, perhaps to finish me off. There is no shelter. All around me is dust and the white walls of the villa. So I start dragging myself, right there through the dirt. Maybe if I get to the end of that wall I'll find freedom. *I'm a survivor, I've got good instincts, and I can think for myself.*

"What's going on?" I hear a woman asking. It's Lydia.

"Blanca fell off the roof."

"Oh God! Is she hurt?"

"Let's hope so," Barbelo growls.

I'm crawling now, up on three limbs, dragging myself away. *I'm a survivor, I've got good instincts, and I can think for myself.*

There's some sort of orchard up in front of me. I see some garden tools. I see a hoe. I grab it.

"What are you doing?" Lydia screams. "Why do you need a gun?"

I'm in the long grass. Curled up under a fruit tree. I've got my hand on the hoe, and I'm waiting. I'm waiting to fight.

"Blanca, dear?" It's Barbelo, coming my way. "Blanca, come out, girl. We need to talk. I need to tell you something. I need you to know your secret."

He can't see me, hidden. So I wait, hoping that the pain won't stop me.

"Your mother, Blanca. Don't you want to know who she was?" Barbelo's voice is stronger. He's closer and closer. "She was a Vestal, like you."

"Stop!" Lydia's here now. "Don't hurt her!"

"Shut up, woman!" There's the sound of flesh hitting together. Then Barbelo's voice goes soft again. "Your mother, Blanca. Do you want to know the truth?"

I'm a survivor, I've got good instincts, and I can think for myself.

I see my chance. Barbelo doesn't see me at all. He's still looking in the wrong direction, and his ankle is a few feet away. So I take every last bit of strength, and I strike him with the hoe. The sharp metal edge bites into his backside. Then, when he's down on the ground, I pull myself up to sitting and bash him one more time. I aim for the head, but the hoe hits his shoulder instead.

That's how Barbelo still gets the chance. That's how he shoots me.

I'm going in and out of consciousness. One instant, I'm looking at the sky, at the white clouds blowing across the blueness; the next, I'm looking at the dirt. Through the grass blades, I see Lydia jump Barbelo and tackle him to the ground.

"No!" she shouts. "I won't let you kill her." They're wrestling together. They're struggling over the gun.

I hear a popping sound and then there's Lydia.

"Blanca, baby. Are you okay?" She lifts up my head, cradling it in her hands. The blood from my shoulder stains her skirt. She takes off her scarf and tries to staunch the bleeding.

"My mother," I whisper. I have to know. I've never cared so much until now.

"My sister," she whispers back. "Barbelo harvested my sister."

"You're my aunt?" I ask, my voice fading.

"I love you so much," Lydia says. "And I am *so sorry*. I never should have brought you here. I ruined everything!"

"No," I whisper.

"You're my daughter now," Lydia says. "I'm going to help you. I'm going to make it better." She's frantic, trying to make me comfortable, trying to stop the bleeding.

I think I hear something. A buzzing sound coming from the sky.

"I need you to know the truth," Lydia says. "Can you forgive me, Blanca?"

"Yes, Aunt Lydia," I say. Even though I'm not sure that's true.

Lydia smiles at me, but she's weeping at the same time. Her heart-shaped face seems almost broken. Then I hear another popping sound. And Lydia's face disappears.

It explodes right in front of me.

Never trust a Vestal. We all have secrets. The secrets people don't find out until after you're dead are the best kind.

I'm dying there in the grass. I know it finally. Maybe I'm not a survivor after all. I look up into the sky and see Barbelo Nemo blocking the light, holding a gun. Maybe he really is my father. Maybe Lydia really was my aunt.

So maybe I didn't succeed in patricide after all. Maybe I didn't put up the ultimate fight. But there is more than one way to fight back. Seth was right about that all along. Sometimes the truth is the best weapon.

Beau knows the truth, because I told him. Vestals aren't the boss of us. We get to choose.

Just like Ms. Lydia got to choose. She could have left Beau locked in his cell to cook to death, or she could have released him, right before she came out of the villa.

Beau stands there now, right behind Barbelo. Beau picks up the hoe and laughs. I see Beau next to the helicopters.

Right next to Barbelo's head, hanging crooked from his neck.

Chapter Twenty

The lion-headed snake is before me, and it's all I see. Every last inch of me is covered in pain, so I focus on that snake. *I'm a survivor, I've got good instincts, and I can think for myself.*

The last time I saw that snake, I was speaking to it on the villa roof. Now I don't know where I am. All I hear is beeping, and the soft whoosh of air-conditioning.

"Her eyes are open," I hear someone whisper.

"Blanca?" somebody asks. Somebody is holding my hand.

"Call the doctor," the snake says. It takes me another minute or two before I realize that it's Seth. He stares at me and wipes his eyes.

"It was real," I whisper.

"What?"

"It was real," I say again. But I can't talk anymore because it hurts too much. My throat feels like it's been ripped to shreds.

"Get her some water," Cal says.

I turn my head and there he is, talking to a nurse. Cal's face looks older, grayer somehow. But he's smiling and crying too.

I'm in a hospital. I can see that now. I look down across the bed, and I'm covered in sheets. Underneath I see bandages and casts. I'm wearing a blue-and-green checked hospital gown. *Blue and green.*

"Get it off!" I say hoarsely. I struggle to lift my arm. It's the only thing that's not hurting. "Take this off!"

"They didn't have white," Seth says. "I asked. Blanca, I promise I asked."

"I'll call the head nurse." Cal springs to his feet. "I'll try again."

"No," I say, fighting to get out the words. "My cuff. Take off my cuff!"

They both look at me, motionless for a second. Then they say "Yes" at exactly the same time.

Seth picks up my wrist and struggles to find the nonexistent clasp. "There's no opening!"

I'm crying now. I can't talk and there are tears rolling down my cheeks. I'll never be free. I've come so far, but it still isn't over. I've been sealed for life.

Cal leans over with a cup of water and a straw. The water tastes good on my throat, like everything might be able to be okay after all.

"I'll find help," Cal says. "We'll take that cuff off for you right away. You're going to be fine, sweetheart. I promise." When he leaves the room, I hear Cal blow his nose, hard.

Then it's just me alone with Seth.

"I'm sorry," I say.

"For what?" Seth holds my hand in both of his.

"For being so crazy. For not telling you the truth."

"Which time?" A hint of a grin floats across Seth's face. He leans down and brushes his lips against mine in a chaste kiss.

I reach for Seth's collar and pull him in for something better. Our lips part, and our tongues touch. I'm transported to sunshine, orange trees, and happiness.

"Real or fake?" he whispers when we finally come up for air.

"Real," I answer. "Definitely real."

The windows are wide open, and all the lights are on. There are about a million doctors and nurses in my hospital room, and almost everyone is filming me. That's why Beau's not here too; he's still camera shy.

"Are you ready?" Cal asks me.

"Yes, Cal. Of course, Cal," I say. Then I laugh at my own joke. I don't mind that nobody else thinks it's funny.

My arm is lying on pillows, ready and waiting for the surgeon to cut off my cuff with a laser. I was the one who wanted the witnesses.

"Hands up, people," I say to the crowd. "I want the whole world to see this."

"But don't send it to *The Lighthouse*," Seth adds. "*Veritas Rex* gets first dibs."

"I'm not so sure about that," says Cal. He holds up a new chip-watch.

"What's that about?" I ask, but they don't have time to answer.

The surgeon is ready. He makes measured cuts through the metal. The whole room erupts in cheers when the cuff splits open.

My tears start when my cuff falls off. They roll down my cheeks, washing away the shame. It's like a window has opened in my heart, releasing all the pressure. I feel joy again. Joy and pride for being free.

Joy and pride for being myself.

My wrist is blank and shriveled. The skin smells funny until the nurse washes it clean with soap. "Do you want this?" She holds up the remnants of my cuff.

"Yes," I say, and I think again about Ms. Lydia. I wonder what has happened to her cuff. I wait until everyone is gone but Seth and Cal, so I can ask. But they don't know.

Seth has stopped filming and is now furiously typing into the air, uploading his latest post. "Can't let *The Lighthouse* beat me to the punch." he says.

"I think it's safe to say *The Lighthouse* won't be posting until later." Cal coughs.

"What do you mean?" I ask.

"Dad's the newest viral blogger in the family."

"It was you?" My eyes open like saucers.

Cal nods his head. "Lydia was right about me. I *was* using our private conversations to find out information about the Vestals. Some of it I posted on *The Lighthouse* and —"

"Some of it he shared with me, for *Veritas Rex*."

"You were working together?" I can't believe it. I thought Ms. Lydia and I drove Seth and Cal apart.

"We figured it was the only way," says Cal. "That's why I started things with Lydia. To get more information."

"We didn't think you would ever leave the Vestals of your own accord, unless you knew the truth about them," says Seth.

Cal takes a deep breath. "But never, Blanca, never would we have ever done any of this if we thought you would get hurt. And Lydia … I'm so sorry about Lydia."

I feel a sharp stab to the heart at the mention of my aunt's name.

Cal fights to keep it together, and Seth slaps him on the back a few times. Then Cal pulls his son in for a hug.

"It wasn't your fault," Seth tells his father. "You couldn't have known she would die."

"I made a mess of things." Cal breaks down and sobs into Seth's shoulder. "I shouldn't have tried to control people so much — Blanca *or* you."

"I made mistakes too." Seth's voice breaks.

"If you want to keep your own apartment, that's fine with me." Cal steps back from the hug and stares Seth in the eyes. "You're all grown up, and I accept that."

Seth wipes tears off his cheek with the back of his hand. "And *you're* right about college. Not earning my degree is something I regret."

But my mind is still stuck on my aunt. "Ms. Lydia was using you too," I say, interrupting their reunion.

Cal and Seth both nod. "We know," says Cal. "But we didn't understand why until now."

"It was me. Ms. Lydia was my aunt. She wanted to get close to me. That was why—" But I stop, midsentence. Color drains from Cal's face and Seth looks awful too. "What's the matter?" My hand reaches for my shriveled wrist where my cuff used to be.

Cal is too choked up to explain.

"Lydia wasn't your aunt," Seth finally manages to say. "She was your mother."

"What? No, that's not right. Ms. Lydia was my *aunt*. Her *sister* was my mom. I don't know how it happened, but Barbelo harvested Ms. Lydia's sister somehow. Barbelo was my father." I shudder, saying the truth.

"No, sweetheart," Cal says, gently. "They've done tests. They've conducted autopsies. Lydia and Barbelo were both your parents. Lydia was your mother."

"No," I cry. "Just no." And then I cannot say anything more at all.

Seth is right about the truth. It hurts, and it digs into you, but once it's finally out there, it ends up making things better. The truth is worth fighting for. It's worth sharing with the whole world. So when Seth finally digs up the whole truth a few weeks later, I let him post all of it on *Veritas Rex*.

Then I write my own response on *The Lighthouse*. Cal has given me his password and handed the site over to me. "You can still be a light in a dark world," he said. "One beacon of light at a time."

So this was my first post:

My name is Blanca McNeal. I grew up an orphan at Tabula Rasa, a school currently under federal investigation. I too was one of the victims of Headmaster Russell's sadistic tyranny. I too was sterilized at fourteen.

Unlike so many students whose parents were under the false impression that their children would have a better life, my parents knew better. My birth parents were Barbelo Nemo and his assistant, Lydia.

My mother, Lydia, was one of the first Tabula Rasa students. When she turned eighteen, my father, Barbelo Nemo, purchased ("harvested") her innocence. Fourteen years later, Lydia became pregnant, which is also when Barbelo began sterilizing Tabula Rasa students.

Rather than abort me, Lydia fled. As soon as I was born, she brought me to Headmaster Russell as a new student, so that she could resume her place with my father.

But as punishment for my mother's perceived transgressions, Barbelo had already taken Lydia's sister, Lilith, as an additional companion. For many years, Lilith continued to make commercial appearances. But seven years ago, she vanished. The circumstances of Lilith's disappearance are only now being investigated.

To my former Vestal Brethren, I say this: I have chosen to free myself from all the lies that were holding me back. You can too. You have everything you need to achieve happiness.

Epilogue

My casts have been off for a few weeks now, and the doctors have finally given me the okay to ride my bike. So Seth and I are heading out to ride along the coast, all the way to the boardwalk. Cal thinks this is a horrible idea, and he's been trying to talk me out of it all morning.

"Do you know what they call motorcycles?" he asks me at breakfast. "Organ donors! Why not let Alan take you guys for a drive —"

"Sorry," I interrupt. "But I've been planning this day for a long time. You're still going to meet us out for dinner tonight to get that hamburger though, right?"

"Of course, sweetheart." Cal throws his napkin on the table. "But I wish you would—"

"Stay safe," I say, finishing for him. "I know. But I've got good instincts, remember? I can think for myself."

"I realize that. But—"

"But what?"

Cal's fighting back tears. I know it. He doesn't have my training, so it's a lot harder for him to stay composed. "I don't want you to get hurt again," he says huskily.

"I won't." I reach over to hug him. The tweed of his coat scratches my cheek.

"And I wish that I could keep you here safe, but I know that I can't, and I know that—"

"You can't keep me locked in my room forever?" I ask, smiling up at him.

"Yes," Cal says. "Something like that." His tanned face reflects warmth.

"I better get going. I need to grab my jacket." I'm still wearing all white; it's a hard habit to break. Fatima and I went shopping the other day, and she bought a bunch of maternity clothes in color, but I couldn't join in. Sometimes I wake up in the middle of the night and freak out that my cuff is gone. But then I call Seth, and he calms me down again.

"One more thing," Cal says, right before I get up to go. "I've got a present for you." He takes a little box out of the pocket of his jacket and hands it to me. It's black velvet with a red bow.

"Nobody's ever given me a present before." My hand shakes as I reach for the gift.

"I'm sure this is the first of many."

I take off the bow and open up the box. It's my own chip-watch, entirely in white leather.

"It's vintage," Cal says. "But it still works."

I slip the watch on my wrist, not knowing what to say. I was supposed to give Cal his watch back, not the other way around. But Cal's watch never came back from Nevada.

"Cal," I say. "About your chip-watch. I'm sorry, but—"

"It's okay." Cal smiles. "The most important thing to come home from that villa was you."

"No," I say, though I can't help smiling a little bit. "It's not only about your watch being lost. Cal, I invaded your privacy. I read all your messages. "

"And did you have a good reason?"

"They kept me going," I say simply.

"Then you don't have anything to apologize for."

"But your wife," I say. "Sophia. I even saw her last message to you. 'But, sweetheart, remember. Remember always—'"

"'—that I love you. You are loved.'" Cal says, finishing Sophia's words for me.

"It almost felt like —"

"Like what?"

"Like she was talking to me too." I sound ridiculous.

Cal's whole face smiles when I say this. "Maybe she was talking to you," he says. "Maybe she was talking to all of us."

"Save any coffee for me?" asks Seth, coming into the breakfast room. His jeans and T-shirt are a clean contrast to his canvas of inked skin. Seth kisses me on the cheek and sits down next to me, grabbing a croissant from the table. "Are you still meeting us for dinner, Dad?"

"I wouldn't miss it." Cal offers his son a cup of coffee.

"Great." Seth reaches for the mug and then pauses when he notices my new chip-watch. "Holy Barbelo, what's that?"

"It's a present," I say. "From your dad."

Seth picks up my wrist gently in his hand. "What, no finger-chips?"

"And infest myself with technology?" I say. "No thank you!"

"Maybe next year," Seth says, grinning. Then he unclasps the watch for a closer look. He turns it over to inspect the back. "Nice, Dad. You did good."

I bend over to see what Seth is looking at. That's when I see the engraving.

Cal had the McNeal family sun etched on the back of my timepiece!

I look up at Cal, but I can't find any words. I just stare at him while Seth slides the watch back on my arm.

Cal clears his throat. "You two better be going. Daylight is calling."

"Exactly," Seth agrees, taking a sip of coffee. "What do you say, Blanca? How about we go have some fun in public?"

I look down at my chip-watch and then up at my new family. "Let's go," I say. "This day is going to make the best post ever."

THE END

ACKNOWLEDGEMENTS

This book would not be in your hands without two pioneering women behind it. My agent, Liza Fleissig, of the Liza Royce Agency, is my friend and champion. Georgia McBride, of Georgia McBride Media Group, makes dreams come true. There is no possible way I could express enough gratitude to these fine ladies.

Jaime Arnold, my excellent publicist, you really are a rockstar in the YA world. Thank you for answering so many questions and entertaining my wild ideas.

I would also like to thank my small army of beta readers, Alana Albertson, Carol Brudnicki, Karyn Brudnicki, Muffie Humphrey, Vanessa Moody, Jennifer Parmenter, Sarah Weston, and Sharman Badgett-Young. You made *Genesis Girl* better.

My LRA siblings, Joshua David Bellin, Darlene Beck-Jacobson, and Sarah J. Schmitt have answered many frantic emails, and provided expert advice on writing. Ginger Harris-Dontzin from LRA, thank you for your work on my behalf.

Jeanne Ryan, not only did you come to my son's school years ago to volunteer your time as an author, you've been my Washington State fairy godmother, swooping in to help when I needed it most. I can't wait to watch *Nerve* on the big screen.

An unseen hand in *Genesis Girl* is the pioneering work of Dale

Carnegie. I based some of the Vestal tactics on ideas first explored in his famous book from 1936 called *How to Win Friends and Influence People*. I also used my experience as a Psychology major at Stanford University where I was taught by the most brilliant researchers in the field.

Thank you to all of my social media friends and followers. I'd like to give a special shout-out to my Delta Gamma sister Claire McCormack Hazlett, who has had my back every step of the way on my blog, TeachingMyBabytoRead.com, and on my Facebook page, The YA Gal. An extra wave goes to my pals from The Sweet Sixteens.

Sixteen to Read sisters, Michelle Andreani, Ashley Herring Blake, Jennie K. Brown, Jennifer DiGiovanni, Laurie Elizabeth Flynn, J. Keller Ford, Catherine Lo, Sarah Glenn Marsh, Sonya Mukherjee, Marisa Reichardt, Meghan Rogers, Shannon M. Parker, Erin L. Schneider, Janet B. Taylor, and Darcy Woods, this journey has been richer because of your friendship.

I live in Edmonds, Washington, and am proud to call Puget Sound my home. Every week I write a column called "I Brake for Moms" for *The Everett Daily Herald*. To my *Herald* readers, it is a privilege spending Sunday mornings with you. To the wonderful people at *The Herald* including Jon Bauer, Sally Birks, Andrea Brown, Gale Fiege, Jessi Loerch, Melanie Munk, Doug Parry, and Aaron Swaney, thank you for developing me as a writer. I owe a special debt of gratitude to executive editor Neal Pattison for taking a chance on an unknown stay-at-home mom.

To my parents, Bruce and Carol Williams, thank you for giving me such a beautiful childhood full of warmth and happy memories. Thank you to my sister, Diane, for making it joyous. My in-laws, Marc and Lynn Bardsley, are the best second set of parents I could ever wish for.

To my husband, Doug, thank you for putting up with the thousands of hours I spent crafting Blanca's world. Bryce and Brenna, I love you with all my heart. When you are old enough to join social media, you can be certain that your mom will be watching your every move. Have fun and be safe.

JENNIFER BARDSLEY

Jennifer Bardsley writes the parenting column "I Brake for Moms" for *The Everett Daily Herald.* You can find Jennifer on her website: http://JenniferBardsley.net or on her Facebook page: The YA Gal. An alumna of Stanford University, Jennifer lives in Edmonds, Washington, with her husband and two children.

PREVIEW:

DAMAGED GOODS

Jennifer Bardsley

Chapter One

All I smell is leather. Seth's arms are around my back, his hands tangled in my long brown hair. My lips devour his, hungry for contact. Beyond us a seagull cries and soars above the waves of Santa Cruz beach.

If I kiss Seth hard enough, my scars fade way into oblivion. Barbelo Nemo and his mind control tricks. My childhood spent in seclusion at Tabula Rasa, hidden from the Internet. I slide my fingers underneath Seth's jacket against the stickiness of his shirt. I begin to undo a button.

"Whoa, Blanca." Seth pulls my hands away. "We're not the only people in the parking lot."

I scan to the left and right of the rest stop. Strangers are everywhere. "Since when did you care about what other people think?"

"Since I started dating a Vestal."

I pull back and look out at the cliffs. "I'm not a Vestal anymore. You know that." I feel the antique chip-watch on my wrist. Seth's dad, Cal, gave it to me as a present after my platinum cuff was removed. Once a Vestal is de-cuffed, they are expelled from the Brethren.

"So those tourists snapping our picture don't bother you?" Seth motions to a small crowd a few cars over.

I look to where he points, and the flash of thumb-cameras blinds me. Vestals must never have their pictures taken by random people. That privilege belongs to the companies that purchase them and market a Vestal's privacy one advertisement at a time. I reach my arms out by instinct, to protect my face from the public. "I'm fine with it," I lie, pulling my hands down. "But we better leave now or we'll be late to the restaurant."

"My dad can wait a few minutes." Seth scoops me in his arms.

"Blanca!" one of the spectators calls. "And Veritas Rex! Is that really you?"

Seth holds up his hand and wiggles his finger-chips. "The one and only!" Then he dips me back for a kiss.

I stiffen like cardboard. "Stop it," I mumble, trying not to squirm. All I can think about is the cameras, my face flashed worldwide and weirdoes slobbering over my private moment with Seth. "We've got to go or we'll be late."

Seth kisses my nose. "I didn't know you were so punctual."

"Yes." I pull myself out of his grasp. "Cal's waiting." The sooner I put my helmet on and get back on my motorcycle, the better.

“Blanca,” a man calls as we ride away. “I love you! I’ve watched you all year!”

Underneath my jacket, I shiver. The fame that surrounds me is chilling.

A few miles of pavement put me in a better mood. The day is radiant, perfect for riding our bikes from Silicon Valley over to the coast and back. It’s our favorite weekend ritual. Seth cruises next to me on his motorcycle with the lion-headed cobra painted on the side, and I zoom along beside him in head-to-toe white.

The speed rushing over me tastes of freedom. When we shift into high gear I can forget—for a moment—that three months ago I was a captive at the Plemora compound in Nevada. The memory of my mother’s face exploding gets sucked away.

But not for long.

The restaurant Cal picked is smothered in shadows. Candles in glass jars at each table are the only source of a hazy glow. As I walk by, other patrons stare up at me.

Their whispers don’t surprise me. Seeing a Vestal in public is unheard of, and I’m the most famous Vestal in history, with the exception of Barbelo, my birth father.

But father isn’t a word I use to describe my tormentor. I don’t think of Ms. Lydia as my mother either, not usually. The closest thing I have to a real parent is Cal McNeal, who paid thirty-two million dollars to purchase me from Tabula Rasa, the school Barbelo founded fifty-one years ago, in 2012, with the ostensible purpose of shielding students from the Internet. Barbelo's real objective was to create a network of Vestals in key positions. Spies all over the world who were devoted to him.

Cal waits for us at the table, a smile on his tanned face. His hair is long around the ears. I need to remind him to trim it. Cal wears his usual tweed jacket with soft brown patches on the elbows. He stands up when we reach the table and hugs us both. "Enjoy your ride, you two?"

"From the mountains to the beach." Seth slides into the booth. He pulls off his jacket and exposes forearms covered with ink. Seth also has tattoos on his face, the most noticeable of which is the lion-headed cobra. That snake was the first thing about Seth I noticed. A year ago he snuck into Tabula Rasa, took my picture days before graduation, and posted it on *Veritas Rex*. Seth is a viral blogger who does anything to break a story even if involves breaking the law.

My own skin is pure white. I've been a consummate rule follower my entire life, with a few notable exceptions. Remaining unmarred by ink or technology tops the Vestal code. It's a hard habit to break.

Cal passes me the bread basket. "So Blanca, I heard from my friend at Stanford today, and I've got good news."

"Yes?" I take a deep whiff of the yeasty aroma and push the basket over to Seth without taking a piece.

Cal butters his slice with a thick slab of butter. "I told the dean about your special circumstance. That you've been out of school for a year, but graduated top of your class."

Seth chokes on his water. "Top of her class? You mean she was auctioned off to the highest bidder at the Vestal Harvest."

"Exactly," Cal says. "Blanca, you're Tabula Rasa's version of a valedictorian. I told the dean that you had a classical education from a different era and that you were being tutored in science and technology so that you'd catch up in STEM by matriculation."

Eagerness glides over me. Six months ago when Cal suggested college I thought he was joking. I dismissed the idea without consideration. But since I returned from Nevada I've made attending college one of my primary goals.

It's not that I don't love being the face of McNeal Solar. Every time I see an advertisement featuring me on a billboard, I get tingles. But representing McNeal Solar and actually understanding how solar power works are two different things. I don't want to be a token bobble head. I want to be a real engineer who designs power systems and imagines new inventions.

Cal wants to help me achieve that dream. Seth is so committed to *Veritas Rex* that there's no way he'll work for his dad's company. But maybe someday I'll join the McNeal Solar board of directors and people will respect my opinion. It'll be another way I can be Cal's daughter. I'll become his intellectual heir.

"What did the dean say?" My knees shake with excitement until I tense my muscles.

Cal puts down his butter knife. "He knows who you are, of course. He watched the news story unfold along with the rest of the world when you were kidnapped."

"And?" I toy with my napkin.

Cal smiles. "Given the special circumstances, he agreed to let you take a private entrance exam with a panel of professors ten weeks from now."

"Yay!" I lean across the booth and hug Cal tight, my face brushing the scratchy fabric of his blazer.

"Awesome, Dad," says Seth. "How the hell did you pull that off? I've never heard of Stanford admitting a student like that before."

"Well that's because they've never had a Vestal apply. Plus, it helps that a dorm is named after your mother, Seth. Being a large donor has its perks."

Cal's wife, Sophia, was an anthropology professor at Stanford until she died of the Brain Cancer Epidemic when Seth was seventeen. It was decades before the world realized cell phones caused cancer. Sophia was one of many victims. Before she died her life work had been researching Barbelo Nemo and the Vestal order he created.

"Mom would have been thrilled to have you as a student," Seth tells me. "She'd probably follow you around and take notes on your well-being."

"To your mother, then!" I lift up my water glass.

"To Mom," Seth answers.

Cal holds up his glass of wine. "To Sophia, a three-way toast."

"Smile, McNeals." A guy with greasy black hair and an ugly smirk holds up finger-chips in our faces. "What a touching moment." The flash pops.

I drop my glass and water drowns the tablecloth.

"Veritas Rex and his Vestal girlfriend. Gotcha!" Another loser creeps up too. The fact that they're both frantically typing their fingers into the air makes me assume they're viral paparazzi, uploading us straight to the net.

"Get out of here," Seth growls, chucking bread at their faces.

A rounded man with a balding head rushes over. "Is there a problem?" He turns to the paparazzi. "I am the maître d' of this establishment and I will notify the police unless you leave this instant."

Seth pelts them with more bread. The one with greasy hair catches a piece and crams some in his mouth. "Thanks, Rex," he mumbles through crumbs, "see you around."

Several waiters rush over to pick up bread and clear off our wet tablecloth. "I sincerely apologize, Ms. Blanca. I don't know how those Viruses got in." The maître d' uses the derogatory term for viral bloggers, the one that Headmaster Russell taught me at Tabula Rasa.

"It's not your fault. Viruses are hard to shake." I slide my foot underneath the table and brush my leg against Seth's.

"They must have seen your white outfit." The maître d' tugs his collar.

"It's okay." I nod. "I'm used to it." I wave off his offer of a meal on the house, but he insists.

Later, over cheeseburgers, Cal brings up my wardrobe again. "You know, Blanca. You don't need to wear white anymore, unless you enjoy the attention."

"Of course I don't want the attention!"

"Then why not change things up a bit?" Cal says. "Shop for new clothes. Try to blend in."

I look at Seth for support, but he nods in agreement with his father.

"Fatima wears colors now," Seth adds, "and she's still a Vestal."

I picture my best friend Fatima. The last time I saw her she wore a silky green dress from her fashion house and looked like a snake that had swallowed a watermelon. Six months pregnant, her figure still says "Babe alert!" Tomorrow night is Fatima's engagement party with Beau.

I, on the other hand, am the proverbial girl-next-door. Brown hair, green eyes, and clear skin. Back at Tabula Rasa they said I had a face that could sell soap.

"I don't want to be a Vestal. I'm a McNeal now. But wearing color seems wrong."

"It's not just the clothes." Seth's finger-chips buzz and he flicks them off. "The only time you leave the house is with me or Dad."

"That's not true!" I insist. "I went to the soundstage last week to shoot a McNeal Solar ad."

"True," Cal admits. "But it's what a Vestal would do."

"What's that supposed to mean? Don't you want me as the face of McNeal Solar?" My stomach feels bubbly, like I ate too many French fries.

"Of course I do, sweetheart. I love your campaign for my company." Cal reaches out and pats my hand. "We're concerned about you though. We want you to get out there and make new friends."

I turn and glare at Seth. "This is about the other night, isn't it? You're still mad because I wouldn't go to that club with you, so you got your dad to take your side."

Seth stares at me hard. "It's not just the other night. It's all the time. Your world is so tiny that it's unhealthy."

"College is a big step," Cal says, "in terms of academics, forming new friendships, and learning to mingle."

"I meet lots of people! I've made a ton of friends online. Every time I write a new post for *The Lighthouse* I get thousands of comments."

Seth looks at me with piercing brown eyes. "Blanca, you're new at this, but online friends are easier than people you meet face to face. It's a different type of interaction."

At that moment a flash makes me jump. But it's not a Virus snatching my picture this time. It's a family in the corner taking a photograph of their kid. "Face to face can be scary," I say.

"Sometimes," Cal nods, "but not normally."

"Normal for me is different."

"Exactly our point," says Seth.

Cal leans forward in his seat. "We think it would be helpful if you could chat with someone, to help you process all you've been through."

"You mean like a psychiatrist? You think I'm crazy?" I twist my chip-watch around and around my wrist where the cuff used to be.

Seth scoots closer and lowers his voice. "We don't think you're crazy. But some really shitty things have happened to you."

"You lost your mother," says Cal.

"Ms. Lydia wasn't my mother! I mean, she gave birth to me. That's it. What do I care what happened to her?"

"You must feel something," Cal says.

"I feel nothing."

"Then why are you talking so loud?" Seth asks.

I take a quick glance of the room and notice stares.

Our waiter rushes over. "Are you ready for dessert now?" he asks.

"Yes," Cal answers. "Please bring the menu."

"No, thank you." I squeeze my fists together, stress coursing through my body like lightening.

When the waiter leaves, Seth touches my elbow. "We've made an appointment for you."

"What?"

"With Dr. Meredith," Cal says. "A therapist."

"You want me to tell my private secrets to a total stranger?" I speak with a steadied calm while a storm builds up inside me.

"She's not a stranger, Blanca. Seth and I started seeing Dr. Meredith when you were kidnapped."

My heartbeat is ragged. "You told her about me? You shared my private life with an outsider?"

"Of course not." Seth's dark hair sticks up in wild tuffs on his head. "Dad and I had our own stuff to work out. You know I spent five years mistakenly thinking Dad cheated on my mom."

Cal flinches. "And you have your issues too, Blanca."

I swallow hard. I reach over and stroke my white leather jacket. Maybe I should get up and go. Ride back to McNeal Manor on my motorcycle. But that would mean going someplace by myself. The last time I rode off into the night, my good friend Ethan was killed and Ms. Lydia kidnapped me.

"Sometimes being an adult means doing things you don't want to do," says Cal.

"I'll drive you to your appointment next week, if that helps," Seth offers.

"No way," I say. "I don't need that type of care."

I can do this if I try hard enough.

I stand up and pick up my jacket. "Thank you for dinner," I snarl.

But as I turn to go I walk smack into dark suits. The man is six foot three, every inch of him as sharp as his buzz-cut hair. The woman is my height, about five foot five, with silver stud earrings.

"Blanca Nemo?" The woman has a steady voice. Both of them hold up their palms to flash electronic badges. "Agents Carter and Marlow with the FBI. We need to bring you in for questioning."

"What the hell?" Seth leaps to his feet.

"Blanca?" Cal springs up. "What's this about?"

"I don't know." I shoot him a frightened look the agents can't see.

"Don't say anything without a lawyer. Okay, sweetheart?" Cal types at his chip-watch. "Hold tight until Nancy gets there."

"Come on, Ms. Nemo." The male agent grabs my arm, "Our car is outside."

"Ouch! Not so tight!"

"Her name's not 'Nemo'," Seth shouts. "It's Blanca McNeal." He and Cal hurry after us out of the restaurant into the night where a black sedan is waiting.

I turn to look at the McNeals one more time. Seth towers over Cal whose face is twisted with worry.

I smile wanly as the agents shove me into the backseat of the car.

The irony kills. I'm going someplace without them after all.

Chapter Two

I force a full breath into my lungs. After my imprisonment in Nevada small spaces grate my nerves. The two large mirrors make the room seem bigger. But I've read enough of Cal's detective novels to assume these are actually one-way windows.

I feel like a butterfly, pinned down for display.

Agent Marlow sits in front of me, his gigantic frame overwhelming a plastic chair. His biceps look like they could crack walnuts. Agent Carter, by contrast, is petite. She has ladybugs tattooed on her left hand that walk across her knuckles. Her boyish hairstyle looks youthful, but she has wrinkles around her eyes.

"Let the record show," Agent Carter says as she clicks her finger-chips to record the interrogation, "that the subject refused to speak until her lawyer was present."

"You know," says Agent Marlow in a kind tone. "You're not in any trouble. You can answer a few of our questions. There's no need for a lawyer."

I look down at my wrist and don't respond. The first thing they did when they brought me into the brick FBI building was take away my chip-watch for "safekeeping."

"We won't access your accounts," said the agent who sealed off my watch in a special box. "This is standard protocol for being escorted into a federal building. Most people hauled in get the lead-lined mitts. We can't let their finger-chips make trouble."

My wrist feels unnaturally smooth. First my cuff and now my watch. Naked skin taunts me.

"I know all about you, Blanca," says Agent Carter. "Every last detail."

I look straight at her. I know all about Margie Carter too. I studied her in the class I took during junior year called Vestal Enemies. She's aged significantly compared to the picture of her in my textbook.

Agent Carter leans into the table. "I've monitored the Vestals for seventeen years. You were in diapers when I first started investigating Barbelo Nemo."

I cross my ankles and fold my hands. I straighten out my spine like I'm being pulled from above. I smooth my expression so all evidence of emotion evaporates. If there's one lesson Ms. Corina taught me, it's that sixty percent of communication is nonverbal. No way am I going to let my body speak while I keep my lips closed.

Agent Carter raps her tattooed fingers on the table and stares back at me. "I have a lot of questions, Blanca. It's time to prove whose side you're actually on."

I answer by not moving one muscle. I could sit like this forever. Headmaster Russell, Ms. Corina, and the other teachers at Tabula Rasa would be proud. Barbelo too, of course, if he was still alive.

The seconds tick away like hours. After an eon, I hear a rustle at the door. I turn to see the McNeal family lawyer, Nancy Robinson, enter in a flurry of worsted wool. Her hair lifts up in an elaborate French twist and her face gleams with determination.

"I'm here now, Blanca." Nancy blusters into the room. "Traffic was awful." She reaches out her hand to shake with the agents. "Nancy Robinson. Pleased to meet you. Now let's get this travesty over with." She sits down in the chair next to me and clicks on her finger-chips. "We'll record this for our own evidence, of course, even though Blanca is here completely voluntarily."

"Yes, well. Let's get started." Agent Carter eyes me closely. "We are here to interview Blanca Nemo about the inner workings of the Vestal order."

"My name's not Nemo."

"Have you been adopted by Mr. Calum McNeal?" asks Agent Marlow. "I was unaware of this."

Nancy nods at me, so I answer. "No," I say. "Not officially."

If we made it official—supposing Cal wanted that—it would be tricky. Legally, Seth would become my brother. Hypothetical incest was more than I could handle at the moment.

"Blanca has the right to use any name she chooses," Nancy says. "Please honor it."

Agent Marlow continues. "Are Barbelo Nemo and Lydia Xavier your birth parents?"

"Lydia Xavier?" I say, before Nancy can stop me. "Where did you hear that name?" I'm angry with myself as soon as the words leave my mouth. I know better than to reveal unnecessary information. But I've never heard Ms. Lydia's last name before.

"We don't reveal our sources," snaps Agent Carter. "Answer the question."

"No, I think not," interjects Nancy. "There's no need for Blanca to cooperate if you're going to be rude. She's not under arrest. And her question is a good one. We've been trying for months to discover Lydia's last name. I need it for probate court. We're working under the assumption that Blanca is Lydia's legal heir."

Agent Marlow's lips twitch. "I'm sorry, but we can't expose our sources. This is an ongoing investigation into the alleged criminal activity of the Vestal order. We thought, given the posts Blanca's made on *The Lighthouse*, that she would be as committed as we were to achieving justice for everyone who was wronged."

"I told you, Marlow," Agent Carter says in her hash, raspy voice, "she'd be as tight lipped as the rest of them. Never trust a lunatic in white."

"I'm not a lunatic!"

"That was uncalled for." Nancy's voice is shrill.

"Prove it." Agent Carter holds out her hand and flashes me a picture. "Do you recognize this person?" She points to a tall Asian man about Seth's age—twenty three. He's naked from the waist up and kicks a punching bag. Sweat drips off chiseled muscles.

Do I recognize him? Of course I do. That's my friend Keung. He's looks older than I remember, and more handsome than ever.

"No," I say. "I don't know who that is."

Agent Carter stares at me sharply. Then she flashes more pictures across her palm. "This person? Or this one?"

I shake my head, but keep the rest of my body perfectly still. I see no benefit in telling them anything.

"What about him?" Agent Marlow shows me another picture.

"Sorry. No idea."

"Damn it, Nemo!" Agent Carter slams her hand on the table. "I know you're lying."

Despite my training, I startle. I jerk back in my chair so hard that the plastic rattles on the linoleum. Then I take a deep breath and focus on my breathing.

Nancy's eyes turn steely. "That was uncalled for. You have no reason whatsoever to question her integrity. Let me remind you that Blanca spent her childhood cooped up in seclusion and has a recent history of being abducted, attacked, and almost murdered."

"All the more reason for her to come forth with information rather than obstructing justice," says Agent Carter.

"No," Nancy replies. "All the more reason for Blanca to be cautious. If she doesn't tell you something for fear of her safety, that's not obstructing justice. What will you do, put her in witness protection? She's been in hiding her whole life."

"Whoa." Agent Marlow lifts up his hands to stop the verbal assault. "Nobody is accusing Blanca of obstructing justice. Let's take a moment to calm down and get back on track."

"Ask me something else." My words are soft and quick. "Ask me a different question."

Nancy raises her tattooed eyebrows at me. Then she turns back to Agents Carter and Marlow. "You heard the girl. Try asking Blanca something in a different way."

"In a different way?" Agent Marlow repeats. "Okay, Blanca. How about this. What can you tell us about the Guardians?"

This, I can do. I know exactly what to say because the textbook answer is engrained in my brain. "Founded in 2028," I begin, "the Guardian order was created in Beijing as a rival to the Vestals. Tabula Rasa was sixteen years old at that point and celebrating its first Harvest of graduates."

"Where your mother was purchased by Barbelo Nemo, your father," Agent Carter interjects.

"I don't consider either of those people to be my parents." I sit up a little straighter and don't say another word.

For a full minute, there is only silence, all four of us staring at each other in a quiet contest of wills.

"Please, Blanca," Agent Marlow finally says, his deep voice rumbling. "Please continue. Agent Carter won't interrupt again." He glares at her.

Nancy nods at me, so I move on to the next memorized line. "Tabula Rasa was gaining international fame as the last bastion of privacy. As the world became aware that lack of a virtual footprint was a commodity, a Chinese businesswoman named Wu Park rushed to copy our success. In the years that followed, the Vestal system Barbelo Nemo established at Tabula Rasa became so popular that it was copied in other countries as well.

The Keiner school in Berlin for example, and the Nadie school in Mexico. As parents began to realize there was financial value in their children's privacy, more and more families begged for placement."

"You said 'ours,'" says Agent Carter.

"What?"

"You said '*our* success.'" She places her hands on the table and the ladybug tattoos make me squirm.

"No, I didn't."

Or did I? I can't remember for sure.

"Ms. Nemo." Agent Carter is expressionless. "Do you still consider yourself to be a Vestal?"

"I'm no longer a Vestal and my name isn't Nemo. It's McNeal. I told you."

"We want to believe you," says Agent Marlow. "But we can't."

"It's hard to trust a liar." Agent Carter sneers.

"A liar?" Nancy exclaims. "Blanca, do not under any circumstance say another word. You are done helping these people without a court order."

"That can be easy to arrange," Agent Marlow says simply.

Agent Carter flicks her fingers and pulls up one more picture. It's grainy and hard to decipher, like the photograph was shot in the mist.

But my white pants are easy to spot. I'm standing on tiptoes leaning up to kiss Seth. We snuggle in front of the doorway of his apartment building.

"So what? Lots of people photograph me every day."

Agent Carter smiles like a panther about to eat fresh meat.

"Look in the corner."

So I do. And what I see stuns me.

Keung is in the picture too. Watching us.

"Blanca," Nancy says. "I highly advise you to not answer any more questions."

I nod my head in agreement and rub my blank wrist.

If there's one thing that Keung inspires, it's silence.

Goose bumps race down my back as my skin touches the evening air. The night is moonless, the stars hidden by the city's ugly glow. My leather jacket hugs me, but offers no protection from the chill. When I see Cal and Seth waiting for me outside, I sprint towards them.

Seth reaches me first, and swings me around in his arms. Cal says a quick goodbye to Nancy, and then leads us to the limo. Our driver, Alan, waits at the front of the parking lot and holds the back door open.

"What happened to my bike?" I ask.

"Don't worry," says Cal. "It's home in one piece."

I sink back into the middle seat of the limo and squeeze my eyes shut. I don't open them again until we're driving to the manor at top speed. Cal and Seth each take one of my hands.

"It's okay now." Cal gives my hand a gentle squeeze, then he releases it.

"What did they want?" Seth pulls me in close so that my head rests against his shoulder.

"They asked me about the Guardians."

"The Chinese Vestals?" Seth asks.

"They're not Vestals." I jerk my head away and shift positions. "Guardians are entirely different."

"How are they different? Lock up your kids in a cyber-safe school for eighteen years and then auction them off to the highest bidder." Seth scratches the back of his neck. "It sounds exactly the same to me."

The irritation that crawls up my throat surprises me. I bite back bile. "It's not the same. Vestals harvest ten people a year—all carefully screened for image, IQ, and likeability. The Guardians churn out hundreds. They have so many graduates of questionable quality that they can't land big contracts. A few lucky ones get placed as spokespeople for multi-million dollar firms, but the rest are assigned to miniscule government positions. It's like a twisted version of the ancient Confucian exam."

"The Con-fu-fu what?" asks Seth.

I turn to look at him. "You don't know who Confucius is?"

"Should I?"

"He was an ancient Chinese philosopher," says Cal. "Starting in the Han dynasty, men who were interested in becoming government bureaucrats either had to know somebody who could offer a recommendation, or pass the imperial examinations, which were based on Confucian classics."

I nod my head in agreement. "It's similar to what the Guardians do now. Graduate the program and get a job. Except with the Guardians, the government can dispose of them at will. Since their family has forsaken them they have no recourse except to do what their bosses say. It's nothing like the Vestals."

"That's exactly like the Vestals," Seth says.

"Vestals don't work for the government!" Sometimes it feels like Seth doesn't listen to me.

"So the FBI is interested in the Guardians?" asks Cal.

"Yes," I say. "Now you know everything."

Well, almost everything. I don't tell them about Keung.

Or the likely reason he's following me.

OTHER MONTH9BOOKS TITLES YOU MIGHT LIKE

LIFER

TEMPER

FACSIMILE

VESSEL

Find more books like this at http://www.Month9Books.com

Connect with Month9Books online:

Facebook: www.Facebook.com/Month9Books

Twitter: https://twitter.com/Month9Books

You Tube: www.youtube.com/user/Month9Books

Blog: www.month9booksblog.com

One slave girl will lead a rebellion.
One nameless boy will discover the truth.
When their paths collide, everything changes.

LIFER

BECK NICHOLAS

FACSIMILE

VICKI L. WEAVIL

THEY ARE NOT ALONE

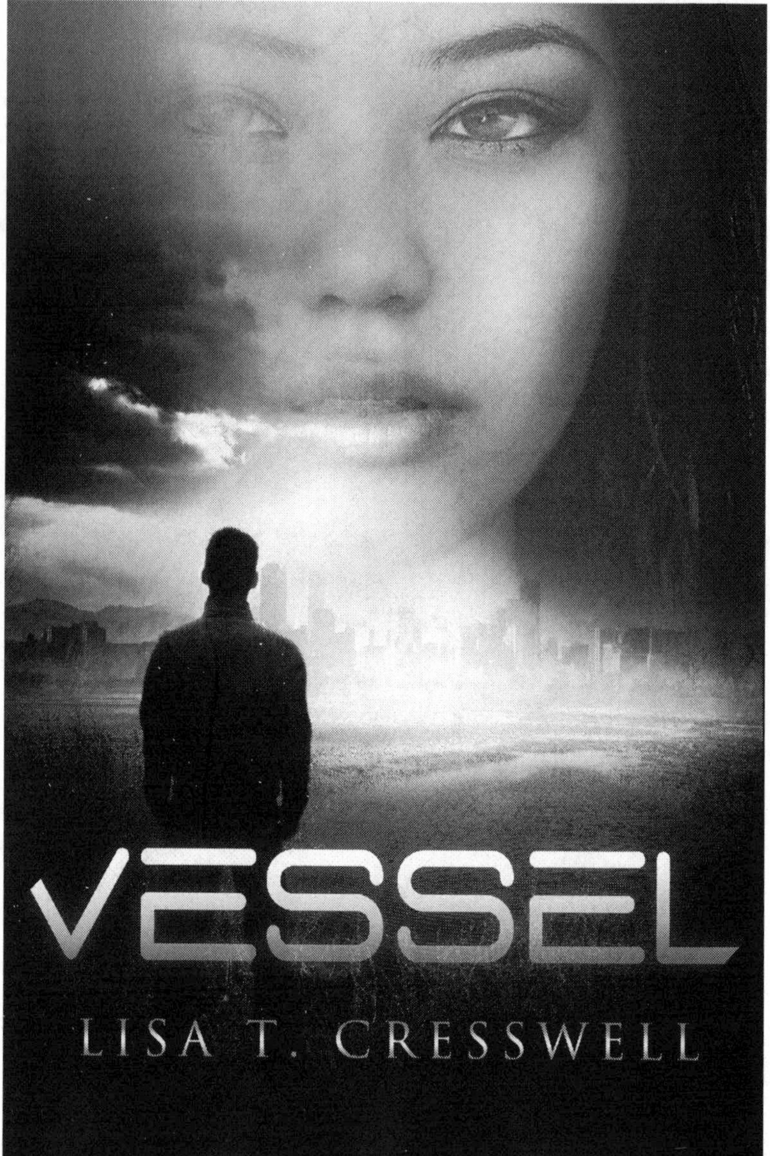
VESSEL
LISA T. CRESSWELL